a quiet life

Also by Kenzaburo Oe
from Grove Press:

A Personal Matter
Teach Us to Outgrow Our Madness
Nip the Buds, Shoot the Kids
Hiroshima Notes

a quiet life

Kenzaburo Oe

Translated from the Japanese by
Kunioki Yanagishita and
William Wetherall

Grove Press
New York

Originally published in Japan in 1990 as *Shizuka-na seikatsu* by
Kodansha, Tokyo
First Grove Press edition published in 1996

Published simultaneously in Canada
Printed in the United States of America

Library of Congress Cataloging-in-Publication Data

Ōe, Kenzaburō, 1935–
    [Shizuka na seikatsu. English]
    A quiet life / by Kenzaburō Ōe; translated from the Japanese by
Kunioki Yanagishita with William Wetherall. — 1st ed.
      p.   cm.
   ISBN 0-8021-1597-7
    I. Yanagishita, Kunioki.   II. Wetherall, William, 1941–
III. Title.
PL858.E14S4913   1990
895.6'35—dc20   96-25795

Design by Laura Hammond Hough

Grove Press
841 Broadway
New York, NY 10003

10 9 8 7 6 5 4 3 2 1

contents

a quiet life

This all happened the year Father was invited to be a writer-in-residence at a university in California, and circumstances required that Mother accompany him. One evening, as their departure drew near, we gathered around the family table and had our meal in an atmosphere slightly more ceremonious than usual. Even on occasions like this, Father is incapable of discussing anything important concerning the family without weaving in some levity. I had just come of age, at twenty, and he started talking about my marriage plans as if they were a topic for light conversation. I had never been much of a talker, and more recently had fallen into the habit of not disclosing my private thoughts to him. So while the table talk now centered on me, I merely listened to it, though attentively.

"At any rate, present your minimum requirements," Father, who had been drinking a beer, suddenly said to me, undaunted by my reticence. Expecting only a perfunctory reply, however,

1

he kept glancing at me with his somewhat impatient smile. Quite inadvertently, I brought myself to tell him about an idea I had now and then entertained.

"My husband has to be someone who can afford at least a two-bedroom apartment, since Eeyore will be living with us. And I want to live a quiet life there," I said, the blunt tone of my own voice ringing in my ears.

I detected bewilderment in both Father and Mother the moment I closed my mouth. Their first reaction was to smother what I had said with laughter, as if to suggest that my idea was merely an amusing, childish fantasy. But this is the way conversation in our family usually proceeds, the way Father orchestrates it, his forte. Eeyore, as my brother is called, is four years older than I, and he works at a welfare workshop that employs people with mental handicaps. Now if I were a new bride, and were to bring someone like Eeyore along to live with us, how would my young husband react? Even if I had told him about my plans before our marriage, wouldn't he simply dismiss them as strange and irrelevant? And then, on the very first day of their life together, his new brother-in-law, a giant of a man, shows up at the small apartment he had gone to such trouble to find—how surprised the inexperienced young man would be.

Sensing that there was some serious motive behind my parents' jocular conversation, I felt tense and hung my head to avert my eyes. What I said may have sounded unreasonable, but having said it, it became all the more important to me.

"I've been told all along that I don't have a sense of humor, and I quite agree," I continued, unable to stay quiet any longer. "Maybe there's a hidden message in what you're saying. . . . In any event, that's what I think. I can't conceive of marriage in concrete terms yet, because I don't have anyone particular in mind. I consider all the possible situations, but run into a dead end, no matter where I start, and that's why I think this way.

"The present conversation, too, tells me that my obsession is ludicrous . . . for I don't think anyone would marry me with Eeyore along. . . . Anyway, Papa, Mama, you're not telling me how to actually get around that dead end, are you?"

This was all I said, though I was abundantly aware I needed to elaborate. Every so often I revert to my childhood habit of standing beside Mother, as though in attendance, and talking to her while she puts on her makeup in her bedroom. I spoke to her the next morning this way, picking up from where I had clammed up the evening before. I had *sort of*—to use my younger brother O-chan's* pet phrase—rehearsed what I would say to her. Or perhaps it would be more accurate to say that something had *made* me rehearse it subconsciously. . . .

I, too, was disappointed with what I had said the night before. I probably would have been better off saying nothing at all. I retreated to my bedroom, but sleep evaded me. I thought about all sorts of things, and with frayed nerves, I was seized by the premonition of a terrible dream, a nightmare in which I saw myself standing all alone in an empty, desolate place. An awareness of the reality that I was still awake lingered within me, and mingled with the dream. I remained in this state of mind—sad, lonely, detached—knowing full well that my body was lying on the bed.

In time I realized that behind and to the side of me in the dream stood another person with feelings the same as mine. Without turning around to look, I knew that this was the *Eeyore-to-be*. This Eeyore-to-be, who at any moment would step out obliquely from behind me, was an attendant to a bride,

Chan is a term of endearment, the diminutive of *san*. Both are suffixes commonly attached to personal names.

and the bride was me. Primly dressed in my wedding gown, I stood lonely in that desolate place with the Eeyore-to-be as my attendant, with no idea who the groom was. Dusk was setting in on that vast, vacuous wasteland. Such was the dream I dreamt. . . .

Deep in the night I awoke. And as I recalled the dream, the loneliness welled back up in me with a vengeance, and with such vividness that I could no longer lie in the darkness of my room. So I went upstairs and turned on the night-light, which Eeyore uses so as not to stumble when he goes to the bathroom, and entered his room, through the door which he lets stand ajar. I hunkered down at the foot of his bed, wrapped my knees in the old beat-up blanket I had unconsciously brought with me—an act reminiscent of my childhood behavior—and listened to the sound of his heavy, deep-sleep breathing, which seemed to surpass the norm for human lungs. Not an hour had passed when, in the pale darkness, he got out of bed and quickly went out to the bathroom just across the hall. He took not the least notice of me, and I felt all the more lonesome.

The loud gurgle of urination seemed to last forever, but when Eeyore returned, he came to me. Like a big dog nuzzling at his master, he crouched and pushed his head against my shoulder and sat down beside me with his knees drawn up, apparently intending to sleep that way. I suddenly felt so happy. After a while, like a discreet adult stifling laughter, yet with a soft, pure, and childlike voice, he said, "Is everything all right with Ma-chan?" Feeling utterly whole again, I helped him back into bed, waited until sleep revisited him, and went back to my room.

The fall semester abroad was about to start, and this took place the last day of summer, just one day before their departure. Father was reading the paper on the sofa by their overstuffed, heavy-looking suitcases when he suddenly exclaimed, "Eeyore's got to start doing something for exercise again! Like swimming!" He was addressing neither Mother, who was working in the kitchen, nor me; rather he sounded like he was talking to himself after a lot of painful deliberation.

"Exercise? I'm a very good swimmer," Eeyore would have replied after a moment of belated thought, evoking laughter from everyone in the family—if, as usual, he had been there beside Father, lying flat on his stomach on the carpet, composing music.

Had Eeyore been there, Father's words would not have come rolling down on me, like a log or something, and just remained there. Eeyore is the buffer in the family—he's not wholly unaware of it—and he plays his role humorously.

But Eeyore wasn't there when Father suddenly mentioned exercise. If I remember correctly, I had already returned home after taking him to the welfare workshop in the morning, and was helping Mother clear the breakfast table when Father, the only one who had slept in, blurted out those words about exercise as he put down the morning paper. As I said, I felt weighed down by an unknown, loglike object. Then, when I started tidying up the living room, soon after Father had gone up to his study, I saw, in the morning paper he had left sprawled on the table, an article reporting that a mentally retarded youth had assaulted a female student at a camp school. The assault appeared to be motivated by sex.

I think the belligerent sensation, the *Hell, no! Hell, no!* that welled up in me, was not really a spontaneous reaction but one I had prepared all along. As a matter of fact, I had recently given vent to it on a number of occasions with those very words—words that Eeyore calls "rough" and reprimands me for using. Still, all too frequently, for some time now, my eyes have caught headlines decrying such sexual "outbursts" by mentally handicapped people. The newspaper we subscribe to, in particular, seemed to be running a covert campaign against such people, and these accounts appeared so often, as in that day's morning edition, that I once suggested to Mother that we take a different paper. Yet Father had reacted with good grace to the paper's campaign denouncing the "outbursts," as though he believed that they were actually taking place. And without even a word about the article, he had stammered that Eeyore should take up something for exercise—an attitude I found repulsive, annoyingly depressing at best.

Eeyore is definitely at a sexually mature age. I see many robust boys, in their twenties like Eeyore, while commuting to classes and on campus. I won't say this for all of them—in particular, I don't at all feel this way about my fellow volunteers—but now and then I detect in a boy's stare a radiation that seems to emanate from something sexual deep inside him. And all those sexy weekly magazine ads that hang everywhere in the commuter trains!

But if Father, from such general preconceptions, had worried about "outbursts" from Eeyore—in the same way the newspaper reporter worried about them—and had claimed that exercise a necessary measure (!?) to prevent them, then wouldn't there be something "banal" about Father that comes from his not seeing the facts clearly? I think I was reacting against this.

There was some talk at Eeyore's welfare facility, too, of several incidents that had almost been "outbursts." But according to what I heard from some of the mothers who had come to pick up their children, these "outbursts" were moderate, even merciful, compared to the glares of robust, able-bodied youngsters. Still, who could have known, as I quietly listened to them from my seat at their side, that a voice rang in me so loud as to almost make me cry, *Hell, no! Hell, no!* In any case, nothing had happened that should have involved the police.

When Eeyore first began commuting to the welfare workshop, I merely accompanied Mother when she took him there; and I recall there was practically nothing near the building at the time, just vacant lots. But since then, many wood-frame apartment houses with beautiful facades have mushroomed in the area, and it's often dangerous to cross the street with those structures blocking the view. So if there had been an assault, surely the new residents would have begun a movement against the welfare workshop.

One windy day early this spring, on my way back from the welfare workshop, where I had taken Eeyore, I turned at the corner of a fenced-in used-car lot to walk along a side street of the always wretchedly busy Koshu Boulevard. Since attendance for the day had been taken and the absence reports had already been submitted to the center office, I knew the boy I had seen wasn't one of Eeyore's workmates. But this seemingly mentally retarded boy had pulled down his pants to his knees to expose his pure white buttocks and was fondling his genitals while gazing at the grimy cars beyond the fence. "My, oh my!" exclaimed Mrs. A, one of the mothers who was walking back with me, a take-charge type of woman, quick in making decisions and taking action. "Ma-chan, you stay right here," she said, "Mrs. M and I will go first!" Having brought me to a halt with these enigmatic words, she briskly headed toward the boy.

Three other women, who happened to be abreast of us on the other side of the street, also began to move to censure the boy's behavior. Reaching him first, though, Mrs. A made him pull up his pants, and helped him with the satchel he had left on the side of the road. She made sure which direction his

school was in, and wasted no time sending him off. The three
women, left standing there with no opportunity to voice their
complaints, reproached us over their shoulders as they resumed
walking.

This is what Mrs. A, who had started toward the station,
said when I caught up with her: "If those neighborhood house-
wives hadn't been there, and if we didn't have to worry about
people mistaking the boy for one of ours, I'd have let him do it
to his heart's content!"

It was then Mrs. M's turn to say, "My, oh my!" Like Mrs.
A, she said this in consideration of a young girl's presence, but
in my heart I concurred with Mrs. A. And this made me repeat
to myself, *Hell, no! Hell, no!* for I had blushed and even become teary-eyed, which seemed somehow indecent, and I grit-
ted my teeth in anger.

While it is not my intention here to fault the boy in any
way, I have never seen Eeyore engaging in the act—at least
not where the eyes of a family member might spot him. We
also know that, unlike the boy, he has never done it elsewhere;
and to be quite honest, I have a hunch he won't ever do it. I
must confess, though, that my feelings regarding this matter
are mixed, for the thought that he will never do it doesn't nec-
essarily ease my mind, much less make me feel happy. . . .

Eeyore has a fundamentally serious streak in him, which
makes him reject all sexual playfulness. Father prefers lighthearted banter about such things, though Mother says he was
seriousness personified when he was a student, that his face-
tiousness is a second nature he acquired with great effort.
Eeyore, however, is of the exacting, stoic sort. So I wonder if,
when he hears "peck," which is frequently uttered in our house,
he consciously endures the word, however much he dislikes it.

"Peck" is Father's four-letter word, which lends itself to
levity like silk off a spool. I know this usage isn't found in the

dictionary, but Father uses it like a wild card, so to speak. Still, if I were to stand in Father's defense, I would say that I understood his need to invent it, for if any impropriety involving sex were to arise, some situation he himself could not well cope with, it would be in his own best interest to treat it more like a scandalous joke than as an embarrassing predicament.

I recall something that happened to Eeyore when he was in the secondary division of a special-care school for the handicapped. One day, at home, he was, as usual, lying on the living room carpet, listening to FM radio and composing music. And then he turned on to his other side, and he did so in such an *awkward* manner, thrusting his hips back, as it were, with obvious embarrassment. Father saw this and said to him, his voice louder—at least as I heard it—than necessary, "Eeyore, your peck's grown. Now go to the bathroom!"

So off he went, wobbling like a woman you might see in a hospital with something abnormal about her underbelly. I thought of his grown "peck" hurting as it brushed against his underwear, and I wished to help him in any way I could. But at such times Eeyore became extremely defensive—to the point that he would have pushed my hand away had I tried to do anything. Mother said she was helpless as far as the grown "peck" was concerned.

There were also times when we would come face to face with Eeyore's "peck." Eeyore has always worn diapers when going to bed. As he grew, the vinyl covers they had in the neighborhood stores became too small for him, so whenever we happened to go downtown, Mother and Father looked for something larger in the department stores. An instructor at the special school said he wanted all bed-wetting problems solved, and suggested that we get Eeyore up at night, between eleven and twelve, and take him to the bathroom. Mother usually did this, sometimes Father, but I took care of everything when Father was away traveling and Mother was too tired to get up. In those days I was up anyway, preparing for my high school entrance exams.

When you turned on the light, Eeyore would immediately awaken, but he wouldn't spontaneously initiate any movement. Seeing him lying there, his form heaving under the blanket, you would think he was a bear in hibernation. You would start by stripping off the blanket, and find him sprawled out every which way. Then you began taking off his pajama pants. While still lying there, totally inert, he would do his bit, making subtle movements to help you with the task.

If his diaper was still dry, you would use it again after taking him to the toilet, so you would carefully remove its adhesive tape to keep its folds and creases the same. You could tell immediately by its sodden warmth if it was already wet, but when you made it in the nick of time, you would be as happy as a hunter who had bagged some game.

Yet it was precisely in this situation that there was a problem. As soon as you removed the adhesive tape, Eeyore's "peck" would spring up with a force that would all but send the diaper flying. But after the diaper was removed and everything below his waist was exposed, there would be little left to do, for Eeyore would raise his upper body, get out of bed, and stand up by himself. No matter how often I did this, though, I could never get used to the smell of his breath, which reeks like some beast, or the foams produced when alloying metals. It's totally different from the sweet smell of his breath during the day; different, too, from the odor of his mouth when he has his attacks. . . .

Thanks to the conscientious instructor, Eeyore's diaper-wetting was cured virtually overnight—a half year after the instructor made his bold suggestion—when Eeyore spent a night at the special school dormitory for a dry run to prepare

the children for camping trips and the like. Since then, I don't
think anyone in the family has seen his "peck" rise as it did
before, with the virility of the serpents on Medusa's pate. Come
to think of it, it's been years since I've seen him double up into
that awkward posture with his elongated "peck." But because
Eeyore is of a serious mettle, and since he's the kind of person
who doesn't allow himself to conceal such things from the eyes
of his family, I wonder if this means that his "peck" has ceased
to grow.

When I told Mother what I thought, she replied, in a lowered tone of voice, "Perhaps that period has passed. A short
youth, wasn't it?" Father was then in the living room, but had
been listening in on our kitchen conversation, and said, "All
in all, it's nothing bad. We don't need to be anxious anymore.
That's the long and short of it." I resented this.

"We don't know if that's good or bad for Eeyore!" I protested in my heart. If his youth is gone, surely he won't do
anything like what that boy was doing on the street. But again,
I don't really know very much about such things. As far as my
feelings go, something makes me want to say that I'd rather
not be spared the anxiety. But more than this, I think to myself,
Hell, no! Hell, no!

Despite the mental preparation I had made for all the things
that might occur, the first week after my parents departed from
Narita presented me with a host of wholly unanticipated events
that set my mind awhirl. Because I was able to sleep only four
or five hours at night, I would lie on my bed a couple of times
a day between my chores and doze off, and sometimes I got so
absentminded that I made two entries in the "Diary as Home"
I had promised Mother I would keep. There was a lot to write
about, though.

a quiet life

Every little thing I had to attend to did, in a way, help forget my loneliness and anxiety. Nonetheless, I was vaguely perturbed by a nagging awareness of two matters, perhaps two persons. Something categorically carnal about them hung suspended in the middle of my body, right above my stomach. I refer to the two men who, at the height of my exasperation, I called "fanatics." Father seemed taken aback by this way of referring to them but was silent, while Mother cautioned me not to speak this way in front of others.

The men started coming to our gate, at least once a week beginning late last year, to bring us presents of a sort. We knew nothing about them, but it was because of their odd behavior that I began calling them fanatics. One of the men brought a bouquet of small flowers, not the kind you find at a florist's, but one that was bunched together in a peculiar fashion. The bouquet was like a cheerless classmate with downcast eyes who one day, when you're not on guard, usurps your inner thoughts. The other man brought water in a half-pint sake bottle stoppered with a cork. This one just went away after leaving the bottle on the brick wall by the gate, but once I confronted him face to face when I went out to receive the delivery of a year-end gift. He was a hefty, muscular person, like a monk who practices rigid religious austerities, and under his broad brow were the light-brown dots of eyes set too far apart.

The bouquet man rang the bell on our gate and offered the flowers to whoever answered. He was a diminutive person with the bearing of a bank teller or a schoolteacher, and always attached to his flowers was a letter in a small envelope. I never read any of them, but because the envelopes bore the letterhead of his workplace, got the impression he was comparatively normal. Father and Mother made little if any mention of him, but come to think of it, I remember there was a big commotion in the house many years back, possibly because of this man. It happened in the small hours of the morning, but oblivious to everything in those days, I had slept through most of it, and only very vaguely remember sensing that there had been some kind of trouble. Now I wanted to know what it was, so I asked Eeyore if he remembered what had happened. "Ah! We really had trouble! A police car came, but I didn't hear any siren!" His reply came in the usual belated fashion, yet he seemed to have a clear memory of the incident. "What kind of trouble was it?" I asked. Eeyore then lowered his eyes and said, with touching sincerity, "I'm in trouble! I'm in trouble!" From the way he tried to skirt my question, I assumed Father had told him to be quiet about it.

The appearance of such visitors was the high point, but there were also letters and phone calls that I felt were of the same nature, and as far as I know they increased after the telecast of a lecture called "The Prayers of a Faithless Man," which Father had given at a women's university. As someone who has had to directly put up with numerous nuisances, I can argue that there was no need for Father to go and tell everyone he was a "faithless man." And though I don't think he meant to offend anyone, for him to talk of *prayers* after admitting he professed no faith was, in my opinion, a breach of common courtesy. In this sense, he did make a social blunder, for which I think he well deserved some minor castigation. "But why do *we* have to go through this!" I protested to Mother once, and I think Father heard about it later. Anyway, that's when I first called the two visitors "fanatics."

Actually, Father seemed to bear all this as a kind of reprimand to himself, but thinking there might be a visitation after he, the person responsible for the family, had gone, and apparently feeling some guilt toward me, he wrote to the bouquet man and implored him to stop visiting. And so the delivery of the small bouquets ended. There was no way to get in touch with the water-bottle man, however, so the week before their departure, Father kept turning his eyes toward the gate as he worked in the living room, and was prepared to hand the man a similar letter, but he never appeared. Then, on Saturday, when dusk had fallen, we found another bottle on the gate, but no trace of the stranger.

After Father and Mother had left for California, I continued to worry about what I would do in the event I was again confronted at the gate by the water-bottle man. It would be depressing enough just to see a bottle there, let alone suffer another encounter with him.

Father's letter to the man rested untouched on a visiting-card tray by the front door. I was aware of its presence, but I let it sit there, for it's never to my liking to pry into someone else's correspondence, whoever its sender or receiver may be. Mother's first phone call to me after they had settled into one of the faculty quarters was to say that Father was anxious about the letter, and that he was having second thoughts about the water-bottle man getting it, for in it he had mentioned that he and Mother would be overseas for some time; this, he worried, might fan a zealous flame in the man, and make him want to see Eeyore protected by the power of his faith. . . . Then Father came on the phone instead of Mother and appeasingly said, "Even so, Ma-chan, I hope you don't become too apprehensive," which left me feeling he was being a bit irresponsible.

We kept the bottles in the corner of our storeroom in the order they were brought to us, for Mother worried that the stranger might ask for them back. The array of bottles, identical in shape, with tight corks fitted evenly on them, presented an awesome sight. The bottling was obviously the handwork of an amateur, and though the water in the bottles didn't look as though it had been boiled to kill the germs, when I picked up one of the earlier ones and gave it a shake, I saw no signs of fermentation, and again I felt the eeriness that gelled right above my stomach. . . .

One evening ten days after my parents' departure, a disturbance erupted on the block right next to ours, which brought a rush of police cars, their sirens ripping the air, unlike the police car in Eeyore's memory. I already know what happened, but I will write as though I am recalling exactly how I felt and what I thought at each point in time. I have already been writing this way about the water-bottle man.

The sirens of patrol cars suddenly began pressing in from all around, and I was so shocked that my mind went completely blank. When I rose from my chair, still without a single thought in my head, all the blood seemed to drain out of my body, and I was forced to slouch down on the dining table, where I had been writing a report. I panicked like this because, at the time, Eeyore was at the barbershop.

The barbershop is on the corner where the bus route meets the street in front of the railway station, and it has always been my job to take Eeyore there, and pay the barber in advance. Eeyore has had his hair cut there for years, so he is familiar with the procedure. He seems to get a kick out of the young proprietor, who asks him repeatedly when his hair is just about done, "Is this all right? Is this all right?" And he loves the slow walk home, I suppose because of the refreshed feeling that a haircut gives. It suited me fine that Eeyore would come home by himself, because it's rather weird for a young girl to sit and wait in a barbershop lounge.

As the patrol car warnings sounded from all directions, I checked to see whether Eeyore had returned home, but he hadn't. O-chan was at cram school for his university entrance exams, and I intensely regretted falling out of the habit of not staying by Eeyore's side until his haircut was done.

Nevertheless, bracing myself, I dashed outside in my jogging shoes. I ran the course Eeyore takes home, and at the third corner, a block just off the route connecting the house and the barbershop, in a quarter where there were a number of stately mansions, their grounds, buildings, and hedges just as they were in the past, I saw four police cars. The passing summer lingered in the twilight air, and its dying light could be seen in the perspiration on the faces and necks of the neighbors who had come out for an evening stroll, and were now milling around watching the policemen go about their work.

My body was already leaning in that direction, but I resisted the urge to start running again, and with a pounding chest, I said to an old man who was standing on the street near our house in calf-length drawers, "A traffic accident, sir?"

The old man turned his face, of classic features, toward me, and from his expression you would have thought he'd been watching a riveting TV serial about the ups and downs of life. This told me, vaguely, that the matter the police were investigating up ahead was nothing so simple as a traffic accident, but something more intimate and involved. With his already sanguine complexion even redder with emotion, the old man said, in a dread-inspiring voice, "It's no traffic accident. A molester, it seems. You'd better not take that road."

I bowed to him, turned with a good swing of my shoulders, and before I knew it, continued running along the route Eeyore should have been taking home. "Well, well!" I said to myself, savoring the rush of relief. "A molester, is it? I haven't heard of a gay molester anywhere in this country. Eeyore's safe! He's safe!" But Eeyore wasn't there at the barbershop; nor were there any customers, in the waiting lounge or in the chairs, but just the barbers cleaning up for the day.

The "Is this all right?" proprietor raised his body, bent over the floor he was sweeping, and said, perplexedly, "Your younger brother left for home some time ago," making the not-uncommon mistake of thinking that Eeyore was younger.

On the way home, I was struck with a new fear. Until then I had optimistically figured Eeyore was safe, since I had never heard of a gay molester. But couldn't it have been the other way around, that Eeyore had victimized someone? He wouldn't, at first, have meant to. He had probably just been trying to be kind to a cute little girl, but had frightened her instead. . . . And Eeyore just hates screaming and wailing. . . .

But Eeyore was home, safe and sound, sitting on the sofa, perusing the coming week's FM program guide in the evening paper. I sat down beside him and calmed the throbbing of my heart. He quickly glanced toward me, with a look of wonder, and quietly continued to mark off titles of classical music compositions with a red pencil. From his closely cropped head came the scent of hair lotion, and from his sport shirt came the green-smelling scent of lush vegetation! I immediately felt relieved, but from the next day on, I keenly recalled this green-leaf scent as material evidence of my *distress*. And then, that evening, when I went outside to close the front gate, there, sitting on the brick wall, was another bottle, the first in some time—not that I longed to see another one—and I felt totally exhausted.

The local page of next morning's paper carried an article about the molester. The report said that an elementary schoolgirl had been victimized, and that a series of assaults identical in nature had been committed since the end of last year—which was news to me—and that the culprit was still at large. And a couple of days later, as I was sweeping the path from our porch to the front gate, I heard two of our neighbors talking: the woman who lives across from us, and another woman her age who always goes shopping with her to the stores in front of the station. I guess they didn't know I was there, because they were standing on the paved street, on the other side of the closed gate and one step down, while I was inside the gate, my body stooped over a short garden broom, sweeping.

"The pervert was lying in wait at the corner of the block where the mansions are. He seized the girl and pushed her into the hollow of a hedge, then grabbed both wrists with one hand and pinned her down. Then he kept moving his other hand where the legs of his pants meet, and squirted something on her face." I think I also heard the words "facial emission." "How dreadful if he has AIDS. The girl's face was drenched, with her tears too." "Why didn't she cry out?" "Perhaps he punched her hard, and she was too frightened." "That reminds me. The other day, I saw someone standing rock-still by the hedge with his back toward me. . . ."

I had to sweep in front of the gate, too, so I stepped out and bowed to the women, whereupon they smiled back at me and promptly changed the subject. Before I was done with the sweeping, one of them went back into her house as the other hastily pedaled away on her bicycle.

The women's conversation imparted an even more ominous vigor to the movements of my floundering heart, which had been possessed by *distress* since the day after the pervert's appearance. The women had started talking about a figure standing by the hedge, but had dropped the subject when they caught sight of my small, round head emerging above the gate. Yet it was this part of their story that had fallen on me with a heavy thud—for the fact is, the *distress* had become so great that, while feeling apologetic toward him, I had tested Eeyore.

The day before, Eeyore and I had gone to a coffee shop on the street in front of the station. Paying the cashier in advance for his coffee, I asked Eeyore to go home alone because I needed to pick up a few things at the supermarket. I then hid in, and watched from, the shade of a pagoda tree whose small, yellowed leaves had already begun to shrivel. Finishing his coffee, Eeyore emerged, and in his placid tension was a soft expression that might, at any moment, have broken into a smile; in other words, he was in a good mood. He was taking delight in carrying out, by himself, the special suggestion he had gotten from me. He waited cautiously for a break in the stream of cars to cross the busy bus route, and then continued walking, slowly, as though on an old-fashioned pleasure stroll.

If he walked the course we always take to and from the station, then my *distress* would prove a needless worry. And indeed he turned the corner as we always do, then continued on the same well-trodden course. I think I already felt very relieved. But when he came to the crossroads where the disturbance had occurred, he turned south, in the opposite direction. His gait was steady, which was unusual in view of the disorder in his legs, and he moved them firmly forward. In time he stopped in front of an old mansion with an untended hedge consisting mainly of a clump of azalea shrubs that had grown thick and scraggly in the summer sun. Then he forcefully thrust his right shoulder into one of the hedge's hollows, and stood there as though hiding himself.

I don't think I stopped to watch him for even a minute. I just couldn't, though there were no passersby. I saw, coming in our direction, only the figures of two uniformed schoolgirls, who in the distance looked like magpies or crows. However, being totally flattened by my *distress*, I desperately ran up to Eeyore's side and said, my voice breaking, "What's the mat-

19

ter? What happened? You took the wrong road. Let's go home!"

While reading over what I had written in the "Diary as Home," I realized that another ten days had passed since then. But it's weird, even mystifying, for at the time, although I must have been overwhelmed by the great mass of my *distress*, not a trace of it remained, its serious weight notwithstanding, once this period had passed. Still, living through those hellish days had made a new person out of me, in a way, I guess. I say this because I, the always withdrawn coward that I am, accomplished something I had never dreamed of.

That day, too, it never cooled off, and in the windless, stagnant air, only the faint evening glow in the western sky was beautiful. Going out to get the evening paper, I saw that another water-filled bottle had been left on top of the wall by the gate. It somberly mirrored the twilight air, and as though a lens had gathered the sunset hues, the confined water surface right below the cork reflected a reddish sheen—which I felt was like the flush on the face of a con artist who has just sold you a bill of goods. If the bottle had been left there only minutes ago, I could run out and give it back to the man, I thought. I then became totally absorbed in this idea, as when one gets excited about something and blood rises to the head.

I returned to the porch-side window to make sure, through the lace curtains, that Eeyore was still lying on the floor, on his stomach, composing music. Then I quietly closed the door and wheeled our bicycle up to the gate. I put the bottle of tepid water in the wire basket attached to the bike's handlebars— carefully setting it on its side to give it some stability, though it rolled this way and that once I started pedaling—and sped off down the road toward the station.

I raced straight to the bus route, turned south, and coasted down the pedestrian walk all the way to the intersection with a traffic light. If I made a left, I would be on the street that meets the one to the station. However, the traffic there was still heavy, despite the time of day, and I wasn't sure if I would be able to make out the water donor even if I did catch up with him. After all, I had seen him only once, and my memory of his face wasn't all that vivid. So I decided that, if possible, I should search for him, one street after another, along the several that few people take at dusk, which run north and south, perpendicular to the one we take from our house to the bus route. And if I saw him on one of them, I would be able to identify him. . . .

When I was a little girl, still free from all cares, we used to spend the summers in our mountain cabin in Gumma, and Father once said I ran like a pony. And now, actually pumping my shoulders like a horse, I pedaled on the bike I hadn't ridden for some time, first north on the street nearest the bus route, and peered up and down the streets whenever I hit an intersection. I turned at the north end and sped along the road running east and west, until I came to the next corner. When I turned south, I spotted two figures, one bigger than the other, entangled in a knot. They were clenched together at the junction of two hedges, the farther one of dense, closely pruned fragrant olives running along the street side of an old mansion, the closer one of dwarf cypresses, poorly cared for, bordering the neighboring mansion.

I jammed on the brakes after I had gone another good five or six meters. The two figures, a man and a girl, seemed to be scuffling. The man had on a dark, grass-colored raincoat, despite the fine weather, and the girl, who wore a light pink one-piece dress, appeared to be in the upper grades of elementary school, or in middle school. He had pushed her down with one hand and forced her to squat between his legs. He had thrust his other hand into the front of his raincoat, and was frantically moving it back and forth. . . .

My immediate course of action was so peculiar that I felt like laughing when I later related my part in the story to the police. I raised myself off the saddle, lowered my head, and quickly pumped the pedals, just like the scout in a game we played when I was a child. Then I raced past the scuffling pair while loudly ringing the bell. Going past them, I caught, out of the corner of my eye, a glimpse of the man in the raincoat glaring at me with his brown-dot eyes.

I stopped some fifteen, sixteen meters ahead, jumped off my bike, turned around, hopped astride the seat again, and with one foot on the ground, looked right at him. All the while I kept ringing the bell. By then the movement of the man's hand where his raincoat parted had ceased, but the other hand continued to restrain the girl with a seemingly strong force. He kept that face with too much space between the eyes turned toward me, and appeared to be busy wondering what to do. Then he raised the hand he had withdrawn from the front of his raincoat and waved it at me as though shooing away a dog.

I furiously shook my head, so mortified I could have burst into a fearful wail. Then I caught sight of a woman, who appeared to be in her mid-thirties, looking down from the second-story window of her boxlike house, which had been built on one of the lots the owner of the mansion beyond the unkempt hedge had divided off and sold.

"Hey!" I hollered. "Please help!" The woman opened the window with a clamor, leaned out to look up and down the street, and with a quick thrust of her head over her shoulder called to someone behind her.

Sensing a new turn of events, I looked back and saw that the man had released the girl. He was about to quickly walk away in the other direction, his shoulders slanted at an oddly

22

acute angle. Finally the girl began crying out loud as she hobbled on her knees to safety. Still ringing the bell, I slipped past her and went after the man. Noticing I was chasing him, he stopped in his tracks and turned to glare at me with those tiny eyes of his. And I stopped, for the most I could do was stare back at him from a distance. Before long, the man dashed into a side street with an incredible vigor, his raincoat fluttering on his back like Batman's cape.

The culprit was caught by the woman's brother, who had quickly wheeled out his motorbike and, unlike me, who had simply followed the molester, beaten him to the bus route. But I was the one—though all I did was belatedly give chase on my bike while furiously ringing the bell—who was able to point out to the police that the pale, perspiring, panting man who pretended to know nothing was indeed the pervert I had seen molesting the girl. In this sense, then, I believe I played my part well enough.

The woman's brother and her husband pinned the man from both sides until the police came, while the woman stayed with the little victim and kept comforting her. I felt uneasy because the man with the brown-dot eyes, which were like those of a febrile catfish, was staring at me, even as he was being held. From what I later heard from the police, though, the man said he didn't make an all-out effort to flee because he knew I had remembered his face.

The man apparently also admitted to bringing all those bottles to our house. Until hearing this, I had felt very queasy about the dampness on the front of my skirt. Then it dawned on me that the cork had come out of the bottle I had put in the basket on the handlebars.

The next day, I came down with a fever and couldn't get out of bed, so Eeyore took a few days off from his work at the welfare workshop, and O-chan prepared our meals. "I took nutrition and balance into consideration, *sort of*," he said as he prepared the table, but the assortment was all instant food he had bought at the supermarket—on sale, for that matter. It was funny, though, since what he set out gave the semblance of well-chosen fare. This was about the only time while I lay in bed that I felt my heart uplifted, for I was possessed by a ponderous fear, morning, noon, and night.

Why had the water-bottle man been a molester? The police said that the bottles of water merely gave him an alibi. If someone had asked why he was loitering around this residential area, he would say he was merely delivering water to our house. To make his alibi even more plausible, he had intentionally chosen a house of a person whose name occasionally appeared in the papers. Still, I think there was something unusual in the way the man kept staring at me while he had the girl pinned down, or when he was trying to get away, and even after he was caught. I sensed those brown-dot eyes had revealed to me, my Father's daughter, the inside of a "fanatic's" mind with an interest in Father's *prayers*.

Even as the night wore on, sleep did not come to me, and in that same half-dreamlike state I often fall into I thought of something even more fearful. Though the man was a molester, he won't be long in prison. So as soon as he gets out, won't he come around the neighborhood, lie in wait for me in one of the hedges, and, remembering me through that stare of his, catch me, and force me down to my knees with that same strength? And like that girl who was hit so hard she couldn't even cry, I, too, would be unable to offer the slightest resistance. That cold water which never becomes stale would be poured from that small bottle into my eyes, my nose. . . .

One day, autumn in the air and my fever finally gone, I went shopping with Eeyore to the supermarket in front of the station. I felt very weak, and so I had Eeyore, who has a strong pair of arms, carry the two shopping bags for me as we slowly walked home. But when we came to the crossroads where one of the streets led to the old mansion hedged with a clump of shrubs, where I had once seen him stand alone, he turned in that direction, and walked on ahead as though leading me there.

"What's the matter, Eeyore? That's the long way home," I protested in undertones as I reluctantly followed him.

Eeyore again pushed one shoulder into the hollow of the azalea bush, and stood there straining his ears with a serious expression on his face. I could hear the restrained notes of some-one practicing the piano. Eeyore listened for a while, then he turned to me with a placid, contented look.

"That's Piano Sonata K. 311," he said. "But it's all right now. The rest shouldn't be difficult. Not at all!"

I realized then that I, too, would be able to rise above the *distress* that possessed me. Sure, there will always be new worries, but what could they amount to, compared to that *distress*. . . .

abandoned
children of
this planet

For as long as I can remember, Father has, on a number of occasions, lived overseas for a period of time. Whether for work or for study, these were always situations in which he would depart for, and reside alone at, a place related to some literary figure he was concerned about at the time. So for Mother to accompany him to a foreign country and live there for eight months, leaving here half the family, namely the children, as we are to them despite our ages, was an unprecedented development in our life. Apparently this wholly new situation came about not only because Father needed Mother with him, but also because Mother resolved to accompany him. Knowing Mother's character, I don't doubt her judgment. If she deemed it important to join him, then it must have been important. In any event, even before I asked her why exactly she was going, I had already volunteered to take care of Eeyore during their absence. O-chan, my younger brother, has college entrance exams to prepare for, but anyway, he's an independent, go-it-alone person.

I then realized the terrifying gravity of the situation I had accepted from the reaction I got when I related it to Father's friend, Mr. Shigeto, who has been looking at Eeyore's music compositions since last year.

Mr. Shigeto sorrowfully returned my gaze, through eyes that shined with a varnishlike transparency, and said, "Life's a sea of troubles for you, too, isn't it, Ma-chan? With Eeyore along and all . . ."

He was trying to comfort me, but his eyes were so painfully sad that I, in turn, felt sorry for him, and had to look away. Yet I could feel my mind turn to the *seriousness* that I had until then avoided thinking about. A case in point: suppose Eeyore were to meet with an accident. Our family situation is to some extent publicly known from what Father writes, and so surely people would criticize my parents if they were to find out that they had gone to the United States, leaving behind a handicapped child and his younger sister and brother to look after themselves—although, as I said, agewise Eeyore was, like me, an adult, and was already duly working, albeit at a welfare workshop for people with handicaps. In any event, if Eeyore was in an accident, that in itself would be a *serious* matter!

When it comes to such *seriousness*, undoubtedly Mother knows more than any of us. She's the kind of person who, once she falls silent, dwells on a problem all by herself until she comes up with a satisfactory solution. So it goes without saying that Mother must have had good reason to decide to leave us here and go to America. I tried not to be too nosy, but I asked her before their departure what it was that had set her heart on accompanying Father.

Father was motivated to go to one of the several campuses of the University of California as a writer-in-residence because, having already attended a number of symposia at UC, he had made friends he respects in the English and history departments there. If this was all that had motivated him, though, he could very well have gone by himself, and lived in the faculty quarters as he had on previous occasions.

Mother's laconic explanation for all this was that Father was in a "pinch." She also said that Father himself had admitted to her that it was a "pinch" such as he had never experienced.

If I detected any change in Father these days, it was only that I sometimes found him distracted. Because I'm the type who doesn't immediately feel shock when I hear something, but who slowly dwells on it afterwards, Mother had already filled me in on Father's condition by first telling me he had previously experienced several "pinches," each of which he had managed to overcome. Once, for instance, by secluding himself in our cabin in Gumma, and another time by taking on an agreeable job at a university in Mexico. What Father needs at such places of shelter is a lush growth of trees. Serious as she was, Mother chuckled when she said that no matter how shattering Father's many pinches had been, he had always taken stock of the trees that were essential to his hideaway: the Erman's white birches in Kita-Karuizawa, the bougainvillea and flame trees in Mexico City, and now the live oaks and redwoods in California. While this was somewhat amusing, at the same time I felt sorry for Father, knowing that he had grown up in a valley enclosed by forests, and so in a pinch would try to return to a place where there were trees.

This time, too, it so happened that Father, to overcome a "pinch," would go to California, a land of trees he himself had already taken measure of. At first he was to have gone alone, as he had until now, but in the meantime Mother began to feel that, in any event, Father was too distracted. . . . First she thought of having Eeyore accompany him. However, an acquaintance of hers at the welfare workshop, a person with some experience, told her that someone with a mental handicap would encounter visa problems. So one morning, a couple of days later, Mother disclosed her intention to go with him. Father himself was there at the breakfast table, as large as life. Father is the kind of person who, whenever he feels he might inconvenience any of us over something about himself, excessively tries to make up for it by carrying everything on his own shoulders. But this day he remained totally distracted.

Reorganizing my thoughts now, I think I embraced two conflicting sentiments when seeing him in that state of mind: one, a feeling of anger at his slack attitude, irrespective of the nature of his "pinch"; the other, an immediate feeling that he was aging. Having seen Father confronted with similar predicaments even before their marriage, Mother said she was used to it, but she gave me no concrete clue as to what the new "pinch" involved. And so mingled in me were the fear and sadness that, despite all the "pinches" Father had overcome by himself, he was now facing one in which a mere seclusion of his person at a place of shelter offered him no solution at all.

The manner in which I have written about things until now should show this, but it seems my character naturally leaves me empathizing with Mother, while I always feel remote about Father. I think I can trace this sentiment back to my childhood, when I saw him always preoccupied with Eeyore and felt that he wasn't really interested in either me or O-chan. Yet fairly recently, Father and I have had several opportunities to talk at some length, and this time, as far as his stay in California goes, he writes to me quite copiously. Still, I often find his letters sitting there unopened on the dining table where I put them. Mother's letters, though, I can hardly wait to open, and I read them with delight.

From Mother's letters, I feel that she's been trying to convey to me more about Father's "pinches" than she did when they were here. "When I thought about it," she wrote in one of them, "I had to admit that Papa's depression—I use this word although I don't like it—started with the sewer-cleaning incident. Don't you, Ma-chan, feel the same way?"

The sewer-cleaning incident, I remember very well, occurred in February this year. The drainpipe connected to our kitchen sink gets clogged up once or twice during the winter. When this happens, Father promptly goes to work with a gadget consisting of some metal bars covered with synthetic resin, which used to be part of the fence around our flower bed and were now connected together with hemp twine—a tool he had made himself. Some fatty substance and mud hardens in the drainpipe, and encrusts it like some kind of brown mortar. Father wields this untrustworthy gadget of his, which looks unreliable even to the casual eye, and goes at it with dogged resolve, until he finally succeeds in opening up a channel for the water to flow. This done, he thoroughly scours the entire pipe to allow the sewage to run more smoothly. When through, he washes his hands and feet well, yet the stench of the sewer is still on him when he starts reading a book on the sofa. And his entire prostrate body, like the sewer stench, clearly gives rise to a sense of satisfaction, however small. . . .

Father has the habit of obsessing over things like this, and he never misses an opportunity for an experiment. When he passes a drugstore and sees an ad or something for a can of drainpipe-cleaning chemicals, he jumps at it. One morning, seeing the breathtaking results of the chemicals he had poured into the pipe the night before, he was beside himself with happiness. All of us had to go out and see the wonder before going to school or the welfare workshop. This was actually the genesis of the sewer-cleaning incident. Above the pipe that runs from the kitchen sink to the back of the house, then along its course all the way to the main sewer system, is a sequence of metal drain covers marked $1, 2, 3 \ldots n$. And what needs cleaning is the whole length of the pipe between lids 1 and 2, 2 and 3, and so forth. On the day the chemicals finally succeeded in loosening up the sewage, the mortarlike globs that the powerful acids had washed out had accumulated under every cover. Father kept furiously ladling out the globs, like an excited farmer reaping his bountiful harvest.

Though Father was very elated at this stage, he appeared to already have sensed an ominous, obscure anxiety, for he had correctly suspected that more globs had been washed away into the long pipe that led to the main system, beyond the last cover, as he then thought it, within our lot. . . . Our fears turned into reality, and the next day water from the sewer gushed out from that very cover. Father's tool no longer served its purpose, and a team of sewer specialists had to come in with a lot of heavy-duty equipment.

The sewer servicemen seemed to have formidable trouble, too. But soon, beneath the dirt, Father found one more cover beyond the one he had thought was the last of the series. Under this cover was a sievelike device that prevented all solid waste from entering the long pipe. This screen had caused the drainpipe to become mercilessly clogged, but the problem was solved once all the globs blocking the waterway were scooped out. Then the sewer service owner, who at first seemed to have no confidence, began to lecture Father to clean everything regularly. Father became despondent, for he had to admit failure. What he had believed to be cover number n was in fact $n-1$. From the start, he should have realized it was strange when his tool hit something at the far end of the pipe. After all, it would have been a simple matter of checking to see if there was another cover hidden under the dirt.

"After the sewer-cleaning incident," Mother wrote, "Papa kept grumbling his remorse for quite some time. 'When the tool hit the end, I should have pulled it out of the pipe and stretched it out on the ground, and then poked along the pipe's perimeters with a metal bar. And why didn't it occur to me that there could have been another cover . . . ?' Inadvertently, I told him rather brusquely to brood over the matter no more, since practiced hands had already taken care of it. Then Papa moaned out loud, 'What better chance was there for a family patriarch to prove himself! And I blew it.' This startled me.

"This time, too, I don't think I can do anything to turn Papa's mind away from what he believes is his 'pinch.' All I can do is stay by his side. Even though, as he admits, his lecturing on faith was the trigger, I don't think he himself knows exactly why everything is piling up on him now and causing him to be so despondent. Nothing about his present 'pinch' is as simple as the sewer-cleaning incident. He has even gone so far as to say that his accumulated evils have caused it. So, Ma-chan, while I know we're causing you a lot of trouble, I'd like to stay at Papa's side and look after him."

I often dream about things that adhere to day-to-day affairs, with only slight distortions. I'm not the kind of person who dreams truly dreamlike dreams; yet the night I read Mother's letter, I did have an elaborate one, though I can't say whether the letter had anything to do with it. Anyway, in the dream, not only had Father written a play—something he has never ventured to do in real life—but he was also on the stage where all this was taking place! Even Mother was there! While doubting that any of this was possible, since neither of them has had any training in acting, and while wondering when they had returned from California, I depart for the theater with Eeyore. . . .

Both Mother and Father are actually on stage, but I can't hear them well. The play has just begun, so Eeyore and I try to move up to a front seat, when a man with a PRESS armband appears and tries to exclude us, saying, "You belong in the cheapest seats, so you can't come here!" That's the dream I had. I had never encountered this man with the PRESS band in real life, and even if I had, we had probably just passed by each other once or twice. Even so, I thought I definitely knew the man, but when I awoke, I just couldn't remember who he was. . . .

At breakfast I told O-chan about the dream, and he said, "Well, I could call this a form of amateur psychology, but it's really only a level of discourse that could reveal as much about me as it does about anything else. But when you see a discomforting, disgusting dream, the guy who appears in such a dream and does something terrible to you is different from the person you regard as the most vicious guy. It's Number Two, so to speak, who appears. Since even in a dream you wouldn't want to encounter the guy you consider the most malicious in real life, wouldn't you make Number Two the executor of the dream? So wouldn't it be simpler to start with the person you now regard as the most vicious in real life, and then consider his proxy?"

When in kindergarten, O-chan was always either putting together Legos or reading science picture books. When talking to my parents, even to me, he spoke as though he were reading from a book, which irritated me so much that I often quarreled with him over it. In middle school and high school he did orienteering, and after he decided he would study natural science in college, I haven't seen him reading even one humanities-related book. Even so, he nonchalantly uses words you find only in such writing. *Malicious? Executor? Proxy?* I stammered to myself, barely able to follow his train of thought. But as I visualized the Chinese characters for these words, each was in its own right quite convincing, and I thought O-chan's diction indeed appropriate. This idiosyncratic way with words, I think, issues from a depth in my younger brother that I don't sense in my everyday life with him. I related all this to Mother, to which not only she but also Father replied.

"Papa appeared to be filled with emotion when I told him about the dream you had, about you and Eeyore going to the theater together.

"I think I, too, can solve the riddle in the dream scene where you and Eeyore sat in the audience seats far separated from the stage that Papa and I were on, and in which you received rude treatment. I would say it represents the situation you and Eeyore have now been put in. Don't you think so, Ma-chan? When I asked Papa about this, he said, 'More than that, I think it portrays their plight after we're dead.' He even went on to say, 'By dreaming such a dream, Ma-chan's rehearsing for the future, hers and Eeyore's future as orphans.' His own strong words seemed to hurt him when he said this. . . . He told me he would write to you about the thoughts your letter evoked, when he can bring himself to feel better."

Just one day after Mother's letter, a letter from Father also arrived.

"When you're in dreamland in Tokyo, Ma-chan, it's either morning or dusk here in California, which means I'm usually up. I remember one day toward evening, I was walking along Strawberry Creek, which is lined with redwood trees and is on the edge of the campus close to where I am now living, and I felt myself in the midst of public observation, but unlike a delusion of persecution, the sensation didn't feel bad. It must have been deep in the night in Tokyo, and you were seeing a dream of us on stage.

"I can think of someone with a malevolent mind, and he's capable of wearing a PRESS armband if he wanted to, but judging from the structure of your dream, I would say this. In your dream you went with Eeyore to see a play you imagined I had written, but before the plot had even unfolded in your head, you paged the insolent man with the PRESS armband, so you could avert your eyes from the stage on the pretext of your relationship with him. Now if this were the case, I would find some relief in what you did, for it could mean that you are preparing yourself for a situation in which you would actually come across men with vicious minds. Because, any day, such people are going to appear not only in your dreams, but in your real life."

The day I received Father's letter, Eeyore had a fit as soon as we reached Mr. Shigeto's house. He hadn't forgotten to take his anticonvulsants, and he neither had a cold nor was feeling bad, yet he had a fit anyway. Not a serious one, though. His movements somehow slowly gave way despite his resistance to it, and when I looked carefully I noticed an expansion of feverish red from his neck to his face. When I explained his condition to Mr. Shigeto and laid him down on the sofa, Mrs. Shigeto brought a blanket that seemed to have a history connected with some country in Eastern Europe. I wrapped Eeyore with it from his chest on down, and placed his head on a cushion, which was also of Polish peasant embroidery. His head was heavy, and because of its uncertain center of gravity, I had difficulty placing it squarely on the cushion. His breath was foul as always when he has his fits, a reek I could never get used to no matter how hard I tried. This made me clearly recall—as did the aura of the blanket and the cushion—a story I had read in kindergarten, a story I now know to be a retelling of a Russian folktale, about a hot-and-foul-breath-spewing devil with legs and arms like those of a small crane fly.

Mr. Shigeto's wife closed the curtains to shut out the sunlight because Eeyore, lying at full length, was shading his eyes with his hand, his shapely fingers straight and tight. "Shall I play a record?" she asked as she drew the curtains, but Eeyore couldn't even gesture a reply, let alone answer her. Mr. Shigeto said nothing. Long-faced, and drooping his head, he looked anguished as if thinking that he, for some reason, had been the cause of Eeyore's fit. A while later I asked Eeyore, "Are you all right now? Do you feel better?" To which he replied, "I'm all right now! I feel better! Thank you!" His voice was still low and hoarse. Perhaps because Eeyore had spoken with the simple seriousness of a small child, Mr. Shigeto's face, which he lifted in relief in the pale darkness, appeared to be stifling tears. I turned my face to look as far away from him as I could. . . .

For this reason, I had to write Mother a letter reporting on the state of Eeyore's fits. I wrote her that toward the end of the following month I would take him to the hospital for a checkup, instead of my going there just for his medicines. I usually just go to a university hospital in Itabashi—the same place he was rushed to in an ambulance immediately after he was born, and where he has received treatment ever since—and drop his medical card in a box labeled PRESCRIPTIONS to get medicines that are issued in four-week quantities.

While writing this letter to Mother, I fondly remembered what each of us did when Eeyore had his fits—especially Father's way of handling it, which I found so repulsive when he was here, but now to some extent condone. Father would make a big thing of it, together with Eeyore, as though it were a game of some sort. But now I'm starting to feel that, in a way, he had the right attitude toward it.

This is what I immediately recall whenever Eeyore has a mild fit: It's morning. Eeyore's just gotten out of bed and is feverish. Sometimes it's just the start of a cold, but Father, with an intuition that comes from long years of experience, can distinguish whether or not it foretells a fit. At such times, Father doesn't go upstairs to his study. Ensconced on the living room sofa, and with a drawing board on his lap, he continues writing, all the while paying mind to Eeyore, who's lying prostrate on the floor, listening to music on FM radio. After a while, Eeyore gets up and starts walking from the living room to the dining room, which is one step higher. And on the way, his batteries die.

When this happens, Eeyore doesn't fall headlong, but there is nothing either Mother or I, with our physical strength, can do. O-chan stands nearby looking worried, but out of reserve he doesn't dare touch him. Enter Father, manifesting an agility that's alien to an adult's dignity; and by the time I notice him, he's already at Eeyore's side. And though I know he's only encouraging him, words I feel as much resistance toward as "peck" fly from Father's mouth one after another.

"Eeyore, it's the 'fit-and-runs,' is it? Well, hang in there and let's go to the toilet. Don't give up now. Don't you let your fit-and-runs come out! . . . Good! You made it! A grand success! Your fit-and-runs!"

Eeyore is already just as tall as Father, and weightwise has surpassed him. And because he's suffering early symptoms of a fit, or is already in the midst of one, his consciousness is blurred and his movements have become dull, and he's on the brink of falling, as Father guides him and takes him to the toilet. Violent diarrhea starts the moment you have him sit on the commode, or even before that. It makes a world of difference for Mother whether or not he makes it there in time, for she's the one who has to do the cleaning. So it's only a matter of course for Father, sensing the beginning of a fit, or one that has just started, to be full of enthusiasm when he plunges into the task of taking Eeyore to the toilet. And I also think it's only natural that he's happy when everything turns out to be a grand success.

Granted, we took delight in this way of talking at the time Eeyore was still going to the special-care school, as we did with "peck." But wasn't it going too far to play it up, as though it were a gay festival, with the seemingly fixed expression *fit-and-runs*? Doesn't Eeyore—just before his fit, or in the midst of one—feel as though hot bubbles were boiling in his bronchioles and esophagus, stomach and bowels? Isn't this condition alone sufficiently disagreeable? And while all this is going on, he's got to listen to Father's relentless banter next to his ears, and move arms and legs that are difficult to move, and head for the toilet, balancing the weight of a body that threatens to fall—and above all bear his fit-and-runs—how excruciating all this must be!

Honestly, it was with such a feeling that I reacted to Father's speech and conduct. Nevertheless, sometime before my parents departed for the United States I began to sympathize with Father, who looked after Eeyore. I remember one Sunday when Father returned home pitifully worn out from a charity event for handicapped people he had taken Eeyore to, a performance by the Metropolitan Orchestra called the Joining of Hearts Concert. By contrast, Eeyore was in high spirits. Come to think of it, Father's "pinch" was clearly apparent to us from about that time. I had taken Eeyore to these concerts twice before, and from these experiences, I worried about Father accompanying him there. It's only my personal impression, but at such charity concerts, the emcee and conductor are oddly spirited, while the members of the orchestra often betray a natural fatigue. So I worried that Father, who was accustomed to concerts of first performances of new works by his composer friends, would be shocked by the slack atmosphere created by such an orchestra. But the night before the Joining of Hearts Concert, he seemed inclined to switch with me and said in his usual sportive manner, "Who're you going to the concert with tomorrow, Eeyore?" Eeyore then pointed his nicely shaped finger shyly, as if to hide it under the table, in Father's direction.

Father had Eeyore wear his old suit to the concert, a suit Father had worn just once or twice a long time ago and saved for Eeyore upon finding that it looked better on him, and they had dinner at a nearby Ikebukuro restaurant afterwards, and came home. His positive attitude seems to have lingered awhile after the concert, for he brought back some ice cream he had bought at the restaurant, but when he got home after sundown, he looked totally frazzled.

The Joining of Hearts Concerts that I have been to have been gatherings of handicapped people with truly diverse idiosyncrasies, and the equally idiosyncratic members of their families. Their different backgrounds are especially apparent in the mothers of mentally retarded children of high school age. They are banded together, and on each is imprinted the dark, indelible mark of the wheel of suffering to which they boldly put their shoulders. I respect them for this, which is why I usually stay with these mothers when I go to these gatherings. But I also feel there is nothing quite like the complex and fervent mood in the assembly of various handicapped people with their families and the volunteers.

But I wonder if Father, who is used to working by himself, didn't find the excitement-echoing atmosphere more enervating than encouraging. When Eeyore and I are in public, at concert halls or on trains, I'm frequently led to reconfirm the oddity of his facial expressions and movements, which are strikingly different from those of ordinary people, though at home they are an integral part of the family and something we like a lot. The oddity is often made more conspicuous in the company of other handicapped people, each of whom unwittingly punctuates their own dissimilarity. So I imagine Father received quite a shock when he began to see unfamiliar impressions in Eeyore at the Joining of Hearts Concert.

And so I felt both sorry for and angry with Father. I possessed no concrete evidence on which to justify my presumptuous intrusion into his inner thoughts when I surmised that his exhaustion was due to his having reconfirmed Eeyore's handicap, which in the presence of other handicapped people had supposedly seemed more obvious to him. I was led to think this way by the various experiences I myself had gone through. Even now, whenever I take Eeyore to these gatherings, or when I help as a university volunteer, I notice that the mothers of handicapped children, however sad they look, appear to have a firm grip on themselves, whereas the fathers, especially those of Father's age, wear expressions of doleful apprehension. Each appears to be nursing a fear that the outline of his own child's handicap, which he has sketched in pencil, is being retraced and accentuated with a magic marker by the other fathers. They also appear to be meditating plaintively on their own future, seeing families caring for handicapped members even older than they are. . . .

At such times, I fix my gaze on these fathers and repeat to myself, "*Hell, no! Hell, no!* The road ahead may be pitch black, but let's brace ourselves and push on!" Were these fathers to see only my exterior, they would merely think that a girl who had been intently looking at them, a skinny girl with a small, round head, had quickly dropped her eyes the moment they had turned to look at her. But the reason I hear such voices calling out within me is because, in the same concert hall, I also notice despondent mothers who, like me, harbor the repelling forces of *Hell, no! Hell, no!*

The honest impression I get at such concerts these days is that time has passed. "Time has passed!" I think to myself. I guess I feel this way because I compare these performances with the ones I used to go to when Eeyore was in the secondary division at the special school for the handicapped. Whenever I accompanied Mother to the school, I felt that not only the students, but the teachers and guardians as well, were in good spirits. And the mothers, especially, were so unaffected: their unconstrained laughter always took me by pleasant surprise. But now I don't hear such laughter ring out in the Joining of Hearts Concerts now. Assuredly, each concert is quite festive with, on the performers' side for example, an elderly musician whistling out—his fingers between his lips—a double-octave, ear-piercing tune, while his daughter trills an Italian folk song, flailing the microphone in pop idol fashion. But during the intermission, which immediately follows this, the mothers keep their eyes fixed on their laps or something, while the fathers look around unnaturally with unsettled eyes.

That's why I feel good when a young person with a handicap sometimes makes a positive, aggressive response at a concert hall. In my heart that voice exclaims, *"Hell, yes! Hell, yes! The road ahead may be pitch black, but let's brace ourselves and push on!"*

My letter to Mother in California. . . . Weekly visitors, mail, and budget report aside, I'll just transcribe the part that pertains to my thoughts and feelings.

abandoned children of this planet

". . . Going to the welfare workshop, where he enjoys the company of his co-workers, and to Mr. Shigeto's music lessons seem to relieve Eeyore of the strain of not having Papa and Mama in Japan. As for his fits, he had two relatively minor ones last week.

"Remember when the whole family was here, he would occasionally become too dependent, and unless someone reminded him, he would forget to take his anticonvulsants? He takes them regularly on his own now—morning, noon, and night—so usually all I have to do every morning is look in the box to see if the medicines for the previous day have disappeared. I plan to take him to the hospital for a checkup when I go there for his medicines at the end of the month, so I have asked the welfare workshop to give him a day off then.

"O-chan's the sort of person who sets up a program for himself and then carries it out alone, so he systematically studies for his entrance exams at the desk in his room. During his breaks he listens to music through headphones at the dining table. I imagine he's working off his stress with this well-coordinated combination of study and music.

"Now about the condition of my stress. As you know, I often burden myself with anxiety, because I'm so clumsy in coping even with matters that, in the eyes of others, might be hilariously simple. I even feel that, in going to America, Mama, next to your worry about Eeyore's *physical* condition, your main concern has been about me sinking into *psychological* stress.

"But now we're stable. The worrywart that I am, though I'm maintaining my usual vigilance, in the event that beyond a higher level of stability might come an even higher level of instability. Please don't be too concerned about this point. Even if something were to come and hit my head with a clunk, it would certainly not be "a clunk from an unexpected blow."

a quiet life

I'm sure Eeyore and I would tide ourselves over pretty well. And though O-chan remains thoroughly reserved, we have his moral support, too."

Now about what happened the following week right after we went to the Shigetos, and Eeyore's music composition lesson started: Mr. Shigeto, who came out of the music room leaving Eeyore to himself, which he usually does not do, approached my side as I was reading a book and said, "Hope I'm not being too inquisitive, but can you answer one question for me?"

These words themselves petrified me. They had been uttered in a manner no different from the way he usually speaks, playfully unconcerned and aloof. But when I looked up, I saw on his face, and in his eyes, which were fixed squarely on the thick staff paper he held in his hands, the ebb and flow of so distressed an ire that a chill came over me. Frightened to the bottom of my heart, I waited for his next words.

Turning toward me a pair of bloodshot eyes that were filled with resentment and agony, he resumed speaking.

"Ma-chan, this is a piece Eeyore started working on immediately after K and Oyu-san left for California, and finished for today's lesson. While he was working on the details, I was thinking more about music theory, which isn't my forte . . . and because I often saw him calmly smiling right before my eyes, it didn't occur to me to think of what was being expressed in the composition in progress. Besides, I was looking forward to the pleasure of playing the piece straight through upon its completion.

"Eeyore made a clean copy of the entire score and showed it to me today, and I played it, only to discover that it's such a dreadfully sad piece! Why is this?"

Mr. Shigeto cut his words short and swallowed, whereupon the blotches on the flesh of his quivering throat appeared to have turned darker and more pronounced, giving the impression of an old man, an impression he usually does not project. My flinching ears heard his voice itself, an echo entreating me, *". . . a dreadfully sad piece. Why is this!"*

I finally took into my dully shaking hands the large sheet of paper that had been thrust before me, and I hesitated as I thought, 'What for? I don't read music.' Yet when I saw in the upper margin of the staff paper the title "Sutego"* in penciled letters, I thought I was able to understand the reason for the painful rage in Mr. Shigeto's voice.

"What," I asked, "is he doing in there now, all alone?"

"He's playing the newly completed piece, using the draft."

"Does he look sad?"

". . . No. Very cool, as usual . . . But Ma-chan, what on earth do you think he means by 'Sutego'?"

"I don't know. I didn't know until now that such a word existed in his mind. . . ."

"Does K have the slightest idea of what Eeyore's going through?" Mr. Shigeto and Father have been friends since before I was born, but the way he bitterly called him by name, without using any honorific, sounded like he was calling down an archenemy or something. "Oyu-san says K's in a 'pinch,' but does this allow her to leave the children to care for themselves? And Ma-chan, you had to go through that molester incident right after they left. You had a very terrifying experience. And now Eeyore's made this very sad piece that seems to wail, and the title he's given it, one he's thought up himself, is 'Sutego' of all things!"

Faint piano chords were coming from the other side of the soundproofed wall beyond the dark, narrow hallway to the

---

*"Abandoned Child."

right of the living room. The hall was further narrowed by bookcases and shelves along the walls, on top of which were stacked more books, one over another. And above them all were handicrafts, woven goods, and toys from Eastern Europe. Eeyore was playing his music just the way he composes it, not by tracing the melody horizontally, as it were, but by playing sound units the way he pencils them on the staff sheets, as though he were assembling building materials, one kind on top of another. Listening to this deliberate, pause-laden way of playing, it didn't sound to me like a "very sad piece that seems to wail," and so I was able to somewhat recover from my restlessness.

Moreover, Mr. Shigeto himself appeared to be regretting his words, which had rung as if he were upbraiding me. Then he continued, this time directing his rage inwardly at himself.

"I hear K's gone to California, with Oyu-san attending to him, in an effort to cope with his pinch," he said. "Oyu-san informed me of the circumstances, and I understand. From the time he was young, K's been more of the forbearing type. When his kind of person reaches a point where, either through action or some other means, he howls that it's dangerous to continue living like he does, then neither Oyu-san nor I could object to his taking emergency refuge. But if his action, which is basically self-centered, causes Eeyore to wonder whether he's become an abandoned child . . . I would be suspicious of the sort of power of observation he's exercised over Eeyore."

The atypical atmosphere had prompted Mrs. Shigeto to come out from the kitchen and listen to her husband, with her head drooping and the silver rim on her glasses mirroring a grayish black. For my part, I sensed a dire need to say something, anything, to lift their heavy hearts.

abandoned children of this planet

"I think there's an element of humor in his usage of an expression like 'abandoned child,'" I said. "It just occurred to me that once, when he was watching a monster film on TV, an infant stegosaur* appeared, and Father explained to him what the name meant.

"*Stegosaur!*" Mr. Shigeto exclaimed, his voice mixed with grief and laughter. ". . . But he *did* entitle it 'Sutego,' knowing very well what an abandoned child is!"

"Mr. Shigeto, why should you be so forward and emotional?" his wife asked, addressing her husband by attaching "Mister" to his family name, which gave me a glimpse into their life in Eastern Europe. "Ma-chan's got it the roughest, shouldering all responsibility for Eeyore, and you shouldn't add to her cares by bursting out like that."

"True," Mr. Shigeto reiterated, "very true."

"If Eeyore titled it 'Sutego,' doesn't this mean he's objectified his feelings through his music? And this very moment, too, he's playing it very calmly. Perhaps he may have a different understanding of 'abandoned child'—the theme itself—from what you, Mr. Shigeto, infer from it. . . . So let's have some tea, shall we, and try to calm down a bit."

With meat-colored streaks of rage remaining on his cheeks and neck, Mr. Shigeto let his head fall and sat at the table, in his usual chair. I helped Mrs. Shigeto carry the black tea and cookies she had made, following her instructions, which she gave with a dignity I hadn't noticed in her until then. Nevertheless, she too appeared to be grieving over "Sutego," Eeyore's composition. We had our tea, which normally Mrs. Shigeto serves me and Eeyore when his lesson is over, in dejection, huddled together as though the three of us were abandoned

Sutegozaurusu in Japanese, hence the play on *stego*saur and *sutego*.

children, and waited in this state until Eeyore came out after playing his newly completed piece to his heart's content.

After a while, because of his strong sense of responsibility, Mr. Shigeto took it upon himself to explain the backdrop of his emotional reaction. He elaborated on what he thought of Father and Mother leaving for California, and on the situation of their having done nothing—whatever their intentions might have been—about Eeyore feeling so forsaken that an expression such as "abandoned child" would enter his mind. I think he wanted to fill me in on things I didn't know very much about: his long friendship with, and personal understanding of, Father.

". . . It's from K himself that I first learned of this 'pinch' he's in. He never said anything more about it, though, and later I heard the details from Oyu-san. Its direct cause, she said, was probably that the novel he was writing wasn't going well, which means that the matter he's been contemplating as the core of his recent theme has entered a difficult stage. If the problem could see a solution in the form of a novel, K would be able to maintain a little distance from the problem itself, and then be able to cope with it. K's a writer who's shaped his life this way. Now, for someone like me, who can only brood when encumbered with a problem, the lengths to which K endeavors to invent a writer's lifestyle sometimes bore me, frankly.

"But looking at it the other way around, having trouble with a novel means to K that a certain period of his life—the whole time he spends structuring, writing, and then rewriting a novel—has come to a full stop. Perhaps it'll remain at a full stop, and he'll be deadlocked forever. K's the type who can't put aside a work he's having trouble writing. That's the way he writes. . . . But I understand the immediate cause of his 'pinch' this time was the lecture he gave, "The Prayers of a Faithless Man." So behind all this, in a way, is a hilariousness that's typical of K.

abandoned children of this planet

"I don't think the lecture was scheduled to be televised," I said. "An upperclassman in the French literature department when Father was going to college asked him to lecture at a women's university, and it just so happens that another former classmate of his, in the same department for that matter, videotaped it, and this got broadcast." Depressed as she was, Mrs. Shigeto faintly smiled when I said this. She probably thought that I had been trying to be fair to Father.

"Yes," Mr. Shigeto said, "and the fact that he hadn't intended it to be on TV was all the more reason he talked so candidly, and so all the deeper the dilemma he's fallen into.

"I watched the program, too. In it, he said that in his life with Eeyore, he had experienced moments in which, even for a faithless man like himself, he felt in his heart a movement, for which the only description was 'prayer.' In line with this, he talked of his own childhood. Now if everything he said in that lecture is true, then K's lived all his life—from about the time he was eleven or twelve—in fear of those who profess faith."

"Father puts his spirit of service to work and tries to make his lectures interesting, but I don't think he says anything untrue when he talks on important matters. Grandma in Shikoku, too, said it was after the wheat-flour incident that he started suffering from insomnia, and this was the onset of the insomnia that has since then frequently revisited him. Something Grandma told me, but which Father didn't broach in the lecture, occurred about the time he learned there was a Christian church in Matsuyama. I understand it was very mystifying, the way he became obsessed with the church. The clan is deeply connected with Buddhism, and it even has its own temple. But Grandma feared he would go to the Christian church by himself, and so she didn't give him any money to make such a visit possible. Then early one morning he left the house without telling anybody. He walked the long trail through the mountains, and at night, when he reached some place near the city, a policeman stopped him. After this, he stopped talking about *matters of the soul*, as though nothing had ever happened. I hear he's even talked about what happened as though it were something to laugh about, telling people that when the policeman stopped him, he, the child that he was then, pleaded with the officer, as a last resort, to call up the church for him, and that when the policeman did call, whoever answered the phone told him the boy should be sent straight back home, which put a total damper on his spirits."

"The nuance of the story I heard from K is a little different," Mr. Shigeto said. "He told me that the portals of churches even in rural Japan were like the gates of impenetrable castles, and the matter-of-fact way he had been denied admittance had come as a relief to him. He said it had assured him that in church there were men who dedicated their entire body and soul to their faith, and that these men were piously engaged in *matters of the soul*. He realized then that it was only natural for them to refuse him, for he was not yet able to abandon everything in order to devote himself to *matters of the soul*. And he was relieved. Evidently, ever since he had furtively read a magazine article on St. Francis of Assisi, at the water mill he spoke of in the lecture, the one deep in the forest where he said the family had their wheat ground, he got to believing that, in order to dedicate himself to *matters of the soul*, he needed to first abandon everything and experience religion. You know, don't you, that St. Francis himself founded three separate levels of monastic orders? But K was only a child then, and he got to thinking that, unless he completely gave up all worldly attachments, he couldn't do anything regarding *matters of the soul*. . . . He sometimes blurted out that everything you did would be flagrant hypocrisy—*mauvaise foi*, he said, as the French students back in our college days used to put it—if you tried to do anything concerning *matters of the soul* without having discarded all attachments to the mundane world, all earthly desires.

"Simplifying things, you could say that K's just added on years of survival without changing a bit, and after reaching his fifties he inadvertently ended up speaking his indiscreet thoughts on *matters of the soul*. So actually, some people with faith quite bluntly told him that they would sanction his faith at face value, no matter how hypocritical it was. Didn't this cause him to lose his cool? K knew he wasn't anywhere near *matters of the soul*. So he reflected upon himself and realized that, so long as Eeyore was by his side, he had a loophole through which he could easily get away with his hypocrisy—which may be exactly what he feared. And perhaps this is why he left for California, to detach himself from Eeyore: reason enough to leave Eeyore behind, however heartrending it would be for them both; and sufficient reason, at the same time, for Eeyore to feel abandoned."

"Eeyore has a mysteriously sensitive side to him, so that may be how he's perceived it. And perhaps because he couldn't express it in words, he let his music say it."

"Not perhaps, but undoubtedly. He's even put it very clearly in words: 'Sutego.' You can't pretend that you didn't see it, or that you didn't hear it."

"What exactly do you think Father's 'pinch' entails? From what you told me now, I wonder if he's going to end up . . ."

"Hanging from a branch of California live oak, one just right for hanging—spurred to the act by taking things too seriously, and everything compounded by the depression of encroaching old age . . . isn't this what Oyu-san is fearing?"

"Mr. Shigeto, I can understand you being upset out of worry for K-chan, and because of Eeyore's music," his wife said in admonition, imparting an even stronger expression around her eyes, which, instead of a smile, were lined with severe wrinkles. "But you're only intimidating Ma-chan with the things you're saying. If K-chan's in a 'pinch,' what you ought to do is explain to her how you think he could get back on his feet. Ranting like that won't get anybody anywhere. If you know K-chan so well that you can say he might hang himself and all that . . . you could do better by saying, for example, that he could use this opportunity to take up religion. . . ."

"I can't know about other people, really," Mr. Shigeto retorted. "The same obviously goes for my understanding of K," he parroted, while repeatedly blinking, and turning red with a flush that was different from before. ". . . Speaking of faith," he continued, "I think it would be harder for K to embrace a faith than to hang himself. For all these years, he's done his best to distance himself, as though with out-thrust arms, from people who have faith.

"I know he'd be offended if he heard me say he'd done his best. I think the question for him is, how is a faithless person to cope with life, staying on this side of the fence? This is where he believes he can find something upon which to establish a literary career. You know, don't you, how often he talks of Yeats? This goes way back, to when he was very young. You hear him mumbling this to himself from time to time, don't you? 'The intellect of man is forced to choose / Perfection of the life, or of the work, / And if it take the second must refuse / A heavenly mansion, raging in the dark.' *Raging in the dark:* that's what it is. But right after he entered the French department in Hongo, he got hung up on the heavenly mansion; he got the Christian paradise into his head, and so fervently sought for his place there that he even volunteered to do menial chores at a monastery. As I've said a number of times, his paradigm of faith is built upon his childhood experience of having imagined St. Francis of Assisi bidding him to devote himself to *matters of the soul*. This means that, unless he abandons everything, and possibly enters a monastery—one that's not too highly institutionalized—he'll never be able to arrive at a faith that gives him true peace of mind. But what he'll have to do then, more than anything else, is to abandon Eeyore! Eeyore's correct in sensing the anxieties of an abandoned child."

"Come, come, Mr. Shigeto. Ma-chan's already nonplussed, and she's all but crying. Is this what gives you pleasure? Making a poor, helpless girl like her cry?"

A redder flush appeared around Mr. Shigeto's blinking eyes and on the tip of his nose, which made him resemble a liquor-loving tailor or cobbler in a European fable—which, in fact, is what I thought about to stifle my tears.

"K is basically of a halfway character. The trouble is, on the more conscious level, he can't stand halfwayness. That's the kind of odd guy he is. By this I mean . . . he believes that he could never enter into a faith only halfway. But being halfway about it, he can't keep from contemplating what it means to pray. Worse yet, he's unscrupulous in talking about it. So in the end this 'pinch' of his is something he himself invited.

"Oyu-san told me that soon after the lecture was televised, K quite unexpectedly received a letter from a Catholic priest he'd held in high esteem. Coming from such a person, it must have been a very serious letter. The priest wrote that he deemed K already a member of the flock. This was a powerful punch for him. K had believed that he'd always been writing from the side of a man without faith, as though thrusting his arms toward the territory of people with faith. But if he'd already unwittingly crossed over to their side, as the priest wrote . . .

a quiet life

Don't you find this a fearful but intriguing summons? The problem, though, is that K himself is blind to the whereabouts of true faith. It's pathetic."

"Really, faith is something Father never talks to me about. He's never said anything to me about the church my university is affiliated with, neither in jest nor as a topic of serious discussion. He once attended a service at the cathedral there when an old friend of his, a literary critic, passed away, but he didn't say anything about the funeral mass when he came home. All he did was read, for several days, the many books he had bought at the bookstore next to the church."

"Mr. Shigeto," his wife put in, "is faith in general really important to K-chan? I never thought it mattered to him all that much. Compared with K-chan, I've always thought that you were in every way poorer at heart."

"Preposterous!" exclaimed Mr. Shigeto, as if to dispel his bewilderment. "But that reminds me of when we were at college. A class had been canceled, so to kill time, we sat by the water fountain in front of the dorm, and chatted as we gnawed at a dry loaf of bread. All of a sudden K blurted out that salvation or damnation of the soul was immaterial to him, that all that mattered to him was whether or not there was life after death. He said he didn't care if he went to heaven or hell, because neither could be more fearful than absolute nothingness; salvation and damnation were one and the same if the only thing out there was total nothingness. It was infantile logic, but it made sense. Anyway, in those days, this was what K kept thinking about.

"But then H, you remember him, don't you, Ma-chan, the guy who became editor after graduation but died of leukemia? H, the level-headed cosmopolitan, needled your father, saying, 'You've got it all wrong, K. What lies beyond us is not, I think, a choice of one or the other. Rather it's been arranged for us to choose one of three. Heaven and purgatory can be lumped together as one. Then you have hell. And the third choice is absolute nothingness. Now should you go to the third place—absolute nothingness—over heaven or hell, which fortunately already exist—well, then, you end up at a place that's tantamount to your not being born. This, too, should appall you.' When K heard this, he became so disheartened that I couldn't bear to look at him. . . ."

Then Eeyore came walking along the hallway from the music room. A somewhat unusual nervousness seemed to tighten his large-featured face. He showed Mr. Shigeto the sheet music he had brought with him, the whole page of which was full of erased and repenciled notes, and he waited for Mr. Shigeto's reaction, which is to say that he ignored both Mrs. Shigeto and me, even though I had primly greeted him. Taking a relaxed breath, the "Sutego" composer pointed to the array of notes—long, thin ones which Father says look like bean sprouts—toward the bottom of the page, and emphatically said, "This part wasn't very good. But I've already corrected it!"

Mr. Shigeto reread the part Eeyore had pointed at, likewise the parts that preceded and followed it, with an expression that was not that of a specialist on Eastern European literature, as when he turns his face to me, but one more typical of a musician. All the while, it seemed as though the common language of music was shuttling between Mr. Shigeto's head and Eeyore's, as Eeyore eagerly waited. The moment Mr. Shigeto acknowledged the validity of the changes Eeyore had made, Eeyore's face fully blossomed into a bright smile. And with the eraser and pencil he had brought in his pocket, he started erasing and rewriting some of the notes on the clean

copy he had given to Mr. Shigeto. I blankly watched the title
"Sutego" tremble, as if in fear, under the eraser's vigorous
movements. And then I blurted, "Eeyore, is that a sad piece?
Is it about the loneliness you feel? It's about an 'abandoned
child,' isn't it?"

"It's in D minor. Is it a sad piece? I wonder," he replied,
with eyes that told me his thoughts still remained on the score.
The pencil he had used to finish making his corrections now
rested on his ear. "I've only just now finished it."

"In time you're going to know very well, Eeyore, whether
it's a sad piece or not," Mrs. Shigeto said with a deep sigh,
squinting her heavy-lidded, thread-thin eyes. I think that in
our hearts Mr. Shigeto and I sighed, in unison, the same deep
sigh she sighed.

When October came, Eeyore and I flew to Father's birthplace
in Shikoku because of a bereavement in the family. Great-
uncle—that's what we called Father's elder brother, using the
title differently from the way it's defined in dictionaries—had
passed away. I was told that cancer had spread from his liver
to his lungs, and even to his brain. And so we were prompted
to pay our condolences on behalf of our parents. Aunt Fusa
sounded calm when she called to inform us of Great-uncle's
passing, probably because he had been in the hospital a long
time, and also because she didn't wish to cause me alarm.

Aunt Fusa asked for the phone number of our parents' quarters in California, and said she would discuss with Father what
we, who were looking after the house in their absence, should
do, and then call back. She added that she would be the information center, for if I also called Mother, not only would this be
redundant, but it might cause some confusion of information,

which would require another overseas call, and this would be uneconomical. Although I didn't have direct, specific memories of Great-uncle, I remembered Aunt Fusa to be a woman who occasionally said a few humorous things, and who could exercise practicality, as she did in the present situation. Other than this, I remembered her as being basically a quiet, reserved person. She was quite different from Father, though they were brother and sister. A half hour later, she called back to tell me she had been able to reach Father at his quarters, for it was early morning here, and the time difference was just right.

The content of Aunt Fusa's second call was that K-chan was shocked, but with Oyu-san with him, he was all right. When he visited Great-uncle in the hospital before leaving for the States, the doctor informed him that his brother's condition was serious, that the cancer had metastasized, which was something everyone in the family already knew. Perhaps the cowardly K-chan had gone to California because he feared he would have to witness the scene of Great-uncle painfully dying of cancer. This was most likely the reason he left. There may have been others, of course, but he became utterly depressed after visiting Great-uncle.

They had talked, she continued, of the possibility of K-chan coming back for the funeral. He said he would, but then they decided that he should remain in California. They would, however, like me to come with Eeyore and attend the funeral ceremony. She told me how much we should bring as a monetary offering to the departed soul. If we came on that day's flight, someone would be there to pick us up at the airport, and we could spend the night at the house in the valley. She wanted me to bring Eeyore along because Grandma was grieving, much more than K-chan, and his coming there would cheer her up a little.

a quiet life

When we arrived at Matsuyama Airport and came out of the boxlike passageway that joined the plane to the airport building, the landscape beyond the window met us with a brightness I thought I hadn't seen in a long, long time. Squinting, and smiling a smile induced by the sun, Eeyore let out a "Hoh!" and kept looking into the light outside. As I stood at the narrow baggage-claim counter, I saw Aunt Fusa—she looked like she had added on a few years—waving at us from beyond the glass partition. Beside her stood a giant of a man, who looked like a fresh sumo recruit. I assumed he must have been Shu-chan, who had visited us once, when he came to Tokyo on his high school excursion. When our baggage came out on the conveyor belt, Eeyore, like another sumo wrestler, vigorously lifted it, taking one deep breath and exclaiming "Yoishoh!" and then carried it for me. Aunt Fusa, who had circled around to the exit and greeted us there, looked sad and serious with the shadow of Great-uncle's death on her face, but the lines around her pale eyes were those of a smile. After obligingly taking the suitcase from Eeyore, the big man, who indeed was Shu-chan, started walking ahead of us to the parking lot. He made the suitcase look like a toy box, carrying it with his arms thrust out at an angle that maintained space between his torso and the case.

"He teaches at a middle school," Aunt Fusa said, as she walked along next to Eeyore and me, exiting the building into the truly dazzling light, "but he's become much more sober, to the point that he's even stifling." The way she quietly said this suggested to me the presence of a nostalgic levity beneath the level to which her feelings had sunk.

"Oh," I replied, politely.

I was in middle school when Shu-chan came to Tokyo on his high school excursion, and in those days, I understood sober to be a generic term referring to suave-looking youngsters. So

I said to Mother, "If anybody is sober, it's Shu-chan!" Father heard me and got a big kick out of it, in the inconsiderate manner so typical of him, and called Aunt Fusa to tell her what I had said. This was what had transpired in connection with *sober*.

Once out of the city area, the well-paved but upward-climbing road continued, on and on. It appeared to wedge its way into a chain of mountains, and the autumn-tinted, broad-leaved trees on the slopes beyond the now-parched rice paddies, and even the forests of cedar and cypress higher above them, glowed calm and bright in the noonday sun. It was through such rural, festive scenery that we sped on, in a small two-door car, with Shu-chan and Eeyore in front, their seatbelts tightly fastened, and Aunt Fusa and me in the back. Treating me the way she would a full-fledged adult, Aunt Fusa told me about how Great-uncle had taken ill, about the pain he had suffered and his last moments. Hefty as both of them are, Shu-chan and Eeyore together looked like a towering wall before us, yet they, too, lent a polite and reverential ear.

What I found most impressive with what Aunt Fusa told me, of course, was the part that pertained to Father. And I feel that Aunt Fusa herself spoke to me especially from that angle. She said that by the time Father had gone to see Great-uncle in the hospital, on the pretext that he was making a courtesy call before leaving for California, Great-uncle had already been taking morphine shots, which made him delirious and drowsy even during the day. Father entered Great-uncle's sickroom, but because all he did was sit deep in the low sofa beside the bed in utter dejection, Aunt Fusa said to Great-uncle, "K-chan's come to see you," to which Great-uncle's knee, the one he had drawn up under the blanket, quivered as if in frightful surprise.

Later, according to Aunt Fusa, Great-uncle let his bare toes touch the floor, saying that his leg was heavy, which in turn made Father's whole body quiver, for he saw where the middle toe should have been on Great-uncle's right foot. Didn't K-chan, who is always shocked when he sees such mutilation of a family member's body, feel rankly enervated just thinking of Big Brother suffering the last stages of terminal cancer and dying? And so did he not, after learning from the doctor about how long Big Brother had left to live, choose to turn tail and fly to California? ". . . I'm not the only one guessing as much," she said. "Grandma feels the same way, and she understands these things."

"It seems that Father told Mother about Great-uncle's toe. He was always thinking of Great-uncle. He felt indebted to him for putting him through college, while Great-uncle himself lived in the forest doing the manual labor that had cost him his toe. The lost toe was a great shock to Father."

"I feel so sorry for K-chan and Big Brother," Aunt Fusa said, her voice sounding angry. When she started talking of how Great-uncle had breathed his last, Eeyore restlessly moved his upper body, secured with the belt of the passenger seat, and clasped his hands in prayer. This startled Aunt Fusa.

"Eeyore does that, and bows in deference, whenever he sees a familiar name in the obituaries," I explained. "When a musician or a sumo stable master dies, for instance." To this Eeyore firmly nodded.

". . . Oh? You've returned to calling him Eeyore again, Ma-chan. Grandma just loves that name. How nice. She'll be relieved to know she can freely call him Eeyore again."

Indeed, in our family, the vicissitudes the name Eeyore has undergone is a story in itself. After enrolling in the secondary division of the special school for the handicapped, Eeyore came home one day after a week of dorm life and training, and when Father called him Eeyore, his usual nickname, he didn't answer. This threw Father into such a dither that we dared not utter a word. After a while, O-chan, who sensed Eeyore's aspiration for independence, discovered that he wished us to use his real name. So we all started calling him Hikari-san, and Grandma followed suit, in her letters and on the phone. But in time we started calling him Eeyore again, and he appears to suffer no discomfort over this. There was a time when Mother became concerned about this, more than ever before, and worried if his frequent fits of epilepsy weren't causing him mental regression. For one fit of epilepsy, she said, is believed to destroy on the order of several hundred thousand brain cells. . . .

Without touching on the part about the effect of epileptic fits on brain cells, for Eeyore was in the front seat listening, I briefed Aunt Fusa on what had made us stop calling him Eeyore for a while, and how we came to use this name again. Aunt Fusa, apparently immersed in quiet thought, said: "I think Eeyore's desire for independence was most prominent when he was in secondary school. Because Shu was the same. But both now possess a most admirable calmness that goes with their age."

It struck me that Aunt Fusa had been very rapidly working her head over all manner of things, even the mental regression that Mother worried about, and that she was also encouraging me. However, she fell silent immediately after she said this, and didn't say anything for quite some time, apparently a character trait she shared with Father.

We drove through a tunnel that had been bored near the top of a big pass, and wound down a tortuous drive into a resplendent ravine matted with the golden and crimson foliage of autumn. When we came out on the flat, wide topography that formed the basin of a town, Aunt Fusa explained that the place had served as a distribution base for all outgoing produce and products from the entire region, and also for the culture that came into the area. We drove on farther, along a sparkling shallow river and into the forest where only a few houses lined the narrow road. And in the distance, on the slope on the other side of the river, we saw the few large and small houses of the village where Father was raised.

In front of Father's childhood home were rows of leafy bamboo trees, floral wreaths to be used at the funeral ceremony, and equipment for votive lanterns. The sight of men in black suits that didn't seem to fit their bodies, busily going about their work, was imposing. Aunt Fusa told Shu-chan to pass them. Sensitive to anything that has to do with death, Eeyore very reverentially clasped his hands toward the funeral paraphernalia as we passed by. We drove upstream for a while, then went back along the levee road. Soon Eeyore and I were ushered into Grandma's detached room through the backyard, where some kiwis hung from a tree. Faint, suppressed voices, like those of spies whispering battle strategy, drifted in from the main house, together with the presence of people moving around nearby.

Grandma was changing into her mourning kimono, but she was standing motionless, in front of the dresser. An age-old, long undergarment, which from its coloration looked like silk, hung from her narrow shoulders. I had stopped at the entrance to the room, in the hallway, and it was in a mirror that I first saw Grandma's small, gray, paperlike face. She was gazing into space with her dark, long-slitted eyes—like Father's—which looked to be all iris, as if blackish water had puddled in them. . . . Eeyore and I stood rooted there in the hallway, and Aunt Fusa didn't goad us on. Sensing our presence, however, Grandma made brisk movements from the seemingly paralyzed posture in which she'd been standing. And as soon as she had donned her black kimono, she straightened the garment around her breasts and turned toward us.

"Welcome," she said, "and thank you for traveling from so far away to come here. . . ."

"You can call him Eeyore," Aunt Fusa said the moment Grandma's words trailed off. "I hear it's back to what it was before."

"Well, Eeyore-san," Grandma resumed, "how nice of you to come. Great-uncle's funeral ceremony is starting soon. Would you please attend it? And Ma-chan, forgive us, please, for the trouble we're causing you. And thank you for coming!"

"I'll have Ma-chan and Eeyore go to the main house," Aunt Fusa said, "and pay their condolences there while you tie your obi, Grandma. . . . Now don't spend so much time putting on your mourning kimono, with the movements of an astronaut swimming in space."

"How true," Grandma replied. "I've been taking too much time, haven't I? . . . Ma-chan and Eeyore-san, you don't have to go up to Great-uncle's coffin when they ask you to! There's an ingenious device, a small window on it, through which you can see him, but I don't think young people need to see the face of the deceased," she said, as though to send us off, standing there with her hands pressed against the pit of her stomach.

I extended my sympathy to Great-uncle's wife and eldest son, and Eeyore reverentially placed the monetary condolence on the altar. Since Aunt Fusa had informed the mourners of Grandma's wish that we not go up to the casket, all we did was bow in the enclosure of white chrysanthemums, before the altar that was set up in the second floor parlor. By the time we returned to the detached room, Grandma was neatly clad in her mourning livery. Her small, entirely gray head rested comfortably on her neck as she sat on the tatami, proper and straight, the epitome of dignity. . . .

a quiet life

Now what words of condolence could I offer this woman who, in her late eighties, had lost a son? I could only hang my head. I depended on Eeyore, who was seated before Grandma, for though the expression on his face was stiff, he was natural, and was answering her questions about the welfare workshop, and about how he was faring with his music composition.

Soon Aunt Fusa started telling Grandma in detail about what I had told her in the car on the way there, about the 'fanatic,' the molester, who kept bringing us bottles of water. While I thought the topic inappropriate for a funeral wake, I felt all the more tense after realizing it was nobody's fault but mine that such a conversation had started. Grandma listened intently to Aunt Fusa's every word, wearing an expression suffused with such force that her eyelids formed a triangle, and a pink flush that made her look somewhat healthier appeared on her ashen countenance.

"Ma-chan," Grandma said, "you were smart to stand on your bicycle and keep watch over the villain before you chased him. The taller one is, the more imposing!"

"Don't tell us we're no different from bears that fight over territory," Aunt Fusa chided Grandma, summarily rejecting her logic. Eeyore still looked serious as he turned his eyes toward me, but those eyes gave a glimpse of his reaction to finding *bears* a humorous word.

The funeral ceremony commenced at three o'clock, although it's customary in the village to have them much earlier in the day. Apparently, they had arranged for it to start later, to accommodate the time of our incoming flight. The procession started in front of Father's home and followed a path downstream to Bodhi Temple. Eeyore and I saw the mourners off, flanking Grandma, who held a walking stick in her left hand. At the head of the procession was Great-uncle's picture, then his mortuary tablet, and following this, in single file, were bamboo poles with baskets hanging from them, and tall floral wreaths, which were trailed by a long line of strangely shaped paper banners. On went the procession, between the villagers, some dressed in black, some in their everyday attire, who were standing under the eaves of the houses along both sides of the road to pay their last respects to the deceased. A bright late-autumn shower crossed over from the mountainside facing the river to the south-facing side, which was dark with the colors of evergreens. Against this backdrop, the whole panorama of the procession presented a strange sight. The way paper flowers were poured from the baskets on the bamboo poles, each time the mourners crowding in on the weighty coffin circled around it, resembled funerals among indigenous peoples in remote areas of Polynesia. It also impressed me as being gentle and nostalgic. Each time small red, blue, and yellow paper flowers flew from the baskets on the bamboo poles, Grandma raised her head on her emaciated neck, and seemed to strain her eyes to see beneath her triangular eyelids.

When the tail end of the procession started off, Grandma, Eeyore, and I retired to the cottage, where we rested for a while, and then headed for the temple, again in Shu-chan's car. Because Grandma can't walk far, Shu-chan took a side road, and we got off at a fork where the precincts of Bodhi Temple and its graveyard meet a woodland trail that climbs into the forest. We entered the temple from its backyard path and found that the funeral services were just about to commence. The monk conducting the funeral and the other monks in attendance were making their entrance into the main sanctuary, while a corpulent undertaker from the basin town, the distribution base, shouted from the housetops to the attending mourners, as though he were giving orders, military fashion—like in an old movie—to sit up straight and correct. Grandma, who sat between me and Eeyore in the middle of the section allocated for surviving members of the family and relatives, stretched her back and began waving for the chief monk to come over. Apparently she had something to say to him. The monk halted in the midst of his procession and sent a young monk to see what she wanted.

The import of what Grandma conveyed was: "Could you please ask that man who's trying to preside over the funeral service to leave?" The chief monk nodded when his disciple returned and repeated Grandma's message, which he in turn relayed to the undertaker. There were no more shouted commands after this, and the ceremony progressed in a natural manner. After the service, as I left the sanctuary and stepped down into the garden, I noticed, in the corner of the wet veranda, the undertaker in his black mourning suit, vest, and bow tie, sitting there hugging his knees, looking at the clintonia leaves on which the rain was spattering.

Great-uncle's eldest son made a brief speech of thanks to the mourners who stood in the garden before the sanctuary. Grandma deemed this to be the end of it all. While we waited for Great-uncle's body to be placed in the hearse and then taken to the crematory upstream, Grandma returned to the antechamber of the sanctuary and talked with the chief monk, who seemed to be an old friend of hers. Watching this, Aunt Fusa remarked, "She's evading her responsibilities. She doesn't like to be greeted by her acquaintances from far away." Soon afterwards, Shu-chan, who looked like the lumpy figure in those Michelin ads, in that his mourning suit was much too small for him, came to tell us that Grandma had left from the rear entrance and was waiting for us at the place where he had dropped us off earlier.

So we went back up the pretty little path lined with small shrubs of various kinds sparkling in their colorful leaves of autumn, and found Grandma seated in the back of the car, pushing the passenger seat forward to help Eeyore get in and sit beside her. On the way to the temple, Grandma, Aunt Fusa, and I had shared the backseat, and though we're all thin, and on the small side, we did feel cramped. But on the way back, Grandma seemed bent on monopolizing the backseat with Eeyore, for as soon as he entered, she pulled the front seat back again.

"I guess you want Eeyore to see the forest, is that it, Grandma?" Aunt Fusa asked, sprinkling the postfuneral purifying salt on the two in the car, and on the three of us, including herself, outside. "If what you've got in mind is a forced march all the way up to the higher places, then three in the rear would indeed be backbreaking. Ma-chan, why don't you sit up front, and I'll do the driving. Shu, you run home on those legs of yours you're so proud of, and help put things back in order there."

We drove down the woodland path, crossed the bridge over the village river, and headed for the road that wound around the mountain beyond. I looked back as we turned the sharp corner at the end of the bridge, and caught sight of Shu-chan, looking exactly like the Michelin man, running firmly and "soberly" down the path along the cliff, rock-bare now that the trees had shed their leaves.

The ever-ascending drive to the top of the mountainside we were headed for was beguilingly tortuous. It's a family joke that the very first time Father took us to his village, I asked O-chan, my intellectual mentor ever since I was small, "Did mammoths still roam this place when Papa was a child?" I don't remember asking this question, but the long stretch of the road up to and down from Father's home before the tunnel was built is vividly etched in my memory. Still, I actually felt that the climb from the road along the river up to the hamlet of the "country"—to put it in the language of the village map—was an even longer journey.

a quiet life

The scenery we glided through was breathtaking beyond measure. After passing through the basin town, I became aware that, on the slopes of the hills on both sides of the road leading to Father's village in the hollow, there were parcels of land where autumn's orange foliage was tinctured with sparkling red. As we climbed farther up into the higher regions of the "country," I realized that the colors were from persimmon patches. Patches, not orchards, is the word. Originally they were farmland, cleared during the postwar years for growing wheat, in the days of food shortages. Grandma, who had once been the proprietor of a "mountain-produce wholesale store," explained to me that after the wheat came chestnut trees, and then the switch to persimmons.

After a while, the road we were driving on was enveloped by a bright crimson-orange: sparkling red-ocher over us, below us, to our right, and to our left. And we got into more of this as we navigated upward. Whenever we came to relatively level topography, we saw stately houses standing on top of firm, solid stone masonry, roofed in part with thatch, in part with tile, unlike the roofing of the houses in the hollow. Such decorous houses lined the road at intervals, and they continued to appear with a certain consistency of style. Eventually, Aunt Fusa stopped the car on a spur from which unrolled a panoramic view. On one side lay a wide, deep-cut valley that sloped down like an enormous earthenware mortar. Beyond the valley, at eye level, across the deep, wide gully, stretched an overlapping range of quiet, somber blue mountains.

"Over there is the Shikoku Range," Aunt Fusa said. "I understand our ancestors finally found refuge from their pursuers in the depths of this forest after trudging over the many trails that meander between those ridges. It's a wonder how, despite all the difficulties, they still dreamed of establishing a new settlement. It's pitiful," she sighed, her eyes traveling over the scenery. Eeyore was helping Grandma out of the car.

"I thought the same thing," Grandma rejoined, "while standing on this high ground, when they wheeled me here on our cart for me to buy chestnuts for the store. But many years have passed since then, and looking at the village in the hollow now, I can see this place is spacious enough—big as it already is—to sustain a sizable community. In any case, just look at those slopes. There're so many of them I don't think human feet could ever walk their every nook and cranny. The place is truly vast! And it's because the place is so vast that a legend such as 'The Marvels of the Forest' has remained in the hearts of the people for so long. But Eeyore-san, you're the only one who's composed music about the legend. . . . I listened to the cassette tape you sent me, right here on this spur. Your music really made me think of 'The Marvels of the Forest.' By the way, Eeyore-san, what's your most recent composition?"

"'Sutego' is its title," Eeyore emphatically replied.

I wasn't the only one startled. Grandma and Aunt Fusa stood there in fearful silence with their bodies and faces petrified in the direction they were looking. Seeing them in that state, I wondered to myself why two women whose ages were so different—granted they were mother and daughter—could react in so much the same way. Then endearing thoughts of Mother far away in California struck my heart. So strong was the emotion that I wanted to cry out, "Help me, too, Mother! Help me with my 'pinch.'" But Eeyore, the source of the ripples in my heart, had nonchalantly walked over to the side of the road, beyond which, a step lower, lay a patch of common persimmon trees pruned short for picking. Holding his face close to a red-and-yellow-studded leaf, he was smelling the sparkling beads the passing rain had caused to form on it. . . .

a quiet life

"If you go so close to the persimmons, Eeyore, they might think you'll pick and eat a few," I exclaimed. The words my mouth uttered were different from those that had welled up from the depths of my heart.

"Nobody's going to think that," Grandma said, recovering her smile. "If this were ten, fifteen years ago, the farmers would have built wire fences around these fields. But everything has changed now. You saw those piles of ripe persimmons in front of every farmer's house, didn't you? They're the ones that were culled as too ripe to ship. With all these persimmons, the children are indifferent toward even those that are just waiting to be picked and eaten. . . . The things children do change at a frightening pace, don't they, Ma-chan? When we were children, we wore straw sandals, had one unlined kimono to wear, and one red, stringy band of cloth for an obi. We used to build a fire on the bare ground with dried branches to bake sweet potatoes, strip down to the waist and catch fish in the river, and scoop them out with a small bamboo basket. You've seen books, haven't you . . . like *Premodern Children's Customs* and *Children's Festivals*? The illustrations in them show exactly the things we used to do."

"You're premodern, Grandma," Aunt Fusa said. "We've already leapt the premodern and are modern. Eeyore and the others are stepping into the future."

"Well, then," Grandma observed, "shall the premodern and future have a relaxed conversation? Eeyore-san, will you tell me about your music composition?"

"Very well," Eeyore replied. Immediately showing interest, he raised his body, which was stooped over the foliage, and returned to where Grandma was.

"Then let us, the contemporary pair, go and talk a little farther up," Aunt Fusa said. "There could very well be an unexpected concurrence of minds if the modern age and the future converse."

As I had suspected, what Aunt Fusa wanted to personally ask me about—as two contemporaries—was "Sutego." She discussed this in the practical manner that was so typical of her. She matter-of-factly told me that if my parents' long-term stay at an American university was making Eeyore feel abandoned, I should call and ask them to come back immediately. What need was there for K-chan, who wrote in Japanese, to be a writer-in-residence in America, and put a burden on that country at a time when the value of the dollar was so low? He claimed that communication with his fellow professors was important, but how much could he accomplish in an English that he confuses with French? K-chan himself, she said, quite honestly admitted this when she last talked to him on the phone.

I didn't think I could tell her about Father's "pinch." I only told her that, although Eeyore did in fact compose a piece he had titled "Sutego," he didn't appear to be suffering the emotions of an abandoned child while working on it. And when it was completed, he was eager about the chords in the final part, and seemed more concerned about the technical results than about its theme.

Because Aunt Fusa had parked the car on one of the topographical overlooks of the delicately undulating mountainside, we could see, after climbing a little farther up, the whole valley below our eyes like the bottom of an earthenware mortar. Upstream the river was as tortuous as the road, and its water sparkled brightly at every short bend. Upriver some distance was a thickly wooded hill of tall, straight cypress trees that protruded like an appendage of the forest, and there a thick congregation of age-old cedars rose fiercely high above the cypresses. Among those trees, quite out of character with the forest, stood a boxlike, concrete structure with a tall chimney. Plumes of white smoke suddenly rose from the chimney with force. Aunt Fusa gazed down on this smoke with a stern expression, and appeared to be immersed in thought.

Alone, I kept looking up at the sky, blue as ever without a trace of the late-autumn shower it had just rained down on us. Confronting the sun, I sneezed: a blessing in disguise, for it unfettered Aunt Fusa from the thoughts that bound her, of Eeyore's "Sutego" or of Great-uncle being burned at the crematory, though most likely a mixture of the two.

"So the sun makes you sneeze, too, Ma-chan!" she said, vigorously raising her head and turning it toward me. "When K-chan was in middle school, he once read a magazine article about that. So he thought of an experiment to see if there was actually any relationship between the sun and sneezing. With only a limited number of subjects, he had me look at the sun every morning, which was no easy task for me. In those days, K-chan was a science nut, just like O-chan."

Aunt Fusa squinted her eyes and gazed at the sun in the western sky, and then sneezed a cute sneeze. We continued to laugh for a while. I then decided to ask her something.

"I guess this happened when Father was even younger," I began. "I heard that after he read about St. Francis, at the water mill where he took some wheat to have it ground, he seriously worried about whether he should immediately begin doing something concerning *matters of the soul*."

"That's right. It's a true story," Aunt Fusa said. "You see down there where the river forks out into two streams, one shining, the other shaded? The water mill is quite a distance up that narrow, darker one, and K-chan came back tightly clutching the bag of flour to his chest, and his face was all white. Fearing that a neighborhood St. Francis of Assisi might appear out of the shade of a nearby tree and lure him to engage in matters of the soul, he began to shed tears, and his eyes looked like those of a raccoon dog. . . .

"From what Father said in the lecture, I understand that you told him he looked like a white monkey. . . ."

"He's embellished his memory a bit because this concerns him personally. A raw-boned raccoon dog, a runty raccoon dog: that's what he looked like. . . . But I expect he's lived his life ever since in fear of the day he would have to abandon everything in order to dedicate himself to *matters of the soul*. At least that's the kind of person he was while he lived with us, until he graduated from high school. He used to get so depressed when his friends invited him to go with them to study the Bible in English. . . .

"Big Brother was also very much concerned about this. He worried whether K-chan would join some religious organization in Tokyo, though he didn't mind political parties. And once he lamented that if this ever happened it would spell the end of K-chan's future, in a social sense. Come to think of it, though, both Big Brother and K-chan were pitiful young men who were constantly hounded by *matters of the soul*. But one of them has already turned into white smoke, without doing anything about *matters of the soul*. . . .

"In connection with this, 'The Marvels of the Forest,' the legend Grandma spoke of when she was talking about Eeyore's composition, is a story Grandma's mother once related to K-chan. Or perhaps I should say that K-chan unearthed the strange legend with his power. The science-minded child that he was in those days, he tried interpreting it all sorts of ways. He once even said that 'The Marvels of the Forest' may have been delivered to Earth by a rocket from either the solar system or from the universe beyond it. Anyway, he said that civilization may have started on this planet with this as its genesis. I've always been a simple-minded girl, and so I imagined a shoal of children from some faraway star, packed like sardines in the 'Marvels of the Forest' rocket, being abandoned here on Earth. And I used to get so lonely. . . .

"When you think of it, though, don't you feel that Eeyore and I share a similar vocabulary of imagination somewhere? And K-chan's probably behind it all. I felt really lonely, thinking about the 'Marvels of the Forest' rocket, probably because he had said something to the effect that we were interplanetary abandoned children. I wouldn't be surprised if he's directed remarks of a similar vein at Eeyore. And then having done something so careless, he himself leaves for California with Oyu-san! It may surprise some people, but that's the kind of person he is."

Grandma and Eeyore had been gently leaning their backs against the stone wall that retained the persimmon patch above them on the upper side of the road. Then Grandma briskly pulled her small shoulders away from the wall. She raised her right hand, in which she again held her cane, and waved at us. Until then, I had thought that both Grandma and Eeyore had been looking in silence at the forest, the sunlight and its reflections on the red-orange foliage of the persimmon trees. But evidently Grandma had, all the while, been very patiently conversing with Eeyore. Half tripping, we ran to her, and heard her voice emphatically ring out.

"The title of 'Sutego' in full," she called out, "is 'Rescuing a Sutego.' Eeyore-san and his co-workers at the welfare workshop clean the park every Tuesday, don't they? He's told me that some of his co-workers once found an abandoned baby there and saved it. Eeyore-san has set his heart on saving such a baby if ever he finds one while he's on duty. That's what he had on his mind while composing his music, and that's why the piece was titled 'Rescuing a Sutego.'"

abandoned children of this planet

"Ah, so that's what it was, Eeyore!" I exclaimed. "Yes, I remember that occasion, when they saved a baby while park cleaning. I should have remembered it as soon as I heard the title . . . but it was so long ago. So that's what it was all about, Eeyore. So it's all right for the melody to be sad. After all, it's about rescuing a *sutego*!" I said, savoring a sensation of quiet happiness.

"Oh, so that's what it was!" Aunt Fusa repeated. Her way of understanding the situation was the same as mine, but in her own characteristic manner, she crowned this understanding with a conclusion. "If we think of all the people on this planet as being abandoned children, then Eeyore's composition expresses something very grand in scale!"

the guide
(stalker)

I saw Tarkovsky's *Stalker*, a movie my younger brother O-chan videotaped for me from a late-night TV broadcast. Eeyore, for a change, watched it with me all the way to the end because its music was interesting. It was a kind my ears weren't used to hearing, though, and to me it sounded Indian. As the movie neared the end, there was a scene in which a mysterious child used the power of her eyes to move three glasses of different sizes. You could also hear the rumble of a train and see the effects of its tremor. While the screen still showed the child's face, Eeyore, who was lying at my feet, flat on the carpet, as usual, raised his body and heaved a sighlike "Hoh!?" In the earlier half of the scene, a dog had become frightened when it sensed the eerie strength—let me call it this for the moment—of the child's eyes, and perhaps Eeyore had reacted to its whining, for more than anything he hates dogs that yelp. Soon after this, when the "Ode to Joy" from Beethoven's Ninth resounded from the sound track, Eeyore

straightened his back and began conducting it, in all seriousness, and with great vigor too.

The film was a good three hours long, and it left me exhausted, so preparation for dinner turned out to be simpler than
what I had planned. O-chan and I sat at the table, where the
dining itself was over very quickly, and talked about the movie,
with my role in the discussion being basically that of a listener.
The night before, despite his preparations for college entrance
exams, O-chan had gone downstairs now and then until the
movie was over, to check if the videotaping was going all right.
And every time he did so, he spared some time to watch parts
of it. He couldn't do much about the commercials, but figuring I wouldn't like it, he did erase the commentary—"It ran a
good five minutes"—by the somewhat heavy, energetic movie
critic I had once seen costumed as an American police officer
in a weekly magazine photograph. In a way, though, I would
have liked to listen to what a person of his kind had to say,
comments by someone who appears to have very little to do
with the general atmosphere of *Stalker*.

To summarize, I believe this is what O-chan said at dinner. I can't in all places reproduce his exact words because I
often became distracted, when my thoughts wandered to other
things. In any case, this is how he began. "I hardly ever watch
movies, and I wasn't watching *Stalker* very closely either, but
it set me thinking about something. . . . What did you think of
it, Ma-chan?"

"I don't think I have what it takes to make an overall comment," I replied. "But in the grassland scene, for example, you
have these people huddled together? With a host of other props
placed unobtrusively at some distance from them? And this
scene goes on and on. With scenes like this, I feel like I'm looking at a stage performance where you can watch each actor or

actress any way you like. These scenes are good for people like me who don't think very quickly."

O-chan *sort of*—to use his pet expression—lent a thoughtful ear to what I said, and then he made this comment: "It seems to me Tarkovsky portrayed a village that had instantly perished when a huge meteor or something fell on it. You could even see it as a village like Chernobyl after a nuclear reactor accident. Of course, with all its radioactivity, you'd be in a sorry plight if somebody took you there now, but I liked the way the guide led his clients, how he zigzagged forward, while hurling into the fields ahead those nuts with the ribbons tied to them. It brought back fond memories of the exploration game we played in Kita-Karuizawa when we were kids, when we followed our own rules, never doubting them, always believing them to be serious promises. Come to think of it, I've gotten old. . . .

"And I also liked the scene where the guide, who is physically and mentally much stronger than the professor and writer he escorts to the Zone, becomes the most exhausted, and a number of times he falls flat on the bare ground and lies there gasping in agony. It reminded me of the orienteering meets I took part in when I was in high school. While running around, I'd slip on some grass and fall, and as though it'd been my good fortune to be there, I'd lie there and exaggerate my fatigue, while clinging, as it were, to the bare ground. I'd be doing this for myself, while nobody was watching, and I would feel I was getting a better grasp of how the earth and I related to each other, and even of my own material body.

"I can't comment on the movie with the kind of formula where one says, 'On the whole, isn't Tarkovsky trying to say something like this?' This, however, is *sort of* what I thought. The 'end of the world' will come. It won't come today or tomorrow. Most likely, it won't come in our time. But it will come creeping along, slowly, as if it didn't want to. And we'll go on living, as if we didn't want to, because all we can do is wait in fearful uncertainty. Now if things were really like this, wouldn't it be natural for us to want to snatch a preview of this 'end of the world' that's so slow in coming? This, after all, is *sort of* what I think the job of an artist is."

Though I thought that my younger brother was truly smarter than me, I sometimes found myself listening only vacantly, for one of the earlier scenes, the one showing the guide's wife in agony, kept running through my mind. The scene had stunned me, for although the guide's wife appeared to be a married woman suffering pangs of lust, as in those "adult movies" you inadvertently see previewed in theaters, she was actually suffering from *matters of the soul*. After all, when the prideful O-chan slips and falls on the grass in his orienteering meets, it's not just physical fatigue that causes him to hug the bare ground, is it?

The guide's wife is a beautiful woman who conceals a dark passion within. Her whole figure, too, is beautiful when, for instance, she endures her suffering by falling and writhing on the floor, as if she were having a fit. Allow O-chan to analyze my unwitting association of this woman with an "adult movie" actress, and he would probably say it's because she possesses a breathtaking carnal beauty. Though I couldn't imagine myself ever having such a beautiful body, I was, in fact, filled more with respect for her than with envy. Moreover, the words this beautiful woman spoke so despairingly to her husband, who had but to herd his charges to a dangerous Zone, captivated me. "Our marriage was a mistake," she says, "and that's why an 'accursed child' was born to us."

The guide, who has managed to return from the Zone safely, and is exhausted, is also in despair, for he has learned that his clients hadn't wished for their souls' happiness, which was to be given them in the Room in the center of the Zone. All in all, he's a serious man—serious to the point of being almost piti-ful—who believes the "zone" could put degenerate mortals back on their feet. After the guide's wife takes him to bed and lulls him to sleep, she suddenly turns to look straight at us, as though replying to the camera in an interview, and starts tell-ing us her innermost thoughts. Whether or not this is a com-mon technique employed in movies of this kind, I don't know. Even though my mother's father was a movie director, and my uncle is one now, like O-chan I have seen only a few movies. Anyway, I really liked this scene a lot. The woman recalls that, as a young man, her husband had been the laughingstock of the town. He had been called a slowpoke and a ne'er-do-well, and at the time of her marriage, her mother had objected that, since the guide was accursed, no child they had could be nor-mal. The woman says she chose to marry the man despite all this, because she preferred a hard life with its few happy mo-ments over a monotonous one. She confesses she may have started thinking this way after the fact, and had glossed things over, but in any event she says she presumes this is what led her to marry him. Here I wanted to cry out, "No, lady! You haven't glossed over things! You've always thought this way! And I believe your way of thinking is correct!"

In connection with this, I asked O-chan the next morning about another related scene I thought was important but didn't understand very well. I asked him about it because his char-acter is such that once he discusses a movie with me, it sets him to thinking, and though it was long, he appeared to have carefully watched this one straight through, using his study time, after Eeyore and I had retired to our bedrooms.

"O-chan," I began, "I want to ask you about the girl who had that gold-colored kerchief around her head. *Platok*, it's called? Remember Papa bought one like that in Moscow? Twice in the movie, her mother calls her an 'accursed child,' and in the scene where her mother comes to the bar to take her husband home, she has crutches with her. So the child must have had some affliction in her legs, but other than this, she didn't seem to have any other handicap. A very beautiful child. . . ."

"I think the child has the power to move objects with just her own consciousness," O-chan remarked. "Psychokinesis, I think it's called. In this sense, I suppose she's endowed with an ability that's newer and stranger than the guide's. The long scene where she moves three glasses with the power of her eyes—it was interesting to watch it in reverse, because then the glasses looked like they were being pulled toward her. And I guess 'accursed child' means she's a child with supernatural powers which neither she herself nor the people around her understand very well."

"The glasses moved in two scenes," I said, "in the beginning and at the end. In the first one, the girl is sleeping. Then the rumble of a train becomes loud. You begin to hear it before this, and it's filmed in a way that makes you think the things on the table slide because of the tremor of the train that's approaching the apartment building. I wonder if this isn't a technique Tarkovsky likes. At first you just can't figure out what he's trying to get across, but as the story develops, important meanings are communicated to you. . . . You can say the same for the scene where the guide tells the professor and writer to tie ribbons to the nuts. Thinking of it this way, don't the glasses move as a result of the train's vibrations?"

"As a science student," O-chan replied, "I'm inclined to see it as due to the vibrations of the train, but isn't it in fact psychokinesis? While watching this scene, I thought, Ah, this must be a precautionary measure against the 'technicians.' You see, Papa once told me that in the Soviet Union it's the 'technicians' who, as representatives of the local masses, write letters to the newspapers criticizing various forms of art, like literature and the movies. Because these 'technicians' strive to construct socialism through scientific practice, they actually occupy a higher place in their society than writers and movie directors. Of course, there would be problems if these 'technicians' wrote letters saying the movie was incomprehensible. And so you have the creation of a means to explain the movement of the glasses as due to the vibrations from the train. Yet somehow I feel that Tarkovsky is showing a child who's able to transmit the power of her mind to objects."

"I half thought so, too," I said, "but I didn't take 'technicians' into account the way you did. .... If you pursue this line of thought, though, couldn't you say that the girl with her head wrapped in the golden kerchief was the image of Jesus Christ in his 'Second Coming?' The guide walks a long distance with the girl on his shoulders, remember? Walks on, makes a sharp left, and then continues walking? Typical of Tarkovsky's style, I guess. And you know about the man who bears Christ on his back? Christopher, is it? I think the scene's alluding to this."

"The Second Coming of Christ! Now that's bewildering. Because then you'd have the Antichrist appearing on the scene to wreak universal havoc."

"Yes," I continued, "but isn't the mere fact that the Zone came into existence after a meteor fell evidence of the havoc, basically? If I were a girl in a farming village in Russia, I would take such a horrible disaster as an omen of Christ's Second Coming."

"Indeed, the woman's mother, who objected to her daughter's marriage to the guide, sensed that their child was an evil omen and called her 'accursed.' Really, though, this movie was a mind-boggler. But it's my fault that I didn't understand it."

a quiet life

"Well, O-chan," I said, "thanks for keeping me company. I'm beginning to feel I understand everything a little better. I guess I'll do some more thinking on my own now."

I'd been thinking about something else in connection with the child's mother in *Stalker*. After our parents left for America, I often thought about them, especially Mother. I associated her with various minor events that occurred in the house, and because of this, I hadn't delved very deeply into anything in particular. Or at least this is what I first thought.

But what I next thought about Mother—or rather what I, the scatterbrain that I am, imagined about her—is as follows. As I now transcribe this thought from "Diary as Home," I realize that its contents are simple and brief, yet it was an idea I'd been quietly nursing in my mind for some time. I had also wondered, while knowing it could never happen in reality, whether Mother had ever thought Eeyore an 'accursed child.' And believing this to be somewhat more probable, I had wondered whether Father, in the habit of carrying his jokes dangerously far, hadn't said to Mother, "You bore me an accursed child." Which is the way he usually unwittingly hurts other people's feelings. And when it backfires he thinks he's been misunderstood, though he's asked for it by being the one who started it. And this, in turn, leads him to indulge in self-pity, and then end up mercilessly angry at the one he offends. My heart sank as I thought of Mother's sorrows and sufferings at the time.

Obviously, it's only a supposition, but if such a thing had actually happened at some point in time, could it be that going to live together alone for the first time in their long married life, twenty-five years after Eeyore was born, was an attempt on their part to heal and restore what had been hurt or broken? . . . I brooded over this, and though I told myself it was only a figment of my imagination, a safety valve on my consciousness, I sank into such a deep abyss of despair, one from which I felt I could not be redeemed by merely sitting quietly beside Eeyore like I usually do, that all I could do was stagger up to my room and bury myself in bed.

Because things like this happened, the next time I took Eeyore to the Shigetos for his music composition lesson I ended up talking with Mr. Shigeto about *Stalker*, which I'd been thinking about all the while. I said nothing about my doubts as to whether my parents had ever thought Eeyore an 'accursed child,' about these suspicions that came to my mind during the night, thoughts that were as vivid as the night's menacing darkness, but which disappeared as evanescent foolishness with the brightness of day. Nevertheless, I talked to him in detail about the little girl whose head was wrapped in the golden kerchief.

"Hmm, *Stalker* . . ." Mr. Shigeto said. "I can't comment on a movie I haven't seen. And I haven't heard of a Russian word like *stalker*. But it's a movie title, so perhaps they're using a new word from English or something. We do that a lot in Japan, too, don't we? If it's *stalker*, then it's a person who pursues game. Couldn't be *stoker*, someone who tends a furnace. . . . This girl, who's protected from the cold air with the golden *platok*, is probably going home, preciously borne on her father's shoulders, so I don't think her parents usually think of her as an 'accursed child.' Such a thought enters the guide's wife's mind only when she's downhearted and wants to reproach her husband. . . . And the guide obviously loves his family, for he says he has no intention of taking his wife and child to the perilous Zone. At the same time, he has a sense of mission to escort those who have a reason to go there. In other words, he's stuck on the Zone. And that's why he can't get a steady job. His wife nags him about this, but she wholeheartedly cares for his well-being. Which is to say, they're a beautiful family."

When, after saying this, Mr. Shigeto noticed his wife by his side smiling at him, the expression on his face suddenly became what you would want to call solemn.

"I believe Tarkovsky expressed his intent very well on the screen," I said. "I feel it's only my limited powers of understanding that leave me unable to decide whether the child who moves those glasses with her stare is Christ in his Second Coming, or the antichrist."

"I'll have to watch the movie to comment on that," Mr. Shigeto replied, ". . . but for the moment, let me think of it this way—though only from what you've told me, mind you. An entire village disappears after a meteor hits it. That's how big the disaster is. After such a calamity, a yearning for the 'millennium' often spreads among the populace, and many so-called messiahs appear. Now if I were to say whether or not the guide represents the existence of one such messiah, I would say no. But couldn't the Room in the Zone where the guide leads the people, the Room itself, be a messiah? For you say that it fulfills the cherished, secret wishes of its visitors; and because it fulfills their wishes, some of the visitors are thrown into such despair that they have to hang themselves. But a place can't be human, can it?

"Looking at it this way, it all comes down to the child. She has yet to make formal use of her powers, but it seems the potential is there. I wouldn't put it past her if she became Stalker Junior. She'll turn out to be a person with ample savvy, unlike her dutiful but slow and benign father. Then the only question becomes: Is she Christ or the antichrist? The part you told me about, where the guide leads his charges through a pool of water, is to me an image of baptism. And so, in the end, the redeeming role of the Room in the Zone is, in itself, an image of Christ. But with a multitude of people rushing to the Zone and dying there, or even with things going well, if the fulfillment of their earthly wishes is merely a matter of desire, then I guess you would have to think of her as the havoc-wreaking antichrist, even if she were to pave the way for Christ's Second Coming. . . . In any event, a child messiah taking charge of the 'millennium' after devastation by a meteor makes an intriguing story."

"A dog anxiously whines," I said, "as the child concentrates on the power of her eyes to move the glasses on the table. Being a dog, perhaps it hears the distant din of the train before the human ear would, especially since it's new to the apartment. Anyway, when the train's rumble becomes loud, one of the glasses that's moved to the edge of the table falls to the floor and breaks into pieces. Up to this point you saw the child's face behind the glass, so now you see it better, and the expression on it appears to be savoring the sound of destruction . . . and then you hear music. Beethoven, wasn't it, Eeyore?"

"Yes," replied Eeyore. "It was the 'Ode to Joy.' It's more than twenty minutes if you play it straight through, but in the movie it was very short!"

Both Mr. Shigeto and his wife appeared happy to hear Eeyore promptly respond to a question about music. Until then he'd been sitting there quietly, though it was highly dubious whether he understood what we were talking about.

"Ma-chan, when Eeyore's with you, you always share your topics of discussion with him, don't you? And it's so natural, the way you do it. Ma-chan is quite a person, don't you think, Eeyore?"

"Does that have a good meaning?" Eeyore thoughtfully asked for assurance.

"The best meaning," replied Mrs. Shigeto. Her husband's face again turned solemn.

"I think Ma-chan is quite a person, too," Eeyore said for me.

a quiet life

There was no music lesson scheduled for the following Thursday, but Mrs. Shigeto phoned to invite us over. Mr. Shigeto seems to truly enjoy teaching Eeyore, and he greeted us with a dash of ceremony, his welcoming mood much happier than usual. Eeyore, too, I know, enjoys his lessons with Mr. Shigeto. But I could tell from the way he sat beside me on the sofa— that day more relaxed, his face thrust forward, all ready to listen to Mr. Shigeto—that he, also, was particularly happy. Mr. Shigeto immediately revealed to us the reason for their invitation.

"I saw *Stalker*, too," he said. "The commercial version. At my friend's place. He's an expert on Russian literature, and he said the version you saw on television must have been more or less the same. First, about the term *stalker*. Just as I thought, it's straight from the English *stalker*. It's just spelled in Russian. This is how it appears on the screen." He printed СТАПКЕР on a piece of paper for me. "Hoh!" Eeyore breathed out in utter amazement at a printed letter with an unusual form. "I checked in some of the modern dictionaries of the Russian language my friend had, but it wasn't listed there," Mr. Shigeto continued. "I looked in both Academy's and Ushanko's four-volume dictionaries. I tried Ozhekov's, too. *Dictionary of New Words of the Seventies* didn't have it either. This means it isn't Russian, but a loanword, and a new one at that. My friend told me he had read, in Russian, the novel on which the movie is based. He said that although СТАПКЕР appeared in it, the title of the book was totally different: *Roadside Picnic* by the Strugatsky brothers. Even as a movie title I think this would have been more chic."

". . . I'm sorry I made you go to so much trouble," I said, feeling much obliged, and Eeyore, who was seated beside me, appeared to stiffen his body. I should have known better than to ask an offhand question of a scholar.

the guide (*stalker*)

"No, no," Mr. Shigeto said. "You see, I'm getting lazy, and I hardly ever go out these days, much less to see a movie. I wouldn't have known about this one if you hadn't told me. But don't you think the actor who played the guide was good, that he did a great job expressing the character's agony? What his wife said about him being derided, being called a slowpoke and a ne'er-do-well, came through very well. His acting also enabled me to quite naturally accept why, even though this man is being so dolefully tormented, a beautiful young girl marries him, and says how much she loves him and can do nothing about it. It reminded me that things like this can happen."

"I especially liked the actress who did the wife's part," Mrs. Shigeto said, while scrupulously rubbing grated garlic into the ribs of lamb she was preparing for Eeyore and me. She had removed the fat on the edges of the bones, and they looked like short comb teeth. "It was great the way she smokes her cigarette like a juvenile delinquent. And she isn't fat like most Russian women. No particular reason, but I wonder if she wasn't Jewish."

"He's so vulnerable," Mr. Shigeto said. "He's the sort of man whose entire heart is exposed on the surface. So I imagine that, until then, his wife protected him quite well. And with that child, too, it must have been tough for her."

I thought of Mrs. Shigeto, who was busily preparing dinner at our side, for although they had no children, she, too, must have a hard time, standing by her husband, encouraging him to do only the kind of work that suited him. When I turned a casual glance in her direction, I saw a slight pink flush come to her face, as if she were feeling abashed, but she kept rubbing garlic into the ribs with her forefinger, which was bent at a charming angle.

Mr. Shigeto, who also had turned to his wife, an expression of surprise on his face compounding his usual solemnity,

89

continued. "I thought the murky and dangerous would-be criminal side of the guide was also very well portrayed. And the irate reaction of one of the clients, who says 'What the hell are you trying to do' when he almost gets a crowbar thrown at him for innocently trying to uproot a tuft of grass, was very true to life. A vulnerable and easily hurt, somber and passion-ate, and ultimately criminal-like guy is really fearsome. . . . And Ma-chan, about this child, I don't think she's Christ in his Second Coming. You can't associate her father's criminal-ity with Christ—though of course you could argue that she was born of a virgin mother. But the child herself, her eyes, struck me as harboring some kind of malevolent force. She could easily grow up to be a person whose role is to destroy everything—in other words, the antichrist—which is my conclusion for the moment."

"Then why," I wondered, "do we hear the 'Ode to Joy' together with the rumble of the train? Eeyore got all excited and started conducting it."

"Exactly!" Eeyore chimed in.

"There could be joy in destruction, too, couldn't there?" Mr. Shigeto said. "Isn't Jesus Christ's Second Coming supposed to occur only after a lot of unmitigated destruction? But again, human history is fraught with tragedies in which man spared no effort to destroy with 'millenarian' joy, only to learn that no messiah appeared afterwards. . . ."

"The story line's getting a little complicated, Mr. Shigeto," his wife said, supplying me with a rescue boat, for actually I was having a hard time trying to follow his thoughts. "You can't tell Ma-chan a realistic story unless you first organize your own ideas better. . . . Well now, Ma-chan, why don't you switch your mind to cooking? I want you to learn the ratio of herbs and salt to pepper. Lamb is readily available these days. Even supermarkets have frozen lamb, and they do a good job of thawing it. Foreigners here say it's the only quality meat they can afford. See how you like it this evening, and if you do, then now and then you could make some for Eeyore."

While Mrs. Shigeto and I busied ourselves in the small but amazingly well-kept kitchen, Mr. Shigeto piled on the table a mountain of old LP records and tapes he had recorded from radio. He and Eeyore, acting very professionally, were preparing to listen to and compare the many versions of the "Ode to Joy."

When dinner started, Mr. Shigeto commended Eeyore for his ability to make accurate, educated guesses on how long each "Ode" was—even on the recordings he had never heard before. As I listened to Mr. Shigeto say to his wife, by way of explanation, that it was all a matter of understanding a conductor's style, I realized he had been so impressed with Eeyore that he had discussed this problem with him as one adult to another.

"The moment you hear the first few notes of some of these versions, you think they're going to be up-tempo," he said. "And sure enough, when you've listened until the end, you tell yourself you were right, and remember them this way. Then there are those you remember as being slow, the way you remember the versions of Furtwängler or Toscanini we usually hear. But very often, these memories become distorted through your own stubborn imagination. Take me, for example. I would have carried such distortions to my grave if not for what Eeyore just pointed out to me. We were comparing only the introductory parts of the 'Ode' by different conductors, and as we discussed the tempo of each one, I learned that the way I perceived the various renditions was different from Eeyore's. He said calmly, but with conviction, that the recording times on this, that, and the other pieces were almost the same. So I picked out a few I believed were of a quite different tempo, and when

I timed them on my stopwatch, it was just as he said. They weren't even thirty seconds apart!"

Mrs. Shigeto rolled at Eeyore her thought-immersed eyes, which watched attentively from deep behind her silver-rimmed glasses, and exclaimed with childlike admiration, "A difference of only thirty seconds is almost no difference at all!"

"I guess it's almost the same," Eeyore cautiously replied.

"Eeyore really has an extraordinary ability to judge music, doesn't he?" Mrs. Shigeto said. "Shigeto-san, you'll have to work hard to teach Eeyore."

"The ideal teacher-student relationship exists when the student is better than the teacher," Mr. Shigeto returned, unperturbed.

While we ate, Eeyore made us laugh with what seemed to be well-calculated jokes. The discussion of *Stalker* continued with Mr. Shigeto at the center, as before. But when we talked again of the scene where the guide piggybacks his daughter back to their apartment, he remarked upon the excellent acting of the dog in the scene, and there followed quite a heated exchange of words between him and his wife. Mrs. Shigeto first directed his attention to the fact that fine acting on the part of dogs is mere coincidence, with the exception of super movie dogs like Lassie or Rin Tin Tin. And even their acting, she claimed, wasn't acting in its truest sense, for their roles were always the same. Her knowledge of the movies, abundant to the point of anarchy, stunned me as she then cited example after example of memorable scenes of dogs acting out their parts. It was also interesting, though, because as she argued, she sometimes unwittingly provided supporting evidence in favor of her husband's contention.

Soon Mr. Shigeto steered the conversation to what I think he wanted to present as a conclusion, at least for the evening.

"To sum it up," he said, "entirely intentional performances

by animals may be limited to the animated films of Disney. By the way, the first Betty Boop was a bitch. I saw it at a private showing by a collector."

"Then you agree with me," Mrs. Shigeto said. ". . . But I don't understand why Betty Boop has to intrude into the discussion," she objected in part, though on the whole she appeared satisfied.

Smiling, she asked Eeyore if he cared for more lamb. But Eeyore, after being cautioned at the welfare workshop about his weight increase, never ate more than what was first apportioned to him, and when I explained his attitude of refusal for him, Mrs. Shigeto promptly changed the subject and asked, "Eeyore, you saw the big dog in the movie too, didn't you?"

"Remember, Eeyore, you were watching it too, beside me, making music?" I said. "You liked the part where the little girl goes home piggybacked on her father's shoulders, because they proceeded across the screen in a crooked way. And there was a dog there, too?"

"Unfortunately, I couldn't observe the dog well," Eeyore replied. "It kept moving around a lot."

"You're right," Mr. Shigeto remarked. "The focus of the dog's role in the scene was to just keep moving around. You have a firm grasp of the meaning of the scene, Eeyore."

Then Eeyore said, "I used to piggyback a lot a long time ago!" He said it as though it was an idea he'd been sitting on for a while. "Yes, I often piggybacked Papa."

"*Papa* piggybacked *you*, Eeyore," I had to put in. "Besides, Papa was fat and heavy in those days."

"I was healthy then," Eeyore said. "My fits hadn't begun yet. I piggybacked very often." We all happily laughed. Eeyore, too, was laughing. He was in high spirits throughout the evening we were there. And because I optimistically saw him as though I were seeing the Eeyore of long ago, I gradually became careless. On our way back from the Shigetos, following Eeyore, who walked hurriedly down the road in front of their house, I actually thought of the days when he was truly able to move very sprightly. Every summer in Kita-Karuizawa, when we jogged, as our daily routine, I could have passed him had I wanted to, but O-chan could never keep up with Eeyore's speed and stamina. Long ago, I reminisced, Eeyore was really very healthy. . . .

But as I now replay that scene of our return home from the Shigetos, I recall that when we reached the station and started going up the stairs to the gate, Eeyore looked unusually tired. We were lucky the train to Shinjuku, where we had to make a transfer, wasn't very crowded, and we were able to sit together, side by side, and rest comfortably for a while. Eeyore no longer talks to anyone in the family when we are out among other people.

That evening, too, he sat beside me in silence, wearing a solemn expression on his face that was somewhat different from Mr. Shigeto's. Even so, I wasn't worried about helping him make the transfer to the crowded outbound Odakyu Line from Shinjuku Station. On the express platform, however, I sensed for the first time, as we stood side by side at the head of a long line, that untoward changes were taking place inside Eeyore's body. Outwardly, his body looked defenseless and unstable, much like a big papier-mâché mannequin propped up against an invisible wall, and on his neck was a flushed face with blood-shot eyes, half-open yet showing no trace of seeing. With blood rushing to my head, and aware of my powerlessness, my inability to do anything, I desperately seized—hung on to—and tried to support Eeyore's body, which was emitting a high, stifling temperature, and was evidently suffering a fit. The upper half of his body, with its uncertain center of gravity, gave me no clue as to which way its weight would fall. At times, though, it would suddenly bear down on me with such force that my shoulder bones creaked. . . .

After all the passengers had gotten off the other side of the incoming commuter train, Shinjuku being the end of the line, I heard the doors on our side open behind me, and my entire body chilled with fear. Immediately, the lines of boarding passengers started moving in, and although I was somehow supporting Eeyore's weight, which had become substantially heavy, the irresistible force of the crowd thrust me back two or three steps. I couldn't even scream at, let alone explain anything to, the passengers who were pushing and shoving to get in and scramble for a seat. I had been holding Eeyore at the front of the line, facing the visibly irate passengers, who merely saw two ostentatious young lovers hugging each other in public, blocking their path. I thought the work-weary, angry people, among whom were several drunks, were going to crush us. They would trample over us, perhaps kick Eeyore in the head with the toes of their hard leather shoes, kick him in the back of his head where his protective plastic plate was embedded. But no voice escaped from my open mouth; only tears of fear and desperation rolled down my cheeks. And all the while, people were gruffly shoving us back toward the end of the queue, and we were barely able to keep ourselves from falling. . . .

Then I noticed that Eeyore's body, which I thought I had been supporting, was in fact shielding me from the procession of the line. Moreover, it had slowly but steadily managed to switch positions with mine. Some clearly vulgar words were hissed beside our ears then, but Eeyore, who was standing so precariously off-balance that I thought he would be crushed at any moment, pushed back with great strength. And holding me with outstretched elbows, he confronted the inrushing passengers, looking them straight in the face. At this point, the pressure of people thrusting and shoving at our sides and backs subsided, and the movement of those who dodged us became in some sense a natural, flowing stream. By this time, passengers who had given up on getting a seat were proceeding through the doors at a calmer pace. Yet as I looked up, my tear-drenched eyes saw Eeyore still staring straight over my head at the people beyond, his face suffused with an expression that reflected less an open, spontaneous hostility toward others and more a sedate, menacing force. . . .

Because Eeyore was soon able to walk on his own, we moved, avoiding the people who were forming new lines, to a place behind the stairs that led to another platform above, and rested there with our backs against the wall. This time, too, Eeyore thrust his arm between me and the wall, and kept it there, enfolding me. His breath was foul with that metallic stench he gives off when he has his fits, but the expression on his face was soft, and he was already his usual self. If there hadn't been any strangers passing us, I would have kidded him with a joke that I myself would be laughing at, for I too was cradled in that sense of relief that comes after riding out a crisis.

Before long, a *peculiar resolve* welled up in my heart. I began wondering if Eeyore, deep inside, embraced a malevolent force like that of the antichrist. Even if he were the antichrist, though, I would follow him wherever he went. As for why I associated the antichrist with Eeyore, the only reason I could think of was that the girl with the golden *platok* in *Stalker* had acted as a catalyst, for in almost all of his childhood pictures, I had seen Eeyore with a bandage or cloth around his head, or sometimes a woolen cap fully covering it. . . .

Still, in the manner of a light that penetrates through my constitution and emanates refracted rays upon leaving it, the joy that came over me then was clearly that of a violent, malicious jubilation. For I no longer had another soul in mind, no one in this whole world but Eeyore and myself. And mingling with the rumble of the express train now departing from the next track, I heard within me, although it could never bear comparison with Beethoven's Ninth, an "Ode to Joy" of a kind that, together with Eeyore's plump earlobe, which nestled just above my head, I seemed to embrace with an overflowing courage.

c

a robot's
nightmare

The crystal-clear morning made me feel, somewhat ceremoniously, that this day and no other was the first day of winter. I busied myself with the laundry to get it dry while the sun was still on the house. A while later, from the kitchen corner where I could see the dining room and beyond, I noticed Eeyore, who had changed out of his nightclothes by himself, standing by the glass door to the terrace. He was gazing out at the array of potted plants in the brick-paved, sunlit terrace beyond the glass door. Though aware that, in this "expressive" state, Eeyore must be pondering something, my head, from low blood pressure, seemed to still be half asleep, and the only thought in it was of having to quickly prepare breakfast if he were hungry.

"Such discipline, Eeyore!" I exclaimed. "Up so early on a Sunday morning. Can you wait till I get the bulk of this laundry done? Then I'll fix you some tea."

a quiet life

Whenever I feel Eeyore's vivacity in the air, I begin to think I'm doing something worthwhile, even in doing my everyday household chores, like the laundry. I went out into the garden with a basket of laundry in my arms, carrying it like a Mexican washerwoman I had seen on TV, hung it up to dry, and prepared breakfast. The aroma of the black tea was nice, and the eggs were fried in such a way that the clear winter day really felt sunny side up.

Returning to the dining room, I found Eeyore still standing there like a guardian deity at a temple gate, looking intently at the plants. Then I realized he'd had the plants on his mind ever since he got up, and he wanted to talk to me about them.

"What is it you want to tell Ma-chan?" I asked. "I'll listen anytime. Or do you want to take your time and talk to me after breakfast?"

"Yes, that's what I will do!"

Whenever Eeyore has something to say, he has trouble saying it, especially if it's a thought he has well deliberated. But this is what I was finally able to get out of him.

"Today's the first Sunday of November!" he began, then nonchalantly added, "Mama puts the plants out in the garden in early May, the eighty-eighth day after spring sets in." I couldn't have remembered this for all my memory was worth. He then went on to remind me that the first Sunday of November was when the plants had to be brought into the house.

Evidently he knew Mother's year-round schedule, and was determined to act as her deputy with me while she was away.

"You're admirable, Eeyore!" I said. "Really!"

"I remembered all along!" he said, looking happy beyond measure.

So after breakfast, I decided to bring in just the plants I could carry from the garden, where I perspired a little in the

sun, and felt more than a bit chilly in the shade. Eeyore, who
had disappeared somewhere, emerged with a bulky loop of
hemp twine bound together, as if entangled, with a wide leather
belt, a device he had probably found in Father's library. Father spares no effort in doing the heavy work around the house,
like that time he tried to clean the sewer. Moreover, he makes
these gadgets himself for each of the tasks, and he really looks
happy when they serve their purpose. The loop of belt-bound
twine that Eeyore had found was a device Father had made to
transport four of the biggest and heaviest potted hemp palms
to and from the garden. Of course, I wasn't going to ask Eeyore
to carry them in. They're all too heavy. The best I can do is
inch them along, zigzag fashion, scraping and screeching them
against the brick floor. Even if my arms were strong enough
to lift them, it would be horrible to drop one on my feet.

But Eeyore had carefully observed how Father went about
the task each year. And though not very adeptly, he had already fastened the belt on to the pot that held the biggest plant.
As a safety measure, he hitched the loop of twine on to the
bottom of the pot, then bent down, hugged the plant, and raised
himself. I quickly ran ahead of him to the front door, opened
it, and cleared the entrance of the shoes and sandals that were
in his way. He couldn't have been able to see ahead very well
with the dense stems obstructing his view, but he proceeded
with a measured gait, mindful of the unevenness in the walkway to the entrance door. Dutifully slipping out of his shoes as
he entered the house, he went into the living room and, without any mishap, set the pot in front of the glass door where
Mother keeps it.

He took not even a moment's rest before bringing in the
next pot, and encouraged by the vigor with which he did this
heavy work, I very carefully watered each plant he brought in.
After bringing in all four pots, Eeyore, unable to otherwise

101

express the sense of satisfaction that takes root in the body after physical labor, stepped back out into the garden again and, with his fingers entwined behind his back, stood in the sun under the colored leaves of the dogwood tree. I went out too, and savoring a rising strength in my heart, tended the potted wild plants, which had shed their bloom long ago and were already preparing for winter. I went around watering all the small potted plants we kept outdoors. Blighted as they were, I pictured their flowers in the spring and summer of their day: the large flowers of the lady's slippers, which were swollen like the bellies of goldfish, and the "snowholders" with the ricecake-like white mound amid their petals. I thought of each flower, and recalled the moments I had squatted beside Mother while she tended them and taught me their names. . . .

Before long, Eeyore came to my side and, while straightening up a tilted pot, he said, reminiscently, "We took flowers of this *grass*, too, to Mr. Shigeto's place!" Apparently we were experiencing the same wandering of minds.

"This is an orchid of the Calanthe family," I said. "Kozucalanthe, I think they call it. I remember it has light brown and white flowers."

"They smelled very sweet!" Eeyore said. "It was the day of Mr. Shigeto's debut!"

"Debut" is typical Eeyore-speak, his way of expressing things slightly off key, which made my recollection of the day more vivid. Eeyore started piano lessons with a tutor—Mrs. T, the wife of one of Father's editor friends—as soon as he entered the secondary division at the special-care school. It was through Mrs. T's patient instruction that he learned chord mechanics as well as how to piece together sequences of melodies. Also thanks to her, he even learned to compose his own music. But then she decided to go to Europe for further study, which left Mother and Eeyore at a total loss. She had left

Japan a number of times before, for the same purpose, but only for short stays. This time, though, she would be gone at least a year.

Then Father, the sort who thinks of actual solutions only when pressed to, hit upon the idea of asking Mr. Shigeto, his friend from college, to take over Eeyore's music education. All I knew of Mr. Shigeto at the time was that he was a specialist on Eastern European literature, but had recently decided to make a career of composing music, which until then he had done strictly for amusement. When asked if he could tutor Eeyore, his reply, I understand, was that, having passed a new turning point, he would first meet with Eeyore to see if he would be interested in working with him. Father said that if he took Eeyore to Mr. Shigeto's place, he might put an undue burden on his old friend. This sounded like he was being considerate, but again, I felt he was really being subtly egocentric. Mother, too, knowing Mr. Shigeto from her youth, genuinely feared his eccentric personality, and at the last minute shied away from the task. So it turned out that I would be making the visit with Eeyore. Mother made a bouquet for Mr. Shigeto's wife with the wildflowers she had lovingly tended, and when she was through, most of the pots were just a mass of green with hardly any flowers left on the plants.

Mrs. Shigeto, whom I met for the first time that day, had a pair of round, silver-rimmed glasses on her plump, round face. I later learned that she had chanced upon these glasses at an antiques fair in Prague. She impressed me as a woman who had grown up among loving folk: a happy, innocent girl turned elderly only with the passage of time. The firm bridge of her nose and the tension in her pliant temples, however, seemed to support the profound weight of her life experiences. With somber eyes, she looked intently at the flowers Eeyore offered her, and quietly spoke.

"The flower of this plant, this bluish-amber one, is very beautiful. It looks like an insect just about to sing, with its wings spread. I'll bet it has a name befitting its beauty."

"I think it's 'jewel beetle,'" I said.

"It'll probably smell like a green bug if you crush it," Mr. Shigeto said, his head peering from behind her, the tall man that he was, and thrust out his hand as though to sink his fingers into the bouquet. Eeyore made a move to stop him, though not in a hostile manner.

"Don't do anything rough with them," Mrs. Shigeto said to her husband as she pulled the bouquet to her bosom. "These are rare wildflowers, each one of them. Thank you very much, Ma-chan, Eeyore. It must've been a bother to carry all this on the train. You can't just bunch them together like an ordinary bouquet. And so many! Your garden must look very lonely now."

"Mother goes to places for some of them; others she buys," I said. "She's the one who looks after them, and it was she who picked them for you."

"She'll have no more flowers this year," Mrs. Shigeto said, "but she's picked them very carefully, so as not to hurt the stems."

Mr. Shigeto appeared a little embarrassed, not only by his wife's reproach but also by Eeyore's gesture. His dignity again intact, however, he returned from the kitchen with a big water-filled jug. And he produced glass bottles, of different colors, from the pockets of a jacket that looked like a painter's work outfit. So we busied ourselves sorting the flowers, which Mrs. Shigeto said were best not bunched together, and put each kind in its respective bottle. As we did this, Mrs. Shigeto said something to this effect: "Ma-chan, your parents are already well aware of this, but the reason Mr. Shigeto can be very particular about and sensitive to such things, and at times be uncouth like he was just a while ago, is because there's angst in his heart these days."

"If I try to be easily cheerful, I can be that way," Mr. Shigeto said. "But I'm the kind of person who aspires to meander into every nook and cranny of his angst, and carefully examine it."

"You certainly are that type," his wife said.

Mrs. Shigeto set the small flower-filled bottles on the table, at intervals, in such a way that they took up its whole surface. Eeyore brought his face close to the bottles to smell each kind of flower, one by one.

"Mr. Shigeto composes music professionally now," his wife said, "but this doesn't earn him much. The translations he did are now out of print. . . . He worked on Milan Kundera, a writer whose father was a specialist in music, and Kundera himself was very much interested in ethnic music. So I think Mr. Shigeto, with his background, produces very good translations of writers of this kind. A few news agencies still ask him to submit translations of important articles from Eastern European newspapers and magazines.

"Mr. Shigeto also attends seminars for young journalists who are interested in the kind of work he does. But because these enthusiastic people, pretending to be specialists"—here Mr. Shigeto corrected her by saying that although the researchers were young, they were, in fact, specialists—"say pessimistic things about the situation in Eastern Europe, Mr. Shigeto became depressed. And at the same time, he suffered a serious illness. That's why he keeps saying these days that perhaps he should sever his ties with the news agencies."

"Well," Mr. Shigeto said, a sigh mingling with his voice, "I have transitions to go through, too." Then, as if to divert himself, he turned to me and asked, "Ma-chan, what do you think?"

"How can anyone answer that?" his wife put in. "You need to elaborate, Mr. Shigeto."

"Well, you see," he said, "the younger researchers have a dismal view of the future of the society they're studying. And they don't seem the least bothered with their pessimism. How do you feel about this, Ma-chan?"

I often recall this question, or perhaps I should call it an oral exam, which Mr. Shigeto asked of me on our first visit there. But it's all the more unforgettable because I felt as though I were going to *robotize.*

. . . I digress from my story about this first visit of ours to the Shigetos, but I think I need to write about my *robotization.* It's a phenomenon I often experience, so I even gave it a name, and here's how I came up with the term. On Eeyore's birthday a long time ago, Father gave him a sumo doll that ran on batteries. We all played with it a long time at the festive dinner table, moving it this way and that. After I helped Mother with the dishes and returned to the living room, I saw Sportsman Asashio on the low table before the sofa, where Eeyore had left him. Eeyore, a sumo aficionado, had given the automatic doll this name, finding humor in the fact that, though the toy moved briskly for a sumo wrestler, the wrestler who actually had the sumo name Asashio was not very agile. With raised arms, and his body twisted in the opposite direction, the mechanized Asashio was hanging rock-still in midair, as it were. When I pushed the button on his back, there was a revving whir, accompanied by a moment's wait. Soon he raised his already-lifted arms still higher above his head, and rolled his eyes around and around. I instinctively turned off the switch, for he looked so much like me. His groaning, mechanical whir continued a few more moments, then suddenly he drooped his head. His twisted body was such a painful sight that I had to lay Sportsman Asashio on his side.

My observations at the time became useful in self-criticism, too. I'm very thin, the opposite of the sumo doll, but whenever I'm in a plight, I hear this revving whir within me. My body assumes this twisted shape, and at some point I suddenly droop my head. This is the phenomenon I call my *robotization*. . . .

I had already half *robotized* at Mr. Shigeto's sudden question. I was somehow able to pull myself together and present an opinion because I was desperately thinking only of Eeyore's well-being.

"Some time ago," I said, "a group of doctors invited Father and me to dinner. We arrived an hour late by mistake, through nobody's fault but ours. Then a young doctor on the host side, who seemed to be an intern, spoke to us, very aggressively, telling us that if we went to his ward, we'd see many babies lying there, whose births were simply tragic, but who cannot be killed. It was clearly a criticism against Father, who's always writing that he finds meaning in Eeyore's existence. . . . I was angry not only at the doctor for saying this, but also at Father for remaining silent. I don't know if I answered your question. . . ."

"Yes, you did," Mr. Shigeto said, blinking his eyes, which made him look much older than he was, old but innocent-looking. "That's exactly what I wanted to hear from you."

"'Whose births were simply tragic, but who cannot be killed,'" Eeyore repeated, with feeling. "How frightening!" This startled both Mr. Shigeto and his wife.

"My brother often chimes in on people's conversations with timely words," I said, "but it's not because he's thinking very seriously. It's just that he . . ."

"Ma-chan," Eeyore said. "Not to worry, please!"

"That's very timely, too, Eeyore . . . ," Mr. Shigeto said. "I guess the only way I can really match you is to look at your sheet music." It then occurred to me that my oral exam was over, and that most probably the two of us had passed.

Mr. Shigeto started Eeyore's first lesson that day with no further ado. Mr. Shigeto has, I think, a generous and practical side to him, not wholly incongruous with his unworldliness. I have written to some extent about how kind he has been, but really, he has helped me in many more ways. Leafing through a few pages of Eeyore's music, he seemed to quickly understand and concur with Mrs. T's teaching methods. He then took Eeyore to his study, which he called his music room. When later they returned, Mrs. Shigeto served everyone tea and cookies she had made with Eastern European patterns on them. I remember Eeyore was thoroughly relaxed by then. I remember, too, that during the course of our conversation in the homey living room, Mrs. Shigeto asked us why our nicknames were so different from our real names. I recall this part very clearly, because I found myself explaining, in earnest, not only the nickname Eeyore, but my nickname as well.

Mr. Shigeto quickly guessed correctly that Eeyore must have come from *Winnie-the-Pooh*, to which his wife said, "The pessimistic donkey, isn't it? These days, Mr. Shigeto is really sensitive to anything pessimistic." She seemed frustrated she hadn't been the first one to guess.

"Well, after all," Mr. Shigeto remarked, "it was the postwar editions of *Selected Poems from the Man'yōshū* and *Winnie-the-Pooh* that helped K develop a closer relationship with Oyu-san. Oyu-san's mother, who then lived in Ashiya, asked him to send her the two books. I happened to know of a secondhand bookseller in Shimo-Kitazawa who had a collection of old Iwanami Press books, and I took him there."

"So," Mrs. Shigeto said proudly, "you've been a connoisseur of old books that long!" Learning how long Father had known Mr. Shigeto, and that their friendship went back to even before Father got to know Mother, I understood, though I felt somewhat remote from it all, why even now Father turned to him in times of trouble. This, I think, is why I explained to them in detail how I got my nickname, and even cited Father's very words. . . .

I have indicated that I'm called Ma-chan, but haven't explained why. Everyone calls me Ma-chan, my family and my friends, but it's got nothing to do with my real name. It's related to the shape of my small, round head. From kindergarten to college, my head has always been the smallest among my friends, in whichever class I was placed. Moreover, it's a perfect sphere. At an outdoor camp I once went to when I was in middle school, every group in each class had to perform a skit by the campfire. Our group decided on a sort of game where we would form a ring and bounce or pass a ball around. They had me wear a black shirt and black tights, which hid my body from my throat on down, all the way to my toes, and covered my head and face with a red ski cap. So who else but me could have been the ball, the *mari*. . . . Ever since then, my nickname has been Mari, hence Ma-chan, through high school and even now at college. Some of my friends think it's my real name, and that's how they address their letters.

Once when I was crabbing to Mother about why my head had to be so small and round, Father explained why. I told Mr. Shigeto and his wife exactly what he said. I remember he was straightforward and serious that day, which was unusual for him. He stuck to the facts, and didn't interlace them with his typical banter. This astounded me so much that I, instead, ended up throwing in a few words of levity. And when I said that I had seen, in a dream, my whole body being cast, subject to a certain system, in some foundrylike place, Father needlessly got angry.

"Four years before you came, Ma-chan, Eeyore was born to us, with a deformity on his head. To be exact, at first he had a minuscule defect in his skull, a small hole. As the skull developed, this defect became larger, which was a matter of course. Then a pouch formed on the outside of the hole to keep what was in the skull from spilling out. In other words, a system was formed whereby the pressure of the spinal fluid flowing into the pouch worked to push back the brain, to keep the brain in the cranium. Amazing, isn't it? In all cases, human genes function in an orderly, predetermined way to create the body. But here was a system quite different from the original design, the bricolage of the organism of the flesh. The pouch took the form of a wen, and grew larger and larger.

"When Eeyore was born, the moment he slipped out of Mama's body, she heard the nurse, who should have received him from the doctor like a rugby pass, cry "Ah!" just before she fainted. Even when I first saw him, he looked like he had two heads.

"Mama's first delivery, and that was the sort of child we had. So she worried whether, the next time, another deformed body would take shape in her dark womb. But she rose above this fear of hers, and decided to have you. Now *that* took some courage. I wonder, though, if apart from her indomitable resolve, her body wasn't likewise bent on self-defense. Mama's womb thought, on its own, that its next delivery should be of a child whose head wasn't too bulky—after all, Eeyore's head was twice the size of an ordinary infant's—and that it should create as small a head as possible. But the brain would have to be of decent size. Isn't that why it chose a sphere, its shape being the least bulky and the most capacious? I think your head, Ma-chan, its shape, is cute. And the brain has decent substance. So I would say that the womb-level control was a success. You were actually a skinny little baby when you were born. I understand your delivery was a very easy one.

"I know it must be revolting to hear a boy in your class call you Ma-chan the *mari*. But I think you have every reason to feel proud of your head, for it's certain that your still-unconscious body cooperated with your mother's womb. So neither Eeyore's wenned head, nor your super small, round head, is in any manner the kind that could have been produced with a die in a factory!"

"That's how carefully K explained things to you," Mr. Shigeto said, after a few moments of silence, "and you carved his words deep in your heart. It's strange, though. K was grumbling to me that he has trouble communicating with you. Yet he's said all this to you, and you understand him quite well. Isn't that enough? I feel he expects too much when it comes to his family relationships."

"It was unusual for Father to talk to me at such length. . . . But I think I was more moved when I learned about Mother's resolve than I was by Father's explanation. In those days, I was more simpleminded than I am now. . . . Besides, my younger brother told me there's no scientific evidence to support the notion that interaction between mother and fetus at the unconscious level can control the physical aspects of the fetus."

"I can't be so sure," Mr. Shigeto rejoined. "There's not much that science has thoroughly resolved—especially when it comes to such a thing as the interaction of minds between a conceived child and its mother."

"Prosaic as he is, Ma-chan, Mr. Shigeto is also a mystic, of the Russian Orthodox kind," his wife wedged in. "No, Ma-chan, you think things out very thoroughly. And I can see that K-chan's life at home hasn't been all that peaceful."

"All I think about is Eeyore and myself, if I do any thinking at all," I said, wondering why I was talking so much at the home of someone I was meeting for the first time.

a quiet life

* * *

The day after Eeyore toted in the heavy potted plants, another incident occurred on our way to the welfare workshop. There is a girls' middle school on the same bus route, and the buses are full. They are even more packed during winter, when everyone wears more. Eeyore, who has a big, bulky satchel hanging from his shoulder, clings to a strap to support himself, but the way he stands reveals the slight abnormality in his legs, which I must admit is obvious to the girls around him. That morning, Eeyore had collided with two female students near the entrance of the bus, one a defiant-looking girl with well-chiseled features, and the other an unassertive type, who seemed to be under her protection. Eeyore's satchel, too, hit the seemingly quiet girl's bosom with a thud. The defiant-looking girl glared at him with the stare of a young tomcat, though Eeyore didn't notice this, for he was concentrating on clinging to a strap with both hands. I finally made my way to his side and apologized to the girls. The seemingly strong-willed girl, with a violence I could feel in the breath she spewed on my face, cursed, "Dropouts!"

I could see Eeyore's face from between his strap-clutching arms. For a moment he appeared to cower at the outburst, yet, unaware of having done anything wrong, he also seemed amused, perhaps because he had never heard the word *dropout* uttered with such malice. Of course, we never used it at home. I had never heard it on my way to or from the special school, at least not when I was with him, and certainly not at the welfare workshop either. The instructors wouldn't possibly use such a word when reprimanding the workers, and I don't think it's ever been spoken among the co-workers. In all fairness, of course, *dropout* is hardly the appropriate word for Eeyore and his co-workers, who work very hard at the workshop.

a robot's nightmare

That's probably why Eeyore found the sound of *dropout* amusing, especially the *-out* part. So thinking, I disengaged my thoughts from the girl, and we made our transfer to the train we had to take. But as we approached the welfare workshop, I saw Tamio-san coming our way. Tamio-san, who is normally a very cheerful person, was walking with his head down, looking painfully dispirited, and an equally dejected-looking woman was trailing him—and *dropout* floated back into my mind.

Tamio-san is one of Eeyore's co-workers, but he is about Father's age. Nevertheless, this woman, his watchdog, sometimes comes with him, as when he isn't feeling well, to see to it that on his way home he doesn't buy and drink sake from the vending machines. I now know that the woman, who I had taken to be as old as Grandma, is Tamio-san's younger sister. And when I saw the two of them that day, I imagined a certain point in our future, when Eeyore would be Tamio-san's age and I would be the age of his younger sister. And both of us would age in such a way that the muscle tissues of our face could only make us look despondent. Despite our age, people would still be calling us the *dropout* duo, *Eeyore* and *Ma-chan*. . . . When I thought about this, I felt wretched and sad for the first time.

I contemplated again, only languidly this time, something I had recalled just the day before, something Father had said about my small, round head. I also regretted having told Mr. Shigeto about it in such detail, which made me say to myself, *You're a fool. Languidly* and *You're a fool*, by the way, are expressions my younger brother O-chan had newly imported from cram school. I need not even think about it to realize that the problem I'm having at present is the small, round head riding on my thin neck. Would Father's dubious psychological explanation serve me in repelling an ignominious individual who might saunter up to me and ask, "Why is your head so small and so round?"?

When I think of the future, for Eeyore and me as a duo, he with his handicap and I with my small, round head, won't the most important thing—not in a universal sense, but in an eminently personal sense, to put it in O-chan's normal way of using words—be the fact that *dropouts*, the word that school-girl uttered, will gradually penetrate even more harshly into our minds?

I made pork cutlet for dinner that evening, for which O-chan commended me with one of his "it's better than just *sort of* good" compliments, and Eeyore, too, ate it with great delight. As for me, though I did sit with them at the dinner table, I just didn't have an appetite. And O-chan got to worrying so much he asked, "Do I detect early symptoms of your *robotization*? I know you have lots to be anxious about!"

What I thought that night, with no energy to log anything in "Diary as Home," was this. Sure O-chan is with us, but I couldn't ask very much of him, the independent, go-it-alone person that he is. Besides, he has college entrance exams to prepare for, his second try at them, after once failing. So at a time like this it must have taken tremendous resolve on Mother's part to entrust Eeyore to someone like me, someone with the sort of character that *robotizes*, and accompany Father to a California university. Could it be that she had perceived the unusual seriousness of Father's inner "pinch"—one that went beyond my imagination and one that he would have to get away from the trivialities of life in Japan to tackle?

That's why I'm holding out, but hard as I try, at times things go awry and I end up, for instance, being called a *dropout* by someone like that female student, a girl who appeared to be the miniature of a woman who stands on her own—by someone who had clearly seen me as the parasitic type, a harmful insect gnawing away at this tree called society. . . . Again I fully *robotized*, and kept gazing into the darkness of my room with unblinking eyes. No need to compare myself with Sportsman Asashio to know that I have become a *robot*, skinny and unworthy of notice —and a faint mechanical whir kept droning in my heart.

During Eeyore's next lesson, after he and Mr. Shigeto had gone into the music room, I talked intermittently with Mrs. Shigeto, and ended up telling her about the *dropout* incident. But I didn't speak with the same sense of depression I had felt when thinking to myself about it. Had I been feeling that heavy-hearted, I think I would have chosen another topic. Eeyore, however, had said something funny on our way there, words that unfettered my heart, and I was prompted to tell her what had happened, as I rode the momentum of this heart.

As for the words Eeyore uttered, I'll just copy what I wrote in "Diary as Home." The Shigetos' house is in a newly developed residential area along the Keio railway line. It stands halfway down the slope from a high ground that leads into a hollow. The station is level with the high ground, and most houses from about where the decline begins have wire-fenced lawns with golf-practice nets hanging over them, flaunting a higher status than the houses in the hollow. And as a rule, there is a dog in the garden.

That day, as Eeyore was retying his shoelace—I had told him it was loose—a spitz in the garden across the road started yelping like crazy, while running about as though it had gone berserk.

"It's really only timid dogs that bark like that," I said to Eeyore before he got angry at the dog and scared the life out of it. "They're weak dogs. You could even feel sorry for them."

a quiet life

Eeyore raised himself and, probably because there was still a good four or five meters to the fence, he called out to the yelping dog with composure, "Ken, Ken!"

"Oh? Do you know him?" I asked.

Eeyore let my question hang in the air, and nonchalantly started walking.

"Today I just thought I'd call him 'dog' in Chinese," he said.

I laughed so loud the dog's yelping turned into a timorous whimper. Going down the road, side by side, I felt that Eeyore had blown away the despondent feeling that had been with me the past few days.

Mrs. Shigeto sank into thought as she listened to me speak of the *dropout* incident. On the dining table, where she sat opposite me, were paper and scissors, and a tube of paste. She was very carefully doing some handwork, and when she rested her hands and raised her eyes, she presented her opinion in the form of two blocks of convincing thought. First she asked me how Eeyore had taken it, if I had detected any sign of hurt in him.

"He appeared to like the sound of the word then," I replied. "But I don't know how he felt afterwards; we never talked about it. . . . If he'd asked any of his instructors what it meant, they would've written something to that effect in the welfare workshop home-correspondence notebook. No, I don't think he asked.

"The incident has left me so depressed that perhaps it's my dejection that's affecting him. My younger brother is the take-things-as-they-come type, and it doesn't seem to matter much if our parents are here or not. Yet even *he* remarked that I must have many things to be anxious about. Perhaps Eeyore sensed my anxieties, and maybe that's why he tried to cheer me up with his Chinese version of *dog*."

116

Mrs. Shigeto relaxed the skin of her feverish cheeks into a soft smile only toward the end of my reply, but from what she said, after tightening the skin again, I realized that her face had flushed simply because she was angry.

"Ma-chan," she said, "the little relief I find in what you told me, if I can call it that, is that you apologized for Eeyore before the girl called you *dropouts* and not afterwards. I wouldn't have gone so far as to slap her in the face, but if I'd been there, I would at least have made her take it back. I wish you had. It's very important for a human being to take such action.

"I told you about the time Mr. Shigeto and I traveled around Europe with our cat, didn't I? We got to Warsaw Airport on a Polish airliner from Dubai on the Arabian Peninsula. Out of an oven, then straight into a refrigerator. We were all shivering as we waited, but our luggage just didn't come out. Then we saw a government official, clad in a suit you could tell was tailored in England, ordering a porter to pick out his suitcases, while luggage for the general passengers was being held up. Mr. Shigeto, as a Japanese visitor who could speak Polish, went up to the gentleman and asked if doing such a thing was socialism. I think it's important to have this kind of courage."

"But this girl was only a middle-school student," I said. "A child yet, and cute, too. . . ."

"All children are cute, Ma-chan," Mrs. Shigeto rejoined. "And cute as they may be, they have certain traits, as yet hidden, that will manifest themselves when they become adults. What I do every time I see a child is to picture him or her in middle age, from whatever outcropping of hidden character I perceive in the child. By doing this, I understand human beings better. What you should have seen, in the girl you say looked cute, was a middle-aged woman with a nicely featured face and a shapely figure, but a discriminatory character. I believe there was a lot of meaning embedded in her disparaging of Eeyore and you as *dropouts*."

Dejected, I felt I was going to *robotize*. I knew that my attitude toward the girl, who in the bus had appeared so much the teacher's-pet type, had been servile. And Mrs. Shigeto's words echoed even more forcefully in my heart, for until then I'd been thinking that, compared to how I had reacted to the word, Eeyore's reserved way of enjoying the ring of *dropouts* in his ears had even been noble. Mrs. Shigeto asked me no further questions, probably because she had clearly seen through my plight.

After Eeyore's lesson, the *dropout* topic cropped up again, this time with Mr. Shigeto entering into the discussion. Mrs. Shigeto began by recapitulating our experience in the bus. Eeyore clearly remembered and vigorously kept nodding his head, and when she came to the part about his satchel hitting the girl's chest, he looked very sorry. Then she reminded her husband about what he had done at Warsaw Airport, to which he, in turn, supplemented her words by telling us what *she* had done there.

"This lady here," he began, "knew very well that summer in Europe could often be very chilly. So after putting a kerchief she'd brought with her around the basket we kept our cat in, she lent a hand-woven muffler to a little girl who was sitting beside her. She's very kind to little girls."

That day Mrs. Shigeto continued with the work she was doing, even after Eeyore joined us, and asked me to bring in the cookies and tea in her stead. She was preparing a draft of a handbill the size of a small notebook, by making a collage of letters she had clipped from an English-language newspaper and other publications. She was going to make copies on a duplicating machine installed at some twenty-four-hour supermarket. Its content was directed toward the chairman of the Polish National Council who would be visiting Napan, and it protested the oppression of the country's poets and writers.

"Why don't you give some copies to Ma-chan to send to K?" Mr. Shigeto said. "There are quite a few expatriate intellectuals from Poland who work on the various UC campuses, like Milosz, for one. I'd like K to know what some Japanese are doing for them."

"K-chan is apathetic," Mrs. Shigeto said emphatically, which made me, and Eeyore too, feel sad. "We've known of Chairman Jaruzelski's visit for quite some time, so I asked K-chan if he'd do something to have the Japan P.E.N. Club protest his coming here, but he didn't do anything. I guess he feels a little guilty about it. That's why he didn't come here himself to ask you about Eeyore's lesson, but got Ma-chan to do it. Don't you think so?"

"K's already issued so many statements, enough to make him sick, all of them ineffective," Mr. Shigeto replied. "Jaruzelski is coming from poverty-stricken Poland to request economic aid of a filthy-rich Japan. At a time when the nation welcoming him has one careful eye directed toward the U.S. and the E.C., while the other's exploiting business opportunities in Poland. Don't you think K shied away from making a statement because he knew it would fall on deaf ears?"

"The privileged few may know it's of no use," Mrs. Shigeto said, "but those of us with no name have to give it all we've got: that's my policy. . . . Mr. Shigeto, could you look over the direct-appeal part for me, the part in Polish? A few copies might fall into the hands of some members of the delegation, you know."

"Anyway, we'll ask Ma-chan to send some to K. He may feel a bit relieved to know that some people are trying to accomplish what he couldn't," Mr. Shigeto said, reading the draft as soon as he got it. "He may suffer a few pangs of guilt for not having done anything, but that can't be helped. . . . I think the Polish here is very good."

"Well then, Ma-chan, I'm going to ask you to send K-chan a few copies when I get it duplicated," Mrs. Shigeto said, happily retrieving the draft. Putting an end to the talk about the handbills, she brought up the *dropout* topic again.

"Of course," she said, "I'm angry at the girl who called you *dropouts*, but that doesn't mean I worry about the kind of person she'll turn out to be. A girl like her is bound to become a fine middle-aged woman who lives robustly in everything she does.

"My feelings go out to those who people of her kind hurt by calling them 'dropouts.' And I wonder how we can become more aware of the unique existence of *dropouts* as individuals. A case in point—I may be jumping to conclusions—but I admire the composure in Eeyore's attitude." ("Thank you very much!" Eeyore happily broke in; to which Mrs. Shigeto gave the rather incoherent reply, "Please don't mention it! The pleasure's mine!")

"As a matter of fact, Ma-chan, I consider myself a *dropout*. I've been one since I was a young girl, I was one during my previous marriage, and I'm one even now with Mr. Shigeto. . . . I'd never thought in terms of *dropout*, but I say *dropout* here because it happens to be the word in question. You see, I feel that I was born a *nobody*. I've lived all my years feeling like this, and I'll live a few more feeling the same way, then die the death of a *nobody*. (Reservedly, so as not to interrupt Mrs. Shigeto's talk, Eeyore, who is sensitive to death, the word itself, sighed "Hoh!"—which took Mrs. Shigeto by surprise, prompting her to say, "Oh, Eeyore! I'm sorry if I caused you alarm.")

"My thoroughly ordinary head thinks that, so long as you refrain from privileging yourself in any manner and live as a *nobody*, you'll have a certain amount of leeway," she continued. "And within its limits, you exert as much energy as you can. Within my limited capacity, exerting energy is not much more than, as Mr. Shigeto just reminded me, lending a muffler to a shivering, tired girl.

"But once you set your mind to living the life of a *nobody*, I feel that—sorry Eeyore, I'm going to frighten you again—even when it's time to die, you can go to zero with some leeway. Which is to say, you return to zero from a point practically next to zero. Isn't being anxious about your soul after death, or about eternal life, privileging yourself? Compared to an insect, for example. . . . Wasn't Abraham the patriarch of the chosen people who made a special contract with some celestial existence? Even in Poland, it's not just the higher-ups in the communist hierarchy who are privileged. Aren't the Catholics there also privileged?—though in a mundane sense they may now be underprivileged. . . ."

"You *are* an anarchist, aren't you—and one who's got absolutely nothing to do with faith . . . ," Mr. Shigeto observed, blinking his eyes in amusement. "But I think your handbill supports the Catholic masses in Poland, too."

"I stand on the side of the *nobodies* there," Mrs. Shigeto said. "I can't support anybody else. I'm a *nobody* down to the marrow, and I rejoice in this. . . . But Ma-chan, when I look through the eyes of a *nobody*, I seem to get a sharper picture of the reality of K-chan's 'pinch.'"

Taking what Mrs. Shigeto said as something she had carefully thought about and wanted to convey through me to Father himself and to Mother as well, I summarized her subsequent comments in "Diary as Home." I knew that I was in no position to say anything about Father's "pinch," let alone do anything to help him overcome it, but if I was going to forward Mrs. Shigeto's handbills to him, I thought I ought to enclose a letter, which would be a verbatim copy from the diary, of the ideas about Father that she had earnestly put together. Another reason I chose to do this was because I feared that, if I sent Father only the handbills, he wouldn't take them seriously, which wouldn't be fair to Mrs. Shigeto. Besides, they would be more meaningful if they came with a letter explaining her thoughts about him, and more so if these thoughts were tied to something within herself.

1. K-chan and Mr. Shigeto became friends when they were both very young, before I got to know either of them. K-chan was already writing novels, and was gaining a reputation. Mr. Shigeto recalls with disgust that K-chan, for the next several years, appeared to be walking a few feet above the ground—a shameful sight, frankly. Didn't he more or less come to himself after Eeyore was born, after experiencing various difficulties? The only thing that had kept Mr. Shigeto from severing ties with K-chan was his tolerance toward a classmate who had come from a rural area, and who, when his writings began to appear in the media, had fallen emotionally ill. I got to know K-chan while he still had traces of that air of self-importance about him, so I don't think Mr. Shigeto was being arrogant when he described young K-chan this way.

2. But isn't K-chan still dragging around some of the scars, or habits, from that period when he thought of himself as constituting a special existence? Doesn't this account for the gall he had in going to California with Oyu-san, monopolizing her, leaving a handicapped child to his daughter's care, under the pretext that he, a full-fledged adult, was

tormented by a "pinch"? Wouldn't his long career of writing about himself for a wide readership have left him unable to spontaneously feel that he's a *nobody*, though in ways that differ from the feelings he had when he was young and didn't reflect upon himself?

3. Let me say that the muddled ideas K-chan sometimes expresses on faith and life after death stem from the fact that he feels he constitutes some sort of privileged existence. I don't know how many billion people are walking this planet today, but those who have religion are, I think, a small minority. Multitudes of *nobodies* live and end their lives without faith, and without any solid assurance of what happens to our souls after we die. If only K-chan realized that he was living in the sea of lives and deaths of all these *nobodies*, he could objectify his own life and death with more leeway. In any case, I don't at all think that leading the life and death of a *nobody* is meaningless. As someone who has lived as a *nobody* for many, many years, I firmly believe this. . . .

I was certainly captivated by Mrs. Shigeto's story. For I, too, long to lead a quiet life with Eeyore as *nobodies*. This was all the more reason that I, feeling a little guilty, thought I needed to put in a few words in Father's defense. Although I didn't write this in "Diary as Home," I told Mrs. Shigeto that Father probably didn't think being a writer made him a privileged person.

"You might refute me," I said, "by saying that, at this very moment, Father is a writer-in-residence, but I think he honestly feels very grateful to have the position. I understand he was grumbling to Mother that if he wasn't suffering this 'pinch,' he'd have declined. He'd accepted the offer, he said, only because he considered himself an unseaworthy old tub that needed shelter from an imminent storm."

Mrs. Shigeto's reply to my words was slightly off the mark, for it seemed she had already thought of putting an end to the discussion. So this is how the long *dropout* talk drew to a close, at least for the day.

"Ma-chan," she said, "a person changes with his or her position, whatever it is—though, of course, you can't ignore the individual's inborn character. . . . Mr. Shigeto's former supervisor, who is still with the news agency, was just recently promoted to director. Mr. Shigeto attended the private party honoring the occasion and came home enervated. He told me the new director's speech was very long, and he got very tired just listening to him. So he drank to recover his vigor, and he overdid it. . . . Remember, Mr. Shigeto, you were still worn out the next morning, and you kept griping about your fatigue, citing some rules of Latin grammar?"

"My Latin grammar doesn't amount to much. It's only elementary stuff everybody knows," Mr. Shigeto said *languidly*. "You see, when accentuating Latin words with vowel clusters," he went on to explain, "the syllables with long vowels are important, and there are two kinds: essentially long, and long due to their position. In other words, *long by nature* and *long by position*.

"My boss was, by nature, a guy who gave long speeches. But after he got the director's position, his speeches became longer. . . ."

Hearing the joke for the first time, I laughed out loud, but Mrs. Shigeto laughed with such vigor that one might have thought it was new to her, too. Eeyore looked on happily as we laughed, while Mr. Shigeto, somewhat dramatically, sat there even more *languidly*.

a robot's nightmare

That night, after finally falling asleep, I had a really sad dream. In the pale glow of a still, seemingly everlasting desert twilight—probably on the Arabian Peninsula, because Mrs. Shigeto had briefly mentioned it—was a multitude of people, some standing, some squatting, but all peering in the same direction. Some were lying down, but they were frantically lifting up their heads, trying to see in that direction. It resembled a scene Father once told me about, in one of Blake's images, just before the Last Judgment. Father went through a period of reading Blake day after day, and he once told me about the scene, while referring to one of the memo cards on which he had written its translation. The powers-that-be had already been arrested in their golden palace, and it seemed they were being tormented. In the desert, the multitude rejoiced and sang as the howlings of the arrestees reached them. The air was fraught with furious energy, charged, as though before the crashing of thunder. . . . "It's just like Blake's desert scene," I reminded myself as I dreamed, as if I had actually been there. . . .

I didn't quite understand what Father's intention had been in telling me about Blake's desert scene, but the focus of his talk was on the babies who, though they had died before being baptized, and their bodies were already cold, were screaming. ". . . the children of six thousand years / Who died in infancy rage furious, a mighty multitude rage furious, / Naked & pale standing on the expecting air to be delivered." And in my dream, too, Eeyore and I were children again, standing quietly in the desert. Perhaps we reverted to childhood because of Eeyore's head disorder, and because I hadn't married. Our desert was different from Blake's in that our Last Judgment wouldn't come for another six thousand years, unlike Blake's

a quiet life

desert, where the Second Coming of Christ is imminent. Which gave me some relief, because this dream meant that Eeyore wasn't the antichrist.

I soon realized that Eeyore and I were truly *nobodies*. I knew that nobody cared about us; nobody, come hell or high water, would come to take us to some other place. And what made it even worse than having nobody to help us, Mrs. Shigeto, who had been on our side that afternoon, was peering over her silver-rimmed glasses, which made her look like an elderly German woman, and was sending us wordless, reproachful glances from across the pale-dark multitude. In her carry-on bag was a thin, hand-woven muffler that, though we were cold, she didn't dare lend us. . . .

It appeared that she was never going to forgive us, for despite the fact that we were *nobodies*, we were pretending otherwise, and she had seen through it. Needless to say, it wasn't because she believed we were self-conscious about Father being a fairly well-known writer. Actually, ever since I was a child, I resented it when someone mentioned his name to me. I tried to maintain as much distance as I could from those who did, even my homeroom teacher. There was no misunderstanding on Mrs. Shigeto's part here. To be sure, she was silently sending a tacit, condemnatory message that the wrong I'd been committing was in taking Eeyore's disorder to be a privilege: cherishing pride in him, believing that his prowess in understanding music, his disorder notwithstanding, had truly made him not a *nobody*; being proud of myself, too, for having decided I would follow him wherever he went. Then I came to this desert on the Arabian Peninsula, and I was thinking that the decision to follow Eeyore there entitled me to be something other than a *nobody*.

"See in the pale glow how you compare with the people around you!" she said. "Look at you two! Retarded Eeyore!

And you, Ma-chan, you can't even hope for marriage! Even among other nobodies, you're a *dead-end dropout*!"

Neither Father nor Mother was beside us. They had gone to California to devote themselves to *matters of the soul*, and later left for some other place to pursue more. O-chan, too, may have been on this desert, but he's such a fundamentally independent and go-it-alone person that he was probably treading his own path somewhere far away from us. And with the expertise he had acquired on the orienteering team, he may have quickly made a map of the desert and could have been running on the sand toward the control points he had set up. I soon *robotized* under Mrs. Shigeto's glare, and could not even turn to see if Eeyore was at my side. I could no longer spot him in the horde of nobodies, and I had the feeling he had long ago forgotten me.

So we were going to stand on the Arabian desert for another six thousand years, the same way we had stood there for the six thousand that had already passed. . . .

As soon as I awoke, I began to weep, and I continued to weep for some time. The twilight desert in my dream was thoroughly arid, and my tears dried even before they welled up in my eyes. I thought of Mrs. Shigeto as I wept. Mrs. Shigeto is never the fear-instilling, inhumane person who appeared in my dream, but there was no denying that the dream portrayed a deep-rooted element in her person. I find her to be a "righteous person," and I have to admit that the reproach, from a "righteous person" like her, had struck home. . . .

I waited until my eyes shed no more tears, then picked up "Diary as Home," which I had put by my pillow, and started reading the part I had written about the fit Eeyore had had on the platform coming home from the Shigetos. Eeyore had protected me from the stampede, though he had been in the midst of a fit, his mind was muddled, and on top of all this, his body was tormenting him. And I wrote then: "I began wondering it Eeyore, deep inside, embraced a malevolent force like that of the antichrist. Even if he were the antichrist, I would follow him wherever he went"—though I had added that even for me this was a *peculair resolve.*

Now why did I so naively think I could follow him wherever he went? I'm a *nobody* in the truest sense of the word. Sheer complacency had led me—a *nobody* and nothing more—to think the way I did, relying solely on Eeyore's handicap. . . . How pitifully sad it is, though, that I'm merely a *nobody*, neither beautiful nor strong, just a *robotizing* coward. . . .

It must have been this sadness, I thought in my weary, frayed heart, that had *substantialized*—that's how O-chan would put it—in my dream of a twilight desert.

In my heart, I apologized to Mrs. Shigeto for dreaming her to be a merciless person. But as the possessor of a mind as perverse as mine, only after the free leap in the dream was I, for the first time, able to associate her with the "righteous person" that she is. Ramifying thoughts of her continued to occupy my mind, making me feel nervous about seeing her the next time I took Eeyore to her place.

While I was having this selfish dream, and was alone ruminating on it, however, the real-life Mrs. Shigeto had met with a calamity totally undeserving of her benign person. What occasioned this, to begin with, was her behavior as a "righteous person." Undue violence had been wrought upon her, an accident in which she had broken her clavicle in a complex way. . . .

Mrs. Shigeto had gone to pass out the handbills, the draft of which she'd been preparing the day I took Eeyore to his lesson, to a place she had discerned would be best for the purpose: the prime minister's official residence, of all places, where the chairman of the Polish National Council was making his formal visit. And she had tried to hand one of her bills directly to Mr. Jaruzelski, the consequence of which was that she was knocked down by a security guard, and broke her clavicle. Mr. Shigeto asked his friend at a news agency to inquire of the police as to why a guard at the prime minister's official residence should exercise such brutality on a middle-aged woman, but both Mr. Shigeto and his wife understood it was not a situation that warranted a tedious protest.

What Mrs. Shigeto had intended to do in front of the official residence was this: since people would be mobilized to welcome Chairman Jaruzelski, as the hour of his visit pressed closer, she would wait behind the welcoming crowd; and if, by any chance, the accompanying representatives came near her, she would hand the fliers to them. To avoid being excluded as a black sheep, she would not yet show the fliers to anyone among the welcomers who had been mobilized. Instead, she would wait until the chairman entered the building, and then get those interested in Japanese-Polish relations to read the fliers.

But Mrs. Shigeto, who surprisingly has an impatient side to her character, arrived there before the guards were stationed. And she saw an elderly Polish woman, evidently lost, walking to the intersection from the street down by the Diet Members' Hall. Mrs. Shigeto asked her if something was wrong, and learned that though she had waited and waited, her interpreter, a woman who had promised to meet her, hadn't come. So Mrs. Shigeto acted as the liaison between this woman and one of the security guards, whereupon she was mistaken for the woman's interpreter and was led in through the gate, together with the woman, who had an invitation card with her. Beside the entrance, a band of media personnel was already waiting for Mr. Jaruzelski's arrival. Mrs. Shigeto asked one of the secretaries to accommodate the woman, while she herself joined the phalanx of media people and waited with them. And when the members of the Polish delegation got out of their limousines, she scrambled out from among the cameramen to hand Mr. Jaruzelski one of her handbills. A security guard, panicking at this unforeseen event—his blunder—thrust her back with his outstretched arms, which hit her clavicle and knocked her down. . . .

The incident was conveyed to me over the phone by Mr. Shigeto. The conscientious person that he is, he called to tell me that an accident had occurred, compelling him to cancel Eeyore's composition lesson that day. When I expressed my wish to immediately visit Mrs. Shigeto with Eeyore, he fell silent for a moment and said, hesitantly, as if speaking the unspeakable, that we didn't have to come, since she was leaving the hospital very soon anyway. He went on to explain that his wife, in a hospital bed from the shock of the accident, was so despondent that she wouldn't give even him a decent answer. He said that the hospital she had been rushed to in an ambulance had five patients to a room, and one of them was rude. He wouldn't want Eeyore to experience something disagreeable.

Having been cussed at on the bus, and seeing a sad dream, paranoia had gotten the better of me. I imagined, for instance, Eeyore passing the rude patient's bed and tripping on the stand from which her IV bottle hung, and she shouting at him in her very fearsome adult voice, *Dropout!* Wouldn't even Mrs. Shigeto, who is so nice to Eeyore when she is healthy, also find it exasperating, when bedridden, to have to receive an unrelated person with a handicap? . . . Isn't this what Mr. Shigeto foresaw, and why he didn't welcome the idea of us visiting her? I was starting to see things with jaundiced eyes.

But no, Mr. Shigeto's tantalizing reserve in speaking his mind had stemmed from his concern for canceling, at his own convenience, a lesson Eeyore looked forward to as a matter of weekly routine.

"My wife's being in the hospital would not ordinarily come in the way of welcoming Eeyore for his lesson," he said apologetically.

Mr. Shigeto added, however, that his wife was concerned about the handbills that she had prepared for distribution, and that he had read in the paper of a return-of-courtesy reception to be hosted by the Polish delegation that evening at the Tokyo Kaikan, a hall by the Imperial Palace moat. He went on to say that his relationship with the petty officials at the Polish embassy had been sour for several years, and that he himself had received no invitation to the party, but that he wished, at least, to go and stand in front of the hall, and pass out fliers to the guests. The most important point of his phone call was that because of this, there was going to be no lesson that day.

It so happened that O-chan had no afternoon classes that day, and had returned home for lunch. So while he ate, I told him about what Mr. Shigeto had said to me. Eeyore, who had already heard me tell him about Mrs. Shigeto's injury, sat beside me listening, occasionally sighing "Hoh!" again, as if the information was new to him. O-chan, for his part, was merely a lunch-munching deadpan. He listened without saying a word and then retreated to his room. A while later, though, he came running downstairs and suggested something that took me by surprise. He knew Mr. Shigeto only from what I had told him, but he conjectured that Mr. Shigeto was currently not affiliated with any political party, or involved in a citizens' movement. So wasn't he intending to do the handbill distribution alone? O-chan's experience in handbill distribution was

a quiet life

limited to an event that his high school orienteering team had
held at a school festival. But he knew that it wasn't easy to get
people to take the fliers, especially if all you did was stand there
absentmindedly. Many people didn't even notice that he was
handing out fliers, he said. So why don't we join Mr. Shigeto's
handbill distribution, and take his injured wife's place?

"What do you mean *we*, O-chan?" I asked.

"I want you to count me in—that's what I mean," he replied, looking offended. "It would be dangerous if Eeyore had a
fit like he did the other time he was in a crowd. You'll need somebody to watch him, won't you, while you pass out the fliers?"

"Yes, please watch carefully, O-chan. It could be dangerous!" Eeyore said authoritatively. The expression on his face,
however, was that of innocent reliance.

So that evening, after duly setting aside some copies for
Father, *we* were going to pass out, in front of the Tokyo Kaikan,
the fliers Mrs. Shigeto had duplicated on a copying machine.
We planned to stand on the corner of the road along the moat,
two of us on each side, in such a way that we could close in on
the pedestrians. We knew that distributing the handbills
in front of the main entrance to the hall was out of the question, because although the reception for the Polish delegation
wouldn't be the only party there, the place would be tightly
guarded by the security personnel the Polish embassy had
requested.

When we got to the Tokyo Kaikan, after taking the Odakyu
Line and then transferring to the subway, we saw Mr. Shigeto
standing some distance from the building, with a bundle of
handbills under his arm and in a state of genuine absentmind-
edness. His explanation of the situation was this: when the
delegation approached the Tokyo Kaikan, a group of young
demonstrators voicing solidarity with the democracy movement

in Poland waited for the delegates' cars to come by. It was a small group, but because it was small, it was very mobile, and the timing went well. The delegates merely slowed down, but after passing the demonstrators, they had to enter the hall through a staff-only passage from the basement parking lot of an adjacent building. Apparently Mr. Jaruzelski's car was the only one able to reenter the hall's driveway, but only after the area was secured by the riot police. In any event, security at the front entrance was tightened, and Mr. Shigeto had no choice but to stand off to the side of the entrance, and try to guess which of the people going into the hall were the invited guests of the Polish embassy. . . .

"Are you *sort of* through with the fliers?" O-chan unreservedly asked Mr. Shigeto, who shook his head. The cap Mr. Shigeto had on, the kind that Irish seamen wear, made his head look awfully flat.

"Those who know my face avoid me," he said. "They probably feel uncomfortable just seeing me. They jaywalk across the street over there to get to the building, and don't use the pedestrian crossing here. . . . In any case, my wife told me not to give any to people who probably wouldn't read them. After all, they're duplicates of a handmade draft, and she made only a hundred copies."

"Please give us a share of the fliers then," O-chan said. "You and Ma-chan can stand on this side of the walkway, and Eeyore and I will be on the other side. And so we will *sort of* surround the people who take the pedestrian crossing. . . . I've checked the information board for today's schedule of parties. There are only two others besides the Polish one: a Japanese chess championship party, and a reception sponsored by a women's apparel company. So it shouldn't be hard to tell who's going to the Polish reception. All right,

Eeyore, let's cross to the other side. There's also the subway exit, you know!"

That's how we started distributing the handbills. But the winter sun had already set, and since the party had commenced some time before, all we could do was hand out a few to the latecomers who trickled by. I wasn't too disappointed, though, for O-chan and I had worked out a strategy on the train going there, which was to wait until after the party broke up, for embassy parties aren't that long anyway, perhaps an hour or so. Mr. Shigeto didn't seem very excited when we told him of our plan, but he stayed with us, standing in his big coat, also a seaman's, though it didn't seem to be staving off the cold. Once, during the wait, he walked into the hall pretending he had some business to attend to. I thought he had gone to the bathroom, but he came back giving off the nice fragrance of distilled spirits from around his reddened nose. . . .

Before long, people you could easily tell had attended the Polish reception started coming out. I started working with the handbills, and when I looked to see how Eeyore, with O-chan beside him, was doing on the walkway across the street, I saw him passing out his share with great composure, bowing courteously, both to those who accepted one and to those who passed without taking any. Some bowed deeply in return, as though infected with Eeyore's bow. I did not, by any means, neglect passing out my share, but really, Eeyore's demeanor was eye-catching. Soon an idea that had never before occurred to me sprang to mind. Though I was his younger sister, I had all along taken it upon myself to be his guardian. And though at times he undoubtedly had been the one protecting me, my heart never rested unless I thought he was within my realm of guardianship. But wasn't it simply wrong of me to think so?

a robot's nightmare

I believe that Mr. Shigeto and I, encouraged by the way the Eeyore–O-chan pair was distributing the fliers, became more aggressive. More people received our handbills, and before I knew it I had finished mine. I asked Mr. Shigeto to give me what he had left, which was soon gone too. Then Eeyore and O-chan, who had come across the pedestrian crossing, reported that they, too, had finished passing out all their bills. O-chan said he had given out even the copy on which he had worked out a math problem—he had used the back, where there had been lots of room to write—while waiting for the party to finish, to a foreign lady who happened to be the last among the party guests coming out of the hall, and who seemed to take a serious interest in what we were doing.

Again the week after we distributed the fliers, there was no music lesson for Eeyore. Instead, he was engrossed in composing a new piece. As for O-chan, I have written a number of times so far that I always considered him an independent, go-it-alone person. So he really did surprise me when he suggested that we help Mr. Shigeto with the handbills. And he actually helped, though he himself had probably thought it the natural thing to do, by giving up some of the precious time he needed to prepare for his exams, sacrificing time that was so precious to him that he worked on his math even while we waited for the party to break up. Moreover, he appeared to have changed somewhat in the way he relates to Eeyore. The day after we went to the Tokyo Kaikan, for example, when I returned home from my errands—shopping for groceries at the supermarket in front of the station, and paying our bills at the bank—I saw not only Eeyore, who was lying flat on the carpet, as usual, composing music, but O-chan, too, studying at the dining table with, at his feet, a bag as big as a medium-size raccoon dog, which is always full of the handouts he gets at cram school.

When I asked him if he had chosen to stay in the dining room after coming downstairs to answer a call, his curt reply was "Not really!" Eeyore then supplemented this by saying, "I answer all phone calls! O-chan has to work hard for his entrance exams!"

What had become an everyday sight, O-chan at the dining table and Eeyore lying on the carpet, and the way each concentrated on his work, revealed to me a similarity the two brothers shared that I hadn't noticed until then. The notes that Eeyore wrote on his staff paper were long, thin, and relaxed, and looked like what Father aptly called "bean sprouts," while the numbers and figures O-chan penciled on his calculation sheets looked like unrestrained processions of eccentric ants devoid of team spirit. . . .

Eeyore completed a new piece during the two weeks he had no lessons with Mr. Shigeto. I didn't ask him about it, though, for I didn't want to dilute the pleasure that I knew he—and I, too, for that matter—would derive from announcing it at Mr. Shigeto's place, at *the right moment.* And when the day came for us to go to the Shigetos, Eeyore was in such high spirits that he got ready for the visit all by himself. On the train, he offered a seat to an elderly gentleman. He stayed calm and turned to look at me, placidly, when suddenly, at the corner of the street where the slope down to the Shigetos begins, the dog he had addressed as Ken scurried to the wire fence and started barking. The irascible small dog kept yelping, but I think it also looked puzzled, as if it had lost confidence in itself.

Mrs. Shigeto, who had just returned from the hospital—her face emaciated and smaller, and her hair, which had lost its perm, bound in a ponytail—reminded me of an upper-class student I knew in the girls' high school I had gone to, a serious girl by nature, who had always been very kind to me. Mrs. Shigeto was preparing ribs of lamb for us, just like the last time. The look on Mr. Shigeto's face was one of solemnity, but he also appeared to be wearing a poker face. In other words, he appeared his usual self, except that he wasn't reading when we visited him that day—he was sitting at the dining table, toying with the bottles of marjoram, whole pepper, and some kind of special salt they use.

"Eeyore, Ma-chan, and even your younger brother did a great job of distributing my handbills," Mrs. Shigeto said. "K-chan, too, wrote me a card as a token of his having received them. Thank you so much. If I didn't have garlic on my hands, I'd give you both a firm handshake this very minute." She imparted her feelings with eyes that, behind her glasses, appeared almost unnaturally clear.

"Why don't you wipe off the garlic?" Mr. Shigeto broke in, handing his wife a napkin with an agility I had rarely seen him exercise; and Mrs. Shigeto obediently complied. While she shook Eeyore's hand and then mine, I was thinking to myself that we were lucky O-chan wasn't there, for he's the sort of person who would have had to smell his fingers to see if the garlic odor had been transferred to them.

"Thank you, Eeyore. Thank you, Ma-chan. Thanks to you, I've already received a response to my handbill from a Polish person," Mrs. Shigeto said as she wiped her hands again with meticulous care to resume the task of rubbing more garlic into the ribs of lamb. Her complexion was paler than usual, and the flush that appeared on her cheeks—I even saw it spread— looked very pink.

"A letter in Polish was addressed here because of the reference I wrote on the handbills," she said. "It's from a female professor at a university in Warsaw. She uses mathematics to analyze contemporary economics, which is unusual. She said in the letter that she was also an adviser to the government, and that she was projecting Poland's agricultural reconstruction while studying Japanese economic policy. . . . She's the one I took to the prime minister's residence, on the occasion of my catastrophe. . . ."

"Perhaps she's the lady who asked Eeyore and O-chan for their last flier," I said.

"Yes, she's the one," Mr. Shigeto said, taking out an envelope from the letter basket that had been shoved to the edge in order that the table could be set. He wasn't going to hand it to me or anything—it was written in Polish anyway—he just kept waving it in circles in front of Eeyore's face, and continued, "When Eeyore was fretting about having no more fliers to give out, O-chan remembered there was one he'd used to work out a math problem. . . . It says here that the calculation on the back has nothing to do with the handbill's message, yet still it's an excellent answer. But I thought O-chan was a humanities person, like K."

"He's a science person," I said, "down to the marrow."

"Evidently," Mrs. Shigeto said, "there are scholars, even among Jaruzelski's delegation, who are seriously concerned about Poland's future. And that's a pleasant surprise, because I've been disgusted with all embassy people."

"At least this woman deserves respect," Mr. Shigeto said. "I guess she's returning to Poland very soon, but I hope the establishment there will change for the better so that people like her can prove their worth. The labor unions at the Gdansk factories are important, of course. But the reconstruction of the nation's agricultural economy, this woman's special field, is more pressing."

"Don't you think Poland will change, too?" Mrs. Shigeto said. "This scholar seems to have that outlook."

"You'll be able to see her when you go to Warsaw next time," I said.

"I don't think so, Ma-chan," Mrs. Shigeto rejoined, and continued with biting seriousness. "Scholars like her may not be in the upper echelons of the privileged, but they are still important people. Really, I don't wish to meet anybody, except the *nobodies*—wherever I go and under whatever regime they are living. . . . I'm sure this woman was happy because she received a handbill from a *nobody* in Japan." Mr. Shigeto blinked at his wife's words and fell into thought.

Then Eeyore, who had been politely sitting there, made a move, as though he'd been waiting for that very moment. He took out a piece of staff paper from his satchel and nonchalantly placed it where Mr. Shigeto had dropped his eyes. From the way he did this, you could clearly see that he had been prompted by unrestrainable joy.

"Huh!? 'Ribs'!?" Mr. Shigeto asked, taken off guard. Eeyore answered by pointing to Mrs. Shigeto with the typical gesture of a concertmaster introducing a soloist.

"Eeyore, did you compose this piece for Mrs. Shigeto, to wish her a quick recovery?" I asked, my brain functioning a little faster than usual. "Mrs. Shigeto, I heard you fractured your clavicle, and I think Eeyore composed it out of worry about your injury. He somehow got ribs and clavicle mixed up. . . . Eeyore, it was her clavicle."

"I think 'Ribs' is more interesting!" Eeyore said.

"You're a naming expert, Eeyore," Mr. Shigeto said contentedly, his eyes carefully perusing the music. "Shall I play it now? It looks like a good one as far as music theory goes. I don't notice any weak points in it."

"Thank you very much!" Eeyore exclaimed.

a quiet life

"The pleasure's ours," Mrs. Shigeto called to Eeyore, bowing to him as he happily followed her husband into the music room.

Then I helped Mrs. Shigeto spice the lamb while she, rather pedantically, taught me the amount of each spice necessary for the mixture. In our spare moments, she continued with the *nobody* topic, which she talked to me about the last time we were there. And what follows is what I have written in "Diary as Home," a recapitulation of what she told me during the moments we rested our busy hands—she appeared to tire easily from the effects that remained of her injury. My replies to her, too, are but a summary.

"Eeyore knew that I'd injured my clavicle, but he decided on 'Ribs' because he found the sound more interesting. Who else but Eeyore could think up such a title? Eeyore has his own world, which he protects in his own way. This doesn't mean he's locked up in his own little niche; he has a channel that's open to the outside world, through music and by communicating with you. I find this delightful."

"Your words are most uplifting. But when I reflect upon myself, I have to admit that, all along, I've been keeping Eeyore locked up in a special place. I realized this when you told me what you had to say about *nobodies*. I was, indeed, putting him someplace where I was treating him as somebody special. And this specialness must be something an outsider would consider lower than nobody, as the word *dropout* so aptly indicates. But the thing is, I grew up thinking, 'So what?' For I love Eeyore despite his handicap; I love him together with his handicap. And from a certain point in time, I even began to brandish his handicap like a banner. . . .

"I still believe there's nothing wrong with such banner-waving in my encounters with the outside world. But I think

I've become too accustomed to accepting him as a wonderfully interesting person at home. And because of this, I wonder if I've neglected to take a more realistic view of him. I've over-looked the fact that, if I disregarded his disorder, he'd be an ordinary *nobody*. Although I often discussed issues like the independence of handicapped people with other volunteers at college, I don't think I've ever imagined a relationship with Eeyore as an independent person.

"The other day, I watched, with one street between us, how Eeyore was passing out handbills to people he didn't know. I'd hardly ever observed him from that far for so long. Then I noticed that, though his movements were too slow, and the expressions on his face too naive, the people who received the fliers from him appeared to take him for an ordinary person. It was Eeyore's first experience in making direct contact with the outside world, but I felt that I'd discovered a genuinely ordinary *nobody* quality in him."

"I don't think you were the only one who felt that way. Didn't the Polish economist receive a handbill from Eeyore? It's apparent from her letter that she thinks he and the math whiz are one and the same person."

"I'm sure that if the lady had had more time to observe him, she'd have noticed his disorder. . . . But it's true that Eeyore does have an ordinary *nobody* side to him."

Trying too hard to understand me, Mrs. Shigeto appeared to have lost track, for I must have caused her undue strain, answering her very haltingly, deliberating every word I spoke. Then I noticed that Mr. Shigeto had opened the music-room door, and I heard him sit at the piano again. The newborn "Ribs" now echoed high and clear, unlike the muffled way we had heard it until then. Mrs. Shigeto tugged at her clavicle cast from over her blouse as though she were scratching herself,

a quiet life

but before long, the piano took told of her. The music evoked a chain of thoughts in me—thoughts that seemingly contradicted, but did not actually contradict, the words I had spoken: Eeyore is a *nobody*, or rather a *nobody* with something about him that's slower than an ordinary *nobody*; in spite of this, though, there's undoubtedly a mystifying side to him, an interesting person. "Ribs"!

sadness of
the novel

With my parents in California, I can think of them with a natural distance between us. Especially Father. One favorable sentiment I have about my relationship with him concerns my memory of the time I read Ende's *Momo*. It was required reading at my middle school, and seeing how excited everyone had gotten, our teacher, perhaps because he felt the need to throw cold water on our childish frenzy, said, "But one little girl saving the whole world—in reality, it just couldn't happen."

As soon as I got home from school, I complained to Mother about it, all but tugging at her sleeve, as she prepared dinner in the kitchen. Mother was discreet, and said she would prefer not to comment, not having read the book yet. But Father, who had been reading on the living room sofa, walked into the kitchen, on the pretext of wanting a glass of the mineral water we kept in the refrigerator, and this is what he said.

143

a quiet life

"Ma-chan, dear, I would think the world's been saved by one little girl a number of times. It's just that no legend of their feats has been handed down to us. In the first place, the girls themselves probably didn't quite understand what they'd accomplished. . . . But, Ma-chan, the moment your heart started beating fast as you lay in bed reading *Momo*, and when you, too, wished to save the world by retrieving time from the men in gray, well, that was the sign, the sign that a little girl could save the entire world. So, Ma-chan, if you ever end up saving the world, remember what you do and tell me about it. If you find it too much of a hassle to tell me, tell Eeyore. He's a better listener than Momo."

Father had written to me about Ende in a couple of his earlier letters from California. And because I'm sure we had also talked about *The Neverending Story*, I regard Ende as a writer who mediates a rare channel of communication between Father and me.

"While walking with Mama through the campus with its big differences in elevation, and looking at the variety of trees, beginning with those originally from Australia, we both draw sketches in our minds of Eeyore, you, and O in our house in Tokyo; and in those moments, my heart sometimes savors a kind of remote calm, a haven from the feelings of urgency that routinely hound me. I feel as though I were looking through a special prism, at a view of us progressing along the natural flow of years, and of your life continuing steadfastly from day to day. I don't think this is just my imagination, because you're already doing a fine job at seeing to it that everything at our home in Tokyo is well. I want you to know, Ma-chan, that I'm really grateful to you for this. I thank you.

"Well, I decided to write to you at some length today. Yet as I prepared to do so, various images of you kept floating into my mind. And it is mainly about these images that I am going to write. One scene is about something that happened when you were around three years old, a scene you couldn't possibly remember. I was reading a book, lying on my side as usual, with my knees sticking out from the sofa, in the shape of a slanted *L*. And you, pressing your underbelly against the lowest part of my bent knees, were standing beside me with a dreamy expression on your face. . . . I had always been preoccupied with the care of Eeyore, and you weren't very attached to me then, so this remains a memory of an almost mystical moment.

"Yet another scene I recall is of when you were already in your late teens, at a time when you had further estranged yourself from me, but surprisingly, you came to me to discuss a book you were reading. I had given you my opinion of *Momo* once before. So I immediately presumed that you would say something along the same lines, for you had Ende's book, the one with the copper-colored silk binding, *The Neverending Story*, pressed firmly to your bosom.

"At the time, I thought that if you were going to ask me something about *The Neverending Story*, in the vein of our discussion of *Momo*, then it had to be about the dialogue between the Old Man of Wandering Mountain and the Childlike Empress, who was in a desperate situation. The Old Man said, 'Do you really intend to entrust everything to the hands of one human child?' And the Childlike Empress replied, 'I do.'

"However, you directed at me not a question, but rather something in the nature of a comment. You had been taken in by Ende's artful buildup to the climax in the middle of the story—of as far as you had read—and were so unable to contain your excitement that you had to talk to somebody about it. You chose to talk to me, and not to Eeyore, because it dawned on you that, in this case, it was more appropriate to talk to your father, a writer of novels. And this is what you said:

a quiet life

"'Bastian is a reader until the middle of the story, then at last he himself enters into the story and becomes part of it, right? He firmly believes that, if the Childlike Empress is to save Fantastica, her new name should be Moon Child. Up to the page before this, I wondered how he'd become part of the story. I really didn't think such a thing would be possible. But as soon as he spoke the name Moon Child, he was already in Fantastica, and everything that took place afterwards seemed so natural. . . . And then I realized that everything about a tale depends on how you tell it.'

"'I agree,' I replied, though to tell you the truth, I was a bit surprised. 'But the same may be said of all manner of novels. From the writer's side, however, you could say that everything depends on how a narration is heard by readers. This is fundamental to writing. I have been writing novels for a long time, and especially when I was young, I was dissatisfied with most of the reviews I got. But these days, whatever evaluation a work gets, if the reader says, "This is how I heard it," I almost always feel that's what I narrated.'

"You then said, again with mystical eyes that reminded me of when you were three, 'It would be nice if you had a reader like Bastian.'

"Almost every day these days, I think of these words you spoke to me. And as I contemplate, in faraway California, the new novel I plan to write, I keep wishing I could become a reader-listener like Bastian, and get him to lend an attentive ear to the story I'm about to tell. I do, in fact, resemble the Bastian who is still on this side of the world, in the sense that I'm short-legged and a bit on the corpulent side."

To my surprise, soon after I received this letter, I learned that Father was going to meet the author of *Momo* and *The Neverending Story* for a Japanese TV station.

"... A large-scale exhibition in memory of Edgar Ende, Michael Ende's father and a painter who suffered oppression in the midst of the rise of Nazi power, was held in San Francisco, and arrangements were made that I would interview Michael Ende on his visit here for the occasion. I am forwarding you the catalogue together with this letter, hoping that you will see the paintings yourself, at least their photographic versions. I say this because, while I was preparing for the interview, which somehow turned out to be a heavy, cheerless one—it's going to be aired in Japan soon—I found these words by Michael Ende in a record of his dialogues: 'But if, because of our discussion, a viewer of a painting were to strive on his own and continue to look at it, and then chance upon a door through which he could enter it, we shouldn't forestall him by offering too many explanations, and otherwise stand in his way to discovery.'

"Although this pertains to something quite different from what I wrote in my previous letter, talking to Ende, I again recalled the words you spoke to me. They concern what *The Neverending Story* started you thinking about. After entering Fantastica, Bastian quickly starts losing memories of this world. For every wish that comes true in the new world, he loses one memory of the old—and he doesn't realize that he's forgetting. You then told me you were afraid, because even if you were going to be reborn in the new world, if in the process you were going to forget all about yourself in the old world, then it would be the same as if you had turned into nothing; and if, in the new world, you didn't know that you had lived in the old one, then it would be the same as if your present self were dead. . . .

"Ma-chan, you said something to this effect, but for some reason or other, I didn't try hard enough give you an adequate answer. Reflecting on this, I tell myself I should have realized that what you had on your mind was the question of death and what comes afterwards: a question that, strangely enough, has frightened me ever since I was a child. I remember that I replied, but it wasn't much of an answer, and now, with a feeling that again depresses me, I apologize, or perhaps I should say, I feel ashamed of myself.

"Ma-chan, what has become of your own discovery of the question of rebirth? I hope that it has changed to a somewhat brighter hue."

At the time, I did indeed spend whole days thinking about the fearfulness of death, however childish these thoughts may have been. But I now know, from what Mr. Shigeto has told me, that this has been the very question Father had been trying to answer since his youth. And I recall an occasion that revealed to me that this question must always have been an inner problem for him. After all, my fear of death is connected with Father's crying over Dr. W's death, his drinking and crying over it every night until early morning, his face beet red. Mother had the habit of scurrying off to her own bedroom and entrenching herself there, instead of keeping Father company while he drank. I slept on a futon spread out beside Mother's bed, and I couldn't sleep, hearing Father moving around in the kitchen when he was drunk. I was furious, thinking that Mother probably couldn't sleep either. Once she told him in a rather stern voice to go upstairs to his study-cum-bedroom, and do his drinking there. To which I heard Father, though definitely trying to control himself, fire back, in a menacing voice, "On one occasion I heard Dr. W say this. . . . He said that with more friends and acquaintances now on the other side, he felt a closer affinity there than here, and was therefore no longer afraid of death, but wished to go without having to suffer too much. But Dr. W died of lung cancer," Father continued, "so he must have tasted excruciating pain!"

There obviously wasn't anything I could do about this, except to sink my head under the pillow, though by the time Mother returned, I was sleeping. *The Neverending Story* reminded me of what I had heard that night, and despite his bewilderment at my question, the very asking of which was a rare occasion, I followed it up with another the next day.

"Oh really?" he replied. "So after Dr. W passed away, it wasn't only Mama who heard me expound on the pain of death. . . . Come to think of it, though, my anxiety over such pain was very vague in those days. The simple fact that Dr. W died a painful death was the sole cause of such fear in me. Beyond this, though, I believe the core of my fear at the time consisted of the thought that, after death, I would turn into nothing."

"Me, too," I said. Frankly, I am no good at communicating with Father, but feeling encouraged by *The Neverending Story*, which I held in my hands, I was ready to at least ask him this, even for the mere sake of asking. "I'm afraid of becoming nothing, too," I said, "but I have a friend who says she shudders at the thought of her having been nothing for billions of years before she was born."

"Oh? That *is* a problem, isn't it?" he said. "For my part, I don't much think about it anymore; not that I have gained any wisdom to encourage you with, but only because age has made me insensitive to the fear of my becoming zero. In terms of the scale of human history, though, I would say that people have always contemplated the rebirth of their dead."

"Even if there were rebirth," I said, "if you remember nothing of your previous existence, it's the same as turning into nothing, isn't it? Bastian in *The Neverending Story* is the same way."

Nevertheless, when I think of rebirth these days, I feel it's better to become a new person—perhaps an animal, some vegetation, or anything that has life—who's totally oblivious to who I am now. I don't feel that if I forget this existence, I'm going to turn into nothing. Rather, I find it comfortable to think that, after being reborn, I won't remember anything of my previous life; and during this lifetime, I'll never know what form of life I'm going to assume next time around. . . .

If there are such rebirths, then Eeyore, O-chan, and I must have experienced many lives before this one, about which we remember nothing. And we're going to chance upon many more that we can't even imagine. If so, there couldn't be any profound meaning in our family feeling mortified over—as though there were no possible atonement for—Eeyore's brain, which had accidentally been destroyed when he came into this world this time.

When Father published Eeyore's music, at his own expense, and distributed copies to his friends and acquaintances, not a few of them said that they had heard in it a mystical voice that transcended the limitations of human beings. Such sentimental impressions, I thought, though as usual these were words I uttered only in my heart. Eeyore starts working on each piece after carefully deliberating what he wants to express in it, which is what he did even for pieces like "Summer in Kita-Karuizawa" or "Requiem for M." He's accumulated his technique through years of listening to FM programs and records, along with Mrs. T's patient instruction. He can't comment on his music the way ordinary musicians so eloquently do about theirs, but I think he creates his music by employing the themes and syntax of the music of the people who walk or have walked this earth, and not at the suggestion of any heavenly will.

To use Father as an example of someone who writes, it was after several years of reading Blake—in his study or on the living room sofa, from morning to night—that he wrote a set of short stories about Eeyore by overlapping images from the poet's Prophecies together with events that delineate Eeyore's growth and development. Characters based on me and O-chan are portrayed in them. So I said to O-chan, "A pain in the neck, don't you think, even if it's been done favorably, that he writes about us from his one-dimensional viewpoint? It's all right with my friends who know me, but it depresses me to think that I'm going to meet some people who, through his stories, will have preconceived ideas of me."

"Just tell them it's fiction," cool-headed O-chan replied.

Neither O-chan nor I read all the stories when it came out as a book, but a woman—a mother of a girl with cerebral palsy who I helped about two years ago through volunteer work at the university—recommended that I read at least the short story that rounds off the anthology, and so I did. I wasn't as impressed with it as I was with the Blake poem he had translated and quoted.

This reminds me: the day Father finished this anthology, he dug a hole in the garden and then burned the bundle of cards he had prepared while reading Blake. When Mother told him he should perhaps keep at least the translations, he gave it some serious thought, and then replied, "A specialist would say it's full of mistakes." That would be *a matter of grave concern to the family*, I thought, and with the branch of a tree I quickly poked away at the mass of cards, so that brisk flames would rise.

"Jesus replied: 'Fear not, Albion: unless I die thou canst not live. / But if I die I shall rise again & thou with me; / This is friendship & brotherhood; without it man is not.' / So Jesus spoke, the Covering Cherub coming on in darkness / Overshadowed them & Jesus said: 'Thus do men in Eternity, / One for another to put off by forgiveness ever sin.'"

151

a quiet life

Father had explained in his story that these lines were from "Jerusalem" in the Prophecies, and so I went to his upstairs library and took out the big facsimile edition from the shelf of his Blake-related books, and looked at the illuminations Blake himself had done. White outlines of a tree float up, silhouetted against the entire blackish background. It's the "Tree of Life." Christ is crucified here. As I understand it, Albion, standing at the foot of the tree, listening to Christ's words, has the role of representing the whole of humanity by himself.

I went to bed after reading these lines over and over, until I could recite them almost by heart, and dreamed I was standing at the foot of the "Tree of Life" in Albion's stead—the story is becoming high-flown, but then I, too, belong to mankind. . . . I can't see Christ very well, for even in our dreams he is too awesome for our eyes to behold, and in the dark only the platinum rays, which the outline of the tree emits, are conspicuous. But when Christ's voice says, "But if I die I shall arise again & thou with me," the covering cherub glides through the pale dark with his accustomed grace, and throws the shadow of a deeper darkness over me. While wondering whether to *act this way* means, in other words, to act with grace, I'm enticed by the form of the familiar shadow; and when I lift my eyes, Eeyore, who has sprouted wings, is floating in the sky with a facial expression that suggests he is stifling a smile.

Christ must have gone through many deaths this way, I thought, and then been reborn many times; and Eeyore has stood witness to each one, which is why he appears so accustomed to them. . . . While I was telling Mother about this dream, Father, who as always was reading a book on the sofa, heard me with his sharp ears. I didn't care how, but I think I actually wanted Father, too, to hear me talk about the dream that Blake had caused me to have. Anyway, he came over and said, "I don't think Christians would accept the thought that Jesus

152

has repeatedly entered into the history of the world—a world bound by time. I should ask you to exercise caution when you speak with your Christian friends. It's an important matter for those who have faith."

I was unable for a while after this to hold my head up when walking past the congregation in front of the cathedral at my university, which I had to pass on the several Sunday mornings our volunteer group met on campus. One morning, a group member, who had been waiting where we were supposed to meet, and was watching me come, perplexedly said, "What happened, Ma-chan? I thought I saw a repentant virgin coming this way!"

Some time after this letter, Father wrote me another one, from which I could tell he was genuinely concerned about the rebirth question I had on my mind.

"Regarding *Stalker*, which you say you and O-chan watched on a late-night TV program, well, I don't have any video equipment here, so I thought I might read the novel it's based on, and went to look for it in a San Francisco bookstore that has a selection of Russian novels in English. Unfortunately, they didn't have *Roadside Picnic* by the Strugatsky brothers, but they had a novel by Aitmatov, a contemporary writer, one that has as its theme the Crucifixion and the question of rebirth. I will forward the book by separate post for you to deliver to Mr. Shigeto, though he may have already read it in Russian.

"Presenting in a novel the philosophical implications of the Crucifixion through Pontius Pilate's interrogation of Christ: I found this arrangement also in Bulgakov's novel, so I wonder if this isn't a technique Russian writers like, including Dostoevsky with his Grand Inquisitor. The setting of Aitmatov's novel is one in which two millennia have passed since Jesus's death and resurrection. The protagonist is a modern young man who has taken it upon himself to worship Jesus Christ in his own way, different from the way churches do—which in itself is nothing new—and who strives to see to it that Christ has not died in vain. The young man is strung from a tree and murdered by some men who hunt elk in a remote area of Russia—men who had come from the city, having been hired to procure meat, and who have a savageness different from that of the local people. This is the central plot.

"Also before this, the young man had once penetrated a gang that illegally procured hallucinogenic plants. His motive was to report the gang's circumstances to a newspaper. But the other gang members found out, and they booted him off a speeding freight train. Though he's had only two such experiences, the young man takes them to be forms of his reliving the drama of Christ's death and rebirth. In the novel, Christ is crucified and reborn three times. In other words, the young man relives each of Christ's sufferings on the cross—the first time in his mind, the two other times as a direct physical experience.

"Come to think of it, no novelist today could write a story on so grand a theme as Christ's Crucifixion and resurrection in one vertical flow. What Aitmatov does with the Crucifixion, therefore, is portray a character who leaps over history in order to experience synchronicity with Christ. This is how the writer traces the original death and rebirth of Christ. As a novelistic technique, it was invented in desperation, but perhaps it runs parallel to what moves in the minds of those who have faith.

"I myself have never written a novel like this, directed toward something that transcends the real world, but I have come to understand the efficacy of this technique through reading many excellent works. And this is what I think of as I reread this work by a Kirgiz-born writer, an Asian writer like myself. . . . Ma-chan, I'm afraid that this letter has ended up a mere confession of a vulnerable writer who has sought emergency refuge in a quiet place in a foreign land, and that it serves no purpose as regards the question on your mind."

Well, from what I have written so far about my relationship with Father, it might strike you as strange when I say that I'm a student of French literature. It's no big deal, though; nothing I meant to hide. Actually I'm a stranger to literature, yet through my own decision, independent of Father, I ended up choosing to pursue it in college. But would I confuse you more to tell you that Céline steered me toward this decision, and that I'm planning to write my graduation thesis on him? My thesis adviser quite frankly told me that Céline's French, with all its slang, would be too difficult for me. He also said he wasn't sure if a girl from today's affluent society could enter into Céline's sensitivity and way of thinking. Blunt as he was, I think his intention was neutral, and his advice—well, pedagogical.

In any case, from about the end of my sophomore year, I started reading Céline every day, making reference cards as I read. When some of my seniors in graduate school found out about this, one flung at me some words laced with toxic implications: "You say 'Céline.' . . . An innocent princess reading Céline, huh? . . . feigning the villain. When did Céline turn into a cute hobbyhorse?" My sheepish reply on such occasions: "I'm not really reading him. I'm a cat lover, and I'm thinking of making a list of quotations of what this writer said about cats."

From the very start, though, I had made up my mind as to how I would approach Céline. I would try to understand him through the children he calls *nos petits cretins, our little idiots*, the children who live under dire circumstances but who live life for all it is worth. And fortunately, I was allowed to participate in the university's volunteer program for handicapped children. I haven't written in "Diary as Home," let alone talked to my family, about the friends I made there, for their privacy is a complex matter. And I intend to live by this ethic, always. But it's through my encounters with handicapped children and their parents—not only with members of the group I belong to, but with people at other colleges as well—that I have been able to somehow re-create my inhibited character, one that's led me to wish always to live like someone who isn't there. ... With the experience I have gained through working with this group—and I've got Eeyore, too, of course—I think I have some idea of what it takes to enter the world of children with handicaps.

Nevertheless, every time I reread the various episodes where Céline vividly portrays *our little idiots*, I always discover, to my amazement, freshly bizarre expressions. For I find truly villain-feigning exaggerations, not so much in the way he addresses the children as in the way he expresses his attendance on them. On the other hand, though my fellow able-bodied countrymen may not express it in words, experience has taught me that they sometimes take a startlingly vicious attitude toward handicapped children, as on the stairs at a railway station, when a child with a handicap desperately reaches out for a helping hand—though granted this may be a situation that reflexively brings out the bigot in them. I believe Céline, in contrast, was a person to whom this sort of meanness, at least, was never to his liking.

I intend to focus on these children and the cat, Bébert, in *Rigadoon*. By way of preparing the general framework of my thesis, I have started by first copying down certain passages from the novel, and then attaching my own translations to them. I have one here that, I think, clearly shows Céline's warm-hearted seriousness. Incidentally, it's in this passage that *our little idiots*, an expression I have written a number of times already, appears for the first time.

"Our little idiots are all where they belong; they've got nothing to do with us anymore; now they're Swedes, all of them—drooling, deaf and dumb Swedes . . . thirty years have passed and I'm thinking: must be grown-ups now, if they lived through it . . . moreover, they aren't drooling, maybe they can hear well, too—thoroughly reeducated . . . the old have nothing more to hope for, those kids, all . . . "

I don't have the ability to comment on French style, but with Céline, I get the impression that he writes in a way that, contrary to what I had imagined, presents a serious subject in a light and straightforward manner—and I like this. I had copied this passage on one of my cards a few days before, and was translating it far into the night, when I realized Father was standing beside me, having snuck up without my noticing—which is another reason this passage, in particular, remains in my heart. Father doesn't dare touch my letters, but he readily picks up the books I read, or the reference cards I make, and looks at them. He does this all the time, and it has irritated me since I was in kindergarten. And that night, while I was copying down some more passages from the book, he picked up a few of the cards and said, "Hmm . . . 'the old have nothing more to hope for, those kids, all . . .' How true." His voice was so unusually earnest and sad that I couldn't make a face at him for having read my cards without asking me.

The next day, however, Father brought me volumes one and two of Céline's *Novels*, from the shelf of the Pléiade editions he especially treasures, and said, "The appendices and annotations should come in handy for the slang and the identities and backgrounds of the models. Take them, they're yours. And you can use volume three and the other reference books too, if you need to." I was actually very grateful for his giving me the two Pléiade books, which would have put too heavy a burden on my meager allowance.

a quiet life

My interest in Céline, in the first place, had been aroused by my meeting an American writer on an errand I once ran for Father. Though I personally believe I chose to major in literature independently of Father's occupation, I have to admit that the occasion has influenced me in many ways.

When I was still in my second year of senior high school, Mr. K. V., a very well-known writer in the United States, came to Japan. Father interviewed him on a TV talk show, and Mr. K. V., when publishing its transcript in a literary magazine, said he wished to donate the proceeds to a hospital for atomic bomb survivors in Hiroshima. In return for his kindness, the publishers said they would pay Mr. K. V. more than the usual fee. But they would first hand the money to him in a special envelope, and after this, he would make the donation. Father said he would gladly act as go-between for Mr. K. V. and the hospital. But then he started saying that he, being the bashful type, would rather not stand in the limelight, and so it turned out that I would go to the ceremony to receive from Mr. K. V. the envelope that would go to the hospital. As I waited in the lobby with a man from the publishing house, Mr. K. V. emerged from the elevator, a tall man with a dignified, winsome head on his shoulders, like a scientist you might see in a cartoon. I had practiced saying, in order to receive the envelope from him, "I shall forward a voucher to your publisher in the United States." I thought *receipt* would have sounded too weak, so I decided, without consulting anyone, to use *voucher*, a word I had found in a Japanese-English dictionary. The word must have rung amusingly odd in Mr. K. V.'s ears, for though he didn't burst out laughing, he vigorously rolled his large eyes.

Mr. K. V. then went to the bookstore in the corner of the lobby to see if they had a pocket edition of his works, but unfortunately he didn't find any. "They have a good selection," he said ruefully, but so seriously that neither the man from the publishing company nor I could help laughing. Encouraged by his sense of humor, I produced a Penguin edition of a Céline book for which Mr. K. V. had written an introduction. Father had told me to look it over before meeting him, and I got him to sign it. The introduction included an illustration of a tombstone that looked like the graffiti of a mischievous boy. The outline sketch he drew next to his signature, of a girl with a small placard hanging from her neck with VOUCHER! written on it, was the same as that of the tombstone, which turns out to bear the writer's pseudonym, his real name as a doctor, and the years of his birth and death: Louis-Ferdinand Céline, Le Docteur Destouches / 1894–1961.

I carried the inscribed book home, impressed by the fact that Mr. K. V. was a gentle and refined American. I made a brief report to Father, gave him the envelope, and continued talking in the kitchen with Mother about my impression of Mr. K. V. Father, who promptly set about sending the money to Hiroshima, heard me with his sharp ears and happily said, "Yes, K. V. is a very *decent* man." Reading Mr. K. V.'s introduction to the book he had inscribed for me, I felt that *decent*, the English word Father used, was the perfect adjective to describe him.

The last passage in Mr. K. V.'s introduction also aroused in me a desire to read Céline. It touched upon an essay Céline, as a doctor, had written in 1924, a treatise on a nineteenth-century Hungarian physicist, entitled "The Life and Work of Ignaz Philipp Semmelweis." Mr. K. V. wrote: "It was written at a time when theses in medicine could still be beautifully literary, since ignorance about diseases and the human body still required that medicine be an art."

Young Destouches penned his essay on Semmelweis with zeal akin to hero worship. Semmelweis was a Vienna hospital obstetrician who devoted his life to preventing the spread of childbed fever. It was largely the poor who were victims of the disease, for in those days people who had houses, which is to say decent dwellings of their own, chose to give birth at home. The essay tells of those times.

"The mortality rate in some wards was sensational—twenty-five percent or more. Semmelweis reasoned that the mothers were being killed by medical students, who often came into the wards immediately after having dissected corpses riddled with the disease. He was able to prove this by having the students wash their hands in soap and water before touching a woman in labor. The mortality rate dropped.

"The jealousy and ignorance of Semmelweis's colleagues, however, caused him to be fired, and the mortality rate went up again.

"The lesson Destouches learned from this true story, in my opinion, if he hadn't learned it from an impoverished childhood and a stretch in the army, is that vanity rather than wisdom determines how the world is run."

I immediately asked Father about this medical treatise, whereupon a look of surprise, which itself he appeared to be relishing, suffused his face. I don't blame him, though, for then I didn't know a word of French. Still, I think he decided to give me his prized Pléiade books because he remembered my asking him about the treatise. Before this, too, when he went to France on some business he had, he bought me, as a souvenir, a Gallimard book entitled *Semmelweis* (*1815–1865*), *thèse.* I put this book on my bookshelf without reading it, and it's still there where I put it. When looking back like this, though, it becomes clear that Father *does* seriously consider the things I inquire about.

I was already a sophomore, and had started taking courses in French literature, when Father gave me the treatise he had gone to the trouble to buy me. So if only I had tried, I would somehow have managed to read it. But I didn't, and there were psychological reasons for this. To begin with, I had recurrent nightmares after reading about the treatise in Mr. K. V.'s introduction. Hands that touch a corpse full of holes, gnawed away by germs that appeared to the naked eye as small bugs; and fingers, wet, slimy, and glimmering with black blood and pus. They take the form of the arms of a doctor of obstetrics you might see in a TV movie, and gloveless and bare, they come closer between my raised knees. . . .

Hands don't appear in my other nightmares, but I see paramecialike germs, a myriad of them, ravaging the back of Eeyore's head—Eeyore the newborn babe lying on the operating table. . . . If my subconscious was causing me to have these shocking dreams, then I detested myself for having such a subconscious. But quite apart from the dream itself, I was overcome with self-hatred, which made me repeatedly shudder. In any event, these were the things that prompted me to read Céline's novels, and go on to French literature in college.

Well, what I want to focus on in my graduation thesis is *Rigadoon*. In this story, Céline does not allow any sentimentalism, though common in such relationships, to come between him and *our little idiots*. Instead of giving them an endearing "oh-you-poor-little-things" embrace, he uses his medical expertise to make the most strenuous efforts to help the children. The children themselves, though handicapped, give it their all, and their actions amid dire circumstances are as shrewd as Céline's. This is what I really like about *Rigadoon*.

The time is toward the end of World War II. The locale is Germany. Air raids by the Allies have virtually paralyzed the railway systems, and multitudes of refugees are fleeing in confusion. The story progresses with the decrepit railway as the main theater of action. Céline is labeled as a Nazi sympathizer who ought to be denounced—though today the prevailing thought seems to be that the French public's denunciation of such individuals, both during the Resistance and after the war, solely because of their antisemitic beliefs, was not appropriate—and because he cannot return to France, or remain in Germany, he tries to make off to Switzerland, or to Denmark, and ends up plying back and forth in Germany, as if he were dancing the rigadoon. And there's his wife, Lili, the cat, Bébert, and his actor friend, La Vigue.

Relying on their uncertain lifeline, an obscure German officer, they continue their narrow escape by trains, on whose tracks bombs repeatedly rain down. To the bitter end, Céline writes, as he would speak, the details of the trips they made back and forth, and of the thoughts that arose in his mind at the time. He freely inserts movements of his mind that occurred to him as he wrote the novel in the French countryside in 1961. And I understand he died the day after he put his last idiosyncratic ellipsis points to the end of this novel. His style, I believe, is really egocentric. Moreover, the novel is full of the practically fanatical self-justifications of an out-and-out egotist. But, of course, this itself represents a spirited charm, which again is the mark of a great writer's work. . . .

But Céline, who runs around amid the flames of war with the sole purpose of saving himself and his retinue, and who spits out cusses and curses everywhere, simply cannot turn a cold shoulder to the abandoned infant or to *our little idiots* he chances upon, which, admittedly, is a rather unnatural thing to do. Nevertheless, he writes with such feeling, and his words pierce the heart. This is what attracts me to *Rigadoon*, and why I think I now know how to help myself rise above the hurt I feel when someone says, "An innocent princess reading Céline, huh? . . . feigning the villain. . . . When did Céline turn into a cute hobbyhorse?" Were I to offer a slightly thorny rebuttal, I would say that those who say such things perhaps haven't read Céline well enough. . . .

With no place to go, Céline, his wife, friend, and cat sneak into a village farm, but then, with a *Reichsbevoll* permit that may already have lost its validity, leave for Norbord on the opposite shore via Denmark—I understand *Reischsbevoll* means Reich plenipotentiary, but I'll have to look it up at the university library to find out more about it. They finally manage to scramble onto a flatcar guarded by a gunner, and halfway through their escape they are forced to disembark from the would-be Berlin-Rostock train. They have to melt into the crowd of evacuees from Berlin to search for another train. Upon learning that the French government has left Vichy for the town of Sigmaringen, near the Swiss border, they decide to mingle with the people returning to France via the same route. . . .

The Ulm-bound train they get on—one passing through Leipzig—is also bombed, forcing them to escape into a tunnel, lest they be roasted by the liquid white-phosphorus shells. The circumstances are frightening, but when Céline sees, on the train, an abandoned infant in its swaddling clothes, he can't just let it be. There's no milk, no diapers; yet he can't keep from doing something for it.

". . . empty . . . nobody! . . . wait! A baby on the middle sofa, in swaddling clothes! . . . a month old, perhaps less . . . not crying . . . abandoned there by its mother . . . I enter . . . I look . . . it's not doing badly . . . not breathing hard . . . a healthy baby . . . now what?"

My stilted translation cannot properly convey the feeling, but as I copy the scene on my card in French—this scene, which starts from where Céline, or rather Dr. Destouches, finds a baby abandoned in the face of hellish circumstances, and then continues until he can entrust it to reliable hands—I feel his warmth directly communicated to me: his spontaneous emotions upon finding the child, his doctor's watchful eye ever on it, and his desperate feelings to want to somehow look after it. And the usage of the Céline-esque ellipsis points is so natural here. Simple though it may be, I imagine the following association: "What if I had been the rescued infant!—found by this diminutive man, who looks ferocious, like a dog, and yet is so kind and unhypocritical! How happy I must have been, picked up by this doctor's big, experienced hands!"

Caught in one impasse after another, they continue their nightmarish railway journey with no alternative but to make repeated changes in course; and amid all this, Céline, who chances upon *our little idiots*, takes them with him, all of them, without a second thought.

Just as I can't explain why he did what he did for the infant, I can't explain his behavior toward *our little idiots*, except to say that it's inborn in his nature. Right before this, too, when he got off at Ulm Station, which had not yet been bombarded, and started walking along the road in front of it, he met an old man with a goatee who claimed to be a fire chief. It was a beautiful May morning, perfect for a leisurely stroll, but Céline went out of his way to walk up to the fourth floor of the station building and examine the fire chief, who stripped naked, except for his helmet, before him. It was as though Céline had been taken by the snout and dragged all over the place, through the caprice of an old man living his second childhood. But the experience didn't make him any wiser. Soon after this, when he is asked to take care of *our little idiots*, he cannot refuse this request, though he has just sustained a head wound in a bombardment.

This is how the story begins: Céline is lying in the Hamburg-bound flatcar, close to the engine, of all places, aware that his shirt is still wet from his bleeding. He embraces an uncertain hope that, upon reaching Hamburg, they will somehow transfer to another train that would take them farther north. Suddenly, a French girl, who says she is qualified to teach German at university level, and had been an instructor at a college in Breslau, comes up to him and confides that she has fled from Berlin, where the Russians are taking over, and that she had been entrusted with the care of forty-two children—idiots all. Twelve of them, maybe thirteen, are left, she says, the rest having succumbed, one after another, to measles during their getaway. Céline immediately wants to go and examine their condition, but they are all on separate cars and cannot be easily found. The girl tells him that their ages range from four to ten, and that they have minds that don't understand a single word. The girl can no longer procure food, for she, too, is running a fever, and is coughing up blood, and so she has only Céline, the doctor, to turn to for the care of the children.

The train arrives at a crippled Hamburg. The children manage to disembark on their own, and come toward him on the platform.

"The kids come closer, boys and girls, they're no different . . . bundled up in the same weird woolen clothes . . . fifteen of them, perhaps . . . isn't hard to tell they're all cabbageheads . . . limping, drooling, and lopsided . . . asylum idiots, positively . . ."

Suppose I were with Eeyore on a welfare workshop excursion, and I heard something like this at a crowded transfer station or wherever: I would feel sick with anger. But Céline doesn't really mean it; for he speaks these words nonchalantly, and tells his wife, Lili, to take the cat, Bébert, out of its bag to let the children see it. And while they wait for the train that should, by midnight, take them to Magdeburg, he goes into a demolished Hamburg building to look for food. He takes the whole train of children with him. "'Now, my children! Let's go! I want you all to follow me . . . I'll take the lead . . .' This 'Hang in there, kid!' spirit, this doggedness, will probably be with me for all time, whether I go mad or remain sane. . . . Really, what you learn when you're young stays with you . . . everything after that is mere imitation, copying, labor, and competing to see who makes the more foolishly obsequious greetings . . ."

In the totally devastated city of Hamburg, where even bodies lie on the streets, the children intrepidly slip into a hollowlike place between the bricks and clay. It's the ruins of a bombarded pharmacy and a grocery store, but from there they haul out round loaves of bread, and jam, and even cans of milk. They nonchalantly return from what Céline had thought was an impenetrable crevasse. While on the train they had sat limply, not a smile crossing anyone's lips, they now stand erect—though they're still drooling—as they head back to the station with the provisions they had procured so well by themselves. . . .

December came, and because I was the person in charge of cooking, and since as I had taken it upon myself to see to the planning and execution of all the housework while our parents were away, I thought of a way to make Christmas enjoyable for Eeyore and O-chan. But before I knew it, there were only ten days left before Christmas, and I still had no idea what I was going to do. I have little talent for housework in the first place, and on top of this, my mind was preoccupied with something that made me feel restless, and I had yet to come up with a practical way to cope with the problem: my graduation thesis on Céline.

The coward that I am, I had managed to acquire all required credits by the end of the first half of my junior year.

And I had planned the second half so that, rather than spend a lot of time in the classroom, I would mainly sign up for courses that required only a term paper, and so be able to concentrate on my thesis. But because something had come up requiring that both Mother and Father go to California, I had to use the time I didn't have to be at the university for household chores, and to take Eeyore to the welfare workshop and back. While admittedly this has given me an opportunity to savor a sense of fulfillment I had never before felt, if it was going to continue until April, when Mother and Father would return, I was sure to be in a "pinch" as far as the writing of my thesis was concerned.

I had the two Pléiade editions Father had given me, and they included annotations for most of the slang my adviser told me would be beyond me. And Father had told me where in his library I could find *Céline's Notes* I through VII. So if I used all the other commentaries, including the several that were in English, I ought to be able to get my thesis done—provided I had the French proficiency of an honor student. And so with the exception of *Rigadoon*, I wanted to follow and quote from any available Japanese translations as material for my thesis. Father had a large collection of studies of Céline in his library, but the books he collected reflected his peculiar leanings, so I wanted to look for something more general. This was why, if possible, I wanted to go to the university a few times a week to use the French literature study room and the library there. The all-around slow-mo that I am, though, I had to begin very early the next year, in fact right after the New Year's holidays, or I would really be in a fix. . . .

I didn't say anything then about the anxiety I felt in my heart, but now I wonder if perhaps I wasn't crying it out in my behavior more eloquently than I could have in words. For despite his being an independent, go-it-alone person, O-chan is very sensitive, and he noticed it. He had probably been asking himself what was hounding me, though even if he'd asked I wouldn't have told him. Or perhaps it was the outcome of sheer coincidence, for it happened on the day the results of the year-end practice test at his cram school were released. He went up to his room after dinner that evening, and a good three hours later—that is, after he had come up with his own idea—he again came down to the dining room. I was, as usual, adding a few more notes to my Céline reference cards, rearranging them, then putting them back in their original order.

"Beginning next year, I'll take Eeyore back and forth to the welfare workshop," he said quite unexpectedly. "I don't need to go to cram school every day anymore. Let me start from tomorrow so I can get the hang of it. Sorry I had you do all the housework all this while, Ma-chan!"

With no further explanation, O-chan headed for the kitchen to look for something to eat, so I immediately called out to him.

"Don't be silly, O-chan! You've got exams coming up! Now's the time for you to be putting on your last spurt. Mama will worry."

He seemed to be first registering my words of objection, then thinking of a way to respond. At the same time, he seemed to be cutting up, and placing on a dish, the imported beef steak that I hadn't finished, that I had only half eaten. Returning to the dining room with it, he *sort of* asked me, by way of being courteous, "Can I have this?" Then, without sitting down, he picked up a piece of the meat with his fingers, and while eating it, he methodically explained the reason for his volunteering to take Eeyore to the welfare workshop, an explanation he had probably thought he could skip.

Judging from the final results released that afternoon, he said, he would be able to enter the university of his choice, so long as he stayed physically fit and did a little more preparation on his own. This, he said, was the diagnosis the cram school had given him. Then he went on to say that their evaluation was not groundless in light of his own assessment of what he had learned after his failure the year before. . . . . He added, however, that he hadn't done any orienteering since the last First Morning OL, a meet held early in the morning on New Year's day, and his basic physical strength was deteriorating. Taking Eeyore on the bus to and from the welfare workshop should put a more effective load on his legs than taking the train to cram school.

I wasn't sure if I should accept his offer, and apparently he took my hesitation for doubt regarding the first half of what he had said, about his score on the practice test, for after he licked his fingers, which were sticky with the juices from the meat, he produced from a trouser pocket a crumpled piece of paper to show me. It was a list of top-ranking examinees, and his name was fifth among those choosing to major in science, in the column titled "Science II for Tokyo University."

"You must have decided this after careful thought," I said, "and you'd easily convince me otherwise, wouldn't you, even if I presented a contrary opinion. So I'll accept your offer without any further resistance. Besides, I'd really appreciate some help now. . . ."

"Good!" O-chan said, sounding just like Father when he brings a discussion to a close, and he took the steak plate back to the kitchen. Now two of the problems that loomed over me were headed for a quick resolution.

"O-chan, what do you say to an early celebration, now that you foresee success in your exams?" I asked. "Why don't we go out for Christmas and have Peking duck? We haven't had that for some time."

a quiet life

Eeyore, who was lying in front of the stereo set, listening to music through the headphones so as not to disturb my card-editing—it seemed he had sensed my tacit irritation and lost some of his composure—suddenly raised his head and kept looking up at me with entirely different, eager eyes.

"Eeyore," I said, "we're going to Madame Chan's. The last time we had Peking duck was at our send-off dinner for Mama and Papa. O-chan's going to pass his college entrance exams, so let's celebrate."

Removing the headphones and carefully winding the leads around them, Eeyore stood up and held out his hand to O-chan.

"Congratulations, O-chan!" he said.

"Thank you," O-chan replied, "but I haven't passed yet. The real tests are next year." Apparently he worried that Eeyore hadn't understood.

"It's a dress rehearsal for when you pass your entrance exams, isn't it?" Eeyore said. He had, after all, correctly perceived the meaning of what O-chan and I had been talking about, through the ears of an aficionado of FM and television music programs.

Eeyore then went upstairs with uncharacteristic vigor, and after spending some time there, returned with a cassette tape, holding it in front of him as when showing his commuter pass at the railway station gate. Skillfully switching the mode on the stereo, he inserted the tape and started playing it for us. It was a recording of the speech O-chan had given at the dinner we had for him to commemorate his success in passing his elementary school entrance exams. I knew we had the tape somewhere, but I hadn't heard it played for at least ten years. At first O-chan looked shocked, but apparently he didn't wish to stand in the way of Eeyore's firm resolve; nor did he retire to his room to demonstrate his feelings in even this passive form of protest.

"Dear Father, Mother, Brother, and Sister. Thank you for your cooperation. Thanks to you, I passed my examinations. Although they were a little difficult, I did my best. There was an intermission, too . . . during the intermission, the quizzes were very interesting. We had fun with riddles, too. . . . My request is, when I pass a test or something, I want you all to say 'Congratulations.' . . . Someday I wish to become a scholar in eleven subjects. I want to know about the stars, the stars and the skies and the oceans; the mountains, rivers, and prairies; about everything that's happened since the Earth was formed; about life in the forest; the plants, that they, too, are living; the life of insects throughout the seasons; about the fishes; the snakes and frogs; the birds; the life of Japanese monkeys. . . . Well, I won't bother with the Japanese monkeys; and I won't bother with the part about the plants being alive. That's eleven already, isn't it? . . . And I want to know about mushrooms, too."

This address, delivered in O-chan's very crystalline voice, is followed by a toast with cola, and then a few congratulatory words from Father. While Father is speaking, O-chan leaves the table to go to the kitchen to see if there is any more cola. Thirteen years have passed, but certain things about him haven't changed at all. With this thought in mind, it was amusing to see him there, with his thin, scrawny beard, listening morosely to the tape—and when he discovers that there's more cola, his voice intrudes, reporting his discovery to all. "Hey, guess what," he says, "there's some cola in the fridge!" He suddenly sounds like a mischievous imp, quite different from the way he usually talks, in his written-language style of speech, which had always irritated me.

"You may have the brains to become a scholar in eleven fields," Father says, taking O-chan to task for interrupting him in the middle of his address, "but you're always thinking only of yourself. You don't think of other people's circumstances. You're going to go to school from now on to meet with children your own age, but who've grown up under different circumstances, and you're going to learn to cooperate with them. This is probably much more important than becoming your so-called scholar in eleven fields. . . ."

"Thank you, Eeyore," I said. "I think that's enough of the cassette. You can get back to your FM. . . . O-chan, I thought you always resisted Father, but in fact you put his advice into practice. In high school, you agreed to become captain of your orienteering team, and you did so much for the team that you even failed your entrance exams."

"I don't fully understand what you're trying to say, and can't, therefore, immediately respond," he said, at first declining my encouragement, still embarrassed at his infantile voice of yesteryear.

". . . Well, it was nice of Eeyore to remember we had the tape," he continued, "and go and find it so quickly. You can tell from the terse replies he gave on the recording that he was fulfilling the role of our big brother very well. If we hadn't been able to hear his voice, the party would've been something like an elite family celebrating their child's entrance into a prestigious school, and the snobbish atmosphere would've been unbearable, don't you think? . . . Anyway, beginning tomorrow, let me take Eeyore to the welfare workshop and back on a trial basis."

"Thank you very much!" Eeyore said, putting the tape back into its box very carefully, as usual.

"The pleasure's mine," O-chan ceremoniously answered.

I took the Chuo Line to Yotsuya Station and went to the university. I hadn't been there for some time, and after seeing some

friends I had promised to meet, I dropped by the French literature study room, then headed for the library, where a
mystifying experience awaited me. After taking a seat in the
reading room, where I planned to make a list of the books I
needed to borrow for an extended period of time, I saw, on
the second empty desk away from mine, the copper-colored,
silk-bound book I so fondly remembered: *The Neverending
Story*. It was noon, and the person who'd been reading it had
probably gone out for lunch, so I excused myself and picked
it up. When I opened it, I saw these words inscribed on the
title page, in a firm handwriting that told me it was no trite
doodle: "Why can't Japan produce writers who can truly
encourage their readers?"

I recalled the excitement I felt when I read Ende, and
empathized with the person who had to write such words. At
the same time, I wondered, with a stifling hesitancy in my chest,
whether, out of personal or even family feelings, I ought to be
agreeing with them. . . . I felt this way because I had read hardly
anything by Father, who was now struggling to ride out his
"pinch." Still, I felt it wouldn't be fair to him if I, as his daughter, were to sympathize with a statement that negated all writers
in Japan, and laud Ende. O-chan might say such a reflection
was meaningless, for were I to interpret such things as his
daughter, this itself would already be attaching an unfair
provision.

So the vigor with which I had taken myself to the library
vanished, and from the index cards that were typed in Japanese, I chose a couple of books that had caught my eye: Céline's
play entitled *Cathedral*, and an American researcher's account
of his visit to Céline in Denmark, where he was still taking refuge; and to the request slip I added Father's novel *M/T and
the Marvels of the Forest*, figuring that he had probably written something in it about "The Marvels of the Forest" that

a quiet life

Aunt Fusa had mentioned in her talk with me. I then hurried out of the library, thinking that I had better go before my neighbor returned. . . .

And so, thanks also to O-chan's trial cooperation, I was able to resume, before the year was over, my visits to the French literature study room and the library, and on top of this, read Father's novel. But O-chan, who was now studying more often in the dining-cum-living room where Eeyore and I spent most of our time, also appeared to take an interest in Céline's novel, his I-wish-to-learn curiosity whetted by the thesis reference cards I had spread all over the place. He said, however, that as someone who would soon be taking college entrance exams, he couldn't be so unscrupulous as to read a novel in Japanese translation. He might sometimes be dropping in at his cram school after taking Eeyore to the welfare workshop, and he wouldn't want his friends to see him reading a novel in Japanese. He wanted to read an English translation, which would benefit him more in terms of study.

So I *sort of* lent O-chan the memorable Penguin edition, my first book by Céline, through which I have come to know him. I have doubts, though, as to whether I have come across the real Céline yet, for in his account of his visit to Céline, the researcher wrote that he had observed a certain ferociousness in Céline's character, a ferociousness I find to be incompatible with the love and dedication to children that I thought ran throughout his writing, from his earlier works to *Rigadoon*.

On Christmas Eve, Madame Chan's, a Chinese restaurant that supposedly has nothing to do with anything Christian, was packed, but thanks to O-chan, who had made a reservation, we were able to secure a table for three. Eeyore in particular, who had long been looking forward to eating Peking duck again, ate everything very skillfully, putting the thinly sliced leeks and miso sauce on the duck skin in a manner close to reverence, then wrapping the ingredients in the thin crêpe. In volume, O-chan ate as much as Eeyore: a good match. I shed my reserve and ate a lot, too. But without Father, who on occasions like this takes his time drinking beer, lao-chu, whatever, the courses were soon over. "Come to think of it," O-chan said as we stood up to leave—the family at the table next to ours had not yet quite finished their second-course dish, the first having been hors d'oeuvres—"our old man, with his drinking habits, was a good pacemaker." Paying the cashier an amount within the limit Mother had approved, I felt lighthearted, and walked in the moonlight, trailing right behind Eeyore on the homeward route he took. We went along with O-chan, who proposed we spend the rest of the evening talking and listening to records, his reason being "because today is the *Sabbath.*" He said it in a manner that suggested he wasn't quite sure of its definition, which was unusual for him, but we let it go at that.

Eeyore had already prepared on a card a list of music he had selected for Christmas, and he had placed the CDs beside the stereo set. I pasted the card in "Diary as Home," just as he had written it: "Jesu, Joy of Man's Desiring"—Bach; "The Magic Flute," selections—Mozart; "Sleepers Awake!"—Bach. . . .

As person in charge of the music, Eeyore seated himself in front of the stereo equipment, while O-chan and I decided to talk at the dining table. We had even prepared ourselves an agenda, for a change. For one thing, O-chan had finished *Rigadoon*, so we could discuss that. For another, I wanted to talk to him about *M/T and the Marvels of the Forest*, something I thought inappropriate to write to our parents about, or in "Diary as Home" for that matter, but which I needed to talk about with somebody. And who would be better than O-chan!

a quiet life

His first comment after reading *Rigadoon:* "This is a kind of 'railway story'!"

O-chan had been jumping all over the country at orienteering meets since he was a middle-school student, so naturally he knows a lot about railways. I hesitated to associate *Rigadoon* with a "railway story," for my image of such stories was one of light reading. But since O-chan was now calling it one, I decided that in a way he was right.

"Of course," he continued, "it's not a leisure-filled 'railway story' as such. Quite the opposite. It's a *clunk from an unexpected blow,* as you often say, and now I know where the expression comes from. It must have been really grueling for him to portray a scene like that."

Just before Céline is asked to look after *our little idiots,* in the Hannover bombardment mentioned earlier, while he is running from the flames of war, in the confusion of an escape journey during a direct bombing, he gets a *clunk from an unexpected blow* and sustains a head injury.

Seeking an escape route from Germany, they head north, piecing together, as it were, the ends of the shredded railway. But at one point they abandon their train to cross the city of Hannover, where the fires that the incendiary bombs had started are still burning. Céline greases the palm of the stationmaster—Eeyore would be shocked at my vulgar expression—to borrow a cart, and after filling it with their luggage, he starts pushing it away from the crippled station, toward another on the opposite side of the city. The other passengers, who have also disembarked but are stuck, swear at him, envious of his guile. Their anger builds to the point where they start going after Céline and his retinue. "Murderers! Murderers! Quick!" he shouts as they flee. A balcony falls to the road, blocking their path, and another bomb explodes. *Clunk!* A brick hits him on the head and he falls. When at length he comes to, he notices blood all over his head, shirt, and trousers. The head wound renders him delirious while he tends to the children, but it doesn't stop him from doing all he can for them.

"It says in K.V.'s introduction, too," O-chan said, "that Céline always worried whether his brain had gone bad, because of the injury he suffered in World War I, and of yet another one he incurred while crossing through Hannover. K.V. writes sympathetically about the injuries, as if they concerned him. I like the part in the introduction where he quotes from the English translation of the novel. Of course, the content is heavy, and I don't think I can do it justice by simply saying I like it, yet my impressions might be different if I read it in French."

So saying, O-chan showed me a card he had put in the leaves of the Penguin book, which made me realize that we shared a common attitude toward reading, a habit we can trace to Father. I read O-chan's translation, contrasting it with the passage in French I had already transcribed.

"Neither death nor suffering," he had written, "could be as serious as I believe them to be. Both are very common, and I must be deranged to treat them as though they deserved my special attention. I must try to be saner."

"O-chan," I said, "you translate much better than I do. I can't put it so straightforwardly in Japanese. Besides, the French has a slightly lighter ring to it. . . . It's the first book by Céline that I read, but I recall that I, too, the first time I read it, was overcome by a strange sensation when I came to this passage."

"You had it underlined in red, I recall."

"This is between you and me, O-chan," I said. "Even then, I hesitate to say it, for it might sound too forward. But I felt sorry for Céline and for Mr. K. V., and for Papa, too, who suggested that I ask Mr. K. V. to autograph this book. . . . And I can't help thinking about Eeyore, you know. Eeyore sustained two head wounds, too—once in Mother's body, and then from the operation, immediately after he was born. When I read these lines, I fully understood why he should be so sensitive to sickness and death."

I already mentioned—when I wrote about Great-uncle's demise—that every time Eeyore sees the name of a sumo stable master or a composer in an obituary, he heaves a deferential sigh, and says, "Oh no, dead again!" And he was truly reverential at Great-uncle's funeral. Any indication of an abnormality in his system—like when he runs a fever from catching a cold, or has diarrhea after his fits—appears to rob him of even his soul, and forces him to lie prostrate on the sofa as though he has been cut down. But on the days of his semiannual checkups at the hospital, he is always in such fine spirits that Mother, bewildered, once said, "He was so happy going there, he was running all over the place." And he has always been like this, even after Dr. M, the doctor who'd been looking after him ever since his first operation, passed away. The reason he is happy to go there, I think, is not so much because he can meet the doctors he likes, as because he wants them to check his state of health, which he is very concerned about.

When the time comes for Eeyore to realize that he is soon going to die, how terrified he's going to be! What agony would compound his fear, were he to die of some pain-ridden illness, like cancer! Wouldn't the torments he goes through be enormously magnified, compared to those of healthy people—of individuals who, to use Mr. K. V.'s expression, are "saner" than he?

I couldn't let such thoughts pass through my lips in Eeyore's presence—he was actually beside me, listening to music—but

I figured that since O-chan had copied this passage from Mr. K. V.'s introduction onto a card, I had enough reason to believe that he felt and thought the same way I did about the novel. So I told him just what I thought about it, linking my words to the feelings that were in my heart.

"Don't you think there's an element of self-abandonment in Céline?" I asked. "In his real life as well as his novels? An attitude similar to the 'desperate, savage courage' of Homei Iwano that Papa once told me about. With Ende, there's something about his work that tells you, before the novel is brought calmly to the end, that Ende himself has arrived at a state of calm. Papa wrote that, when he met Ende in San Francisco, he found him to be precisely this kind of harmonious person.

"I consciously thought of Father as I read him this time, which is something I'd never done before. And though it's a work of fiction, I got the impression that Papa, the storyteller, has thrust himself out into an ever-harsher reality. Putting it more bluntly, I suppose the big question for him now is the question of faith. Unlike Ende, neither Papa nor his protagonist knows salvation; nor is he like Céline, who takes a devil-may-care attitude toward both his novels and the real world. Despite the kind of person he himself may be, Céline pulls no punches when he fights for 'our little idiots'; whereas Papa, in my opinion, is lukewarm when it comes to action. . . . He's always fondly reminiscing on the hollow deep in the forest, to the point that he even writes a novel based on its legends. After writing it, though, he realizes he can't live in the forest the way Grandma and Aunt Fusa have so naturally done—and die there. . . . So I can certainly see why he should be in a 'pinch' after writing that novel."

"That *is* a problem, isn't it!" O-chan remarked, in a manner that again made me recall Father's way of talking. "If a difficult problem on the side of reality is to be clarified by writing a novel, and yet the problem can't be hurdled in the novel, then things are really going to be hard for him."

"I don't understand Papa's 'pinch' very well," I said, "but from what I can tell, I guess that's what it's all about. And in his case, from what Grandma told me, he himself didn't choose to make a career of writing. Apparently his family's position in the village gave him no choice but to become the one to remember and pass on the legends of the deep forest. The people around him had high hopes for him from the time he was a child. . . ."

"O-chan," I said, "you were good at talking the way people write, even before you entered elementary school. I wonder if Papa was the same when he was little—though, of course, he spoke with the accent of his village."

"That was a close call," O-chan rejoined. "Has someone been trying to make a storyteller out of me, too?"

"Remember when I went to Papa's village to attend Great-uncle's funeral?" I said. "As I listened to what Grandma had to say, I felt that it'd been planned for someone in our family to become a creator of stories, and for someone else to become a composer of music, and that someday they would give expression to 'The Marvels of the Forest.' Reading *M/T and the Marvels of the Forest* led me to reconfirm this."

"Which means," O-chan said, "that Papa and Eeyore saved us from acting out those roles. I guess we've been lucky, as far as that goes! But this doesn't mean we can be optimistic about the future."

Having heard his name and the words "composer of music," Eeyore, who had redirected his attention toward us, joined our conversation.

"No, I don't think we should be optimistic!" he said.

"Oh, Eeyore, do you know the word *optimistic*?" I asked.

"I don't think it has anything to do with intercostal neuralgia, and it doesn't boil water, either,"* he said, holding on to his side and expressively gazing at the red kettle on the gas stove, in which water was boiling. I laughed, momentarily cut loose from the depression that had been tying me down. But O-chan, to my surprise, flew into a rage, perhaps because *Rigadoon* had started him thinking deep in his heart about something serious; or simply because he had endured, or recalled having endured, listening to the tape, which he didn't want to hear—the recording of the speech he gave when we celebrated his acceptance into elementary school.

"Eeyore," he said, "I think puns like that are a bore. There's nothing productive in such puns. Father is pleased when you make them, and he writes about them in his novels, but I don't think they're a good idea. Puns don't bring about realistic solutions. . . . I dislike an Eeyore who's always amusing himself by saying such things. So tomorrow I'm not going to take you!"

His face pale with anger, O-chan brusquely left the living room. Both Eeyore and I became silent and glum. I wanted to comfort Eeyore, tell him not to worry. But I couldn't, for I felt that O-chan had reprimanded me for the way I'd been treating Eeyore. Moreover, I felt that his rebuke was fair—and then for the first time in a long while, I *robotized*, and I remained in this state. But even before he reached his room, O-chan came downstairs again, and his face, still pale, peered in from the door he had opened halfway.

*A play on the words *rakkan* (optimism), *rokkan shinkeitsu* (intercostal neuralgia), and *yakan* (kettle).

a quiet life

"Pardon me. Nothing I said was coherent . . . ," he said, taking back what he had said. "Eeyore, tomorrow let's go to the welfare workshop together!"

Once more, this time quietly, O-chan closed the door and went upstairs. Eeyore, who nodded his head instead of replying by raising his voice, kept his head down as if in fearsome awe. It took some time for me to recover from my robotization, and I thought how I would be robbing O-chan of his precious time if I let him take Eeyore to the welfare workshop and back. For although O-chan *sort of* sees the light ahead in terms of his entrance exams, he undoubtedly has his anxieties, there being no absolute guarantee he will pass. . . .

As the person responsible for doing the chores, though, I couldn't just sit there forever despondent. The moment we finished listening to Bach's short cantata, I took Eeyore to his bedroom. I stood by his side and watched him change into his nightclothes and lie on his bed. I then covered his large body with a blanket, and put the bedspread over him. Eeyore, as always, hooked his finger on to the switch of his bedside lamp and waited for me to go out into the glow of the night-light in the hallway. He was still very sad, and his head was turned the other way. As I exited the room, I heard the click of the switch behind me, and all was black. And from that darkness, I heard Eeyore's words, spoken in a suppressed tone of voice, as though in a quiet monologue: "I've been optimistic all along!"

diary as home

My younger brother, O-chan, made a thorough daily schedule, to start from January, which focused on home preparation for his college entrance exams. As for me, I decided to go to the university library and my French literature study room twice a week. I even had time to seriously think about Eeyore's physical exercise, the idea of which I had reacted to when Father declared Eeyore's need for it in connection with sexual "outbursts." So Eeyore and I decided to go swimming. From my experience as a volunteer for handicapped people, however, one thing worried me. If I wanted to register Eeyore as a family member at the health club, where Father has a full-time membership, wouldn't he—admittedly a *sort of* mentally handicapped person—have to go through a troublesome interview? Nevertheless, the two of us, Eeyore and I, headed for the club in Nakano, where I remember Father had once taken me when I was in elementary school.

a quiet life

My apprehensions were allayed by the membership sales manager, a certain Mr. Osawa, who went out of his way to ensure that everything went smoothly for us. Mr. Osawa's face was pale—probably from overwork—and attached to this face were a pair of expansive shoulders and a big chest, both of which were proportionately a size larger. He had originally started at the club as a gymnastics instructor, he said, but was now part of the management. He kindly showed us around the building and explained each facility, and by the time we returned to the lounge the required paperwork had been taken care of, and all Eeyore had to do was write his name and affix his seal to it.

I immediately reported to Mother that I had registered Eeyore at the club. I wrote that the only worry I had—because I couldn't enter the men's locker room—was whether Eeyore would be able to go through the whole procedure, from changing into his swimming trunks to putting his clothes in the locker, in a timely manner. In an international phone call he made in reply to my letter, Father told me about the men's locker room, so that I would be able to utilize his own knowledge of it. He also supplied a meticulous explanation of the dos and don'ts therein—earnestly. Eeyore should use one of the lockers way back in the corner, for he would always find an empty one there, and be least in the way of the other members. He should be careful of the locker door, as it is a bare metal sheet whose edges have been bent inward, and so be especially careful, for some of the edges haven't been properly burnished, and he could cut his fingers on them. Always bring a ten-yen coin to insert into the slot in the locker. He would receive two towels at the entrance, a large one and a small one. Take the small one to the swimming pool downstairs. Use it in the drying room to wipe off the perspiration. . . .

But Father said nothing directly about the decision I had made to have Eeyore take up swimming—an attitude I thought to be very typical of him. He was having scruples about having done nothing before his departure to deal with the matter that had been on his mind: Eeyore's exercise, the need for which he had deliberated on and declared in my presence. Using the bathroom at home, I gave Eeyore some practice in changing. O-chan, who was playing a video game with a device he had hooked up to the TV set in the living room, an unusual diversion for him, commented that the overly enthusiastic tone of my voice in addressing Eeyore was the same as Father's when he was trying to get Eeyore to do something difficult. How right he was.

"Let's be quick now, Eeyore! There's nothing to be ashamed of, but if you stand there naked too long, they'll take you for a helpless old geezer. Now let's see you get into your swimming trunks in three minutes! Then check and see if you've put your clothes and stuff in the locker. Remember to put a ten-yen coin into the slot. Then you turn the key, right? I'll be waiting for you in front of the locker room with your smaller towel, goggles, and swim cap."

Would Eeyore be able to properly do all this? At first, of course, he'll be confused and very slow, but I am firmly convinced he'll eventually master it. My activities in looking after children with heavier handicaps than Eeyore's have gradually led me to a certain way of thinking, which I keep only in my heart. I call it the "Hang in there, kid!" method, from an expression I found while reading Céline. Little Céline is walking with his mother to the shop where she works. He's going there with the intention of helping her. His uncle, who happens to pass by, encourages the little boy. "*Hardi petit*—Hang in there, kid!" he shouts at him. The expression has a double meaning, but it's the positive, encouraging connotation that projects a vivid image in my mind. Céline must have felt the same way when he unearthed it from his *Rigadoon* memories.

The handicapped children I have become friends with through volunteer activities at first had trouble with their apparently slow and uncertain movements. Yet they seemed to be shouting, "Hang in there, kid!" in their hearts, and in the end they succeeded in accomplishing things. Couldn't I expect the same from Eeyore?

So long as Eeyore is at home, no one in the family finds his movements odd. Admittedly there have been incidents like the one that occurred on the bus, which I have already written about. But when we go out for a Christmas dinner or something, for example, Eeyore gets so excited that he walks ahead of everyone. He also displays a certain social consciousness, as when he offers a seat to an old person, though he does this only when he is not too tired, and only after he has discerned that the person, agewise, deserves to sit down. At the club, everybody is athletic. And I have seen a few young people who move their bodies in very rough ways. Couldn't Eeyore's more relaxed behavior become the cause of an annoying congestion in the men's locker room? Even if such things happened, though, I would hope he'd deal with the problem by showing a "Hang in there, kid!" spirit.

In fact, Eeyore conducted himself admirably well from his first day at the pool. After rehearsing the procedure, I sent him into the men's locker room, went into the women's side where I quickly changed, and then waited for him in the hallway opposite the beverage vending machines, where a flight of stairs leads down to the pool. Then I saw Mr. Osawa come down the stairs from the workout room on the upper floor, and with him was a man who appeared to be in his thirties, wearing a jersey, the front of which was dark and wet with perspiration. I bowed to them, then immediately turned my gaze back to the swinging door of the men's locker room, worried that Eeyore might be having trouble changing. I thought the two men would go on their way, but they continued to stand beside me. And when I looked at them again—this time my eyes must have sharpened with disapproval, for I was in my bathing suit—I saw them looking at me with truly virtuous eyes.

"This is Mr. Mochizuki, a member of the club's Social Committee," Mr. Osawa said, introducing the man to me.

"I run a printing shop," Mr. Mochizuki said. "Oh, and that was very nice of your father." He seemed the sort of man best suited for a cameo role in a TV soap, the hail-fellow-well-met type, but he sounded very sincere in the way he addressed me. The "that was very nice of your father" seemed to be about a letter Father had written him in order to introduce us to him, after I had written to California about us taking up swimming for exercise. The words he spoke next, and the way he said them, though he made the familiar mistake about Eeyore, revealed his relaxed and good-natured personality.

"Your younger brother is in the locker room? Shall I go and look in on him?"

"He needs time," I replied, "but he should be here very shortly."

Mr. Osawa went back to his office, looking the very symbol of business efficiency while Mr. Mochizuki stayed on, standing beside me, smiling brightly. But when Eeyore came out, pushing the swinging door with exaggerated inertia, trailed by a young man who seemed to be protecting him, a look of bewilderment appeared on Mr. Mochizuki's face. My head had been turned toward him just then, for I thought he was going to say something to me, but seeing his smile freeze into a frown, evidently from the consternation he felt when he spotted the young man, I directed my eyes toward Eeyore and the man. I was compelled to become defensive, for I thought that

a quiet life

Mr. Mochizuki may have been shocked at seeing Eeyore naked. Mr. Mochizuki appeared genuinely troubled, yet at the same time his eyes, like those of a spoiled, mischievous child, were fixed on Eeyore's walking, and he seemed to be rapidly thinking how best to deal with the awkward situation—which is to say, there seemed to be something about the young man that spelled trouble.

The young man had well-developed muscles, and fair skin tightly hugged his body. His swimming trunks, almost excessively short, complemented the muscles around his loins, as if they had been tailored for them. With bewilderment still on his face, Mr. Mochizuki introduced the young man who approached me with Eeyore.

"This is Mr. Arai. He's one of the swimmers your father used to swim with for some time, when he frequented this place."

"I swam with this man, too," Eeyore said. "I never forgot."

"Myself, I'm free now," said Mr. Arai. "Myself, I can coach you, if you wish."

"Yes, please coach me," Eeyore said firmly, deciding by himself. He also appeared to remember where the pool was, and stood before us as if to lead us down the stairs toward it.

In the brief moment that Mr. Arai looked at me, I noticed between his lips, which he parted slightly like a girl would, a set of white teeth too straight for a boy, and rose-pink gums, which did not become his firm masculine figure. Even while he looked at me this way, his attention seemed directed also at Eeyore. For my part, I could only say, "I'd be much obliged!" Then he pursed his lips and hurried off to catch up with Eeyore, firmly treading the floor with limbs that seemed to have springs in them.

Downstairs, there were three pools in all: one for racing, one for high dives, and a dark one—with a net over it—for deep diving. Swimming classes were in session in the racing pool, and children were enthusiastically receiving coaching. Beside this pool was the high-dive pool, which, with its tiered bottom, resembled a tabernacle submerged in deep Nile waters; and in it was an armada of middle-aged women in aqua suits that resembled life jackets, leisurely moving their arms and legs to music from a radio–cassette player.

The pool for regular members lay beyond sliding glass doors along the high-dive pool, a few steps lower, and at the poolside Mr. Arai was already having Eeyore do some warm-up exercises. They immediately entered the lane farthest from the entrance to the pool, where nobody was swimming, and began practicing. I decided to swim in the lane next to theirs, so that if anything went wrong I could act as their interpreter. The place was off-limits to swimming-class pupils, and it being a weekday afternoon, there were only one or two swimmers in each lane. Someone awfully small, like a child, stood resting against the wall in one corner at the other end of the lane I had chosen to swim in.

I did the crawl to the other end, and slowly turned. The woman who was resting against a lane marker was clad in a lackluster swimsuit, and all I thought of as I swam back was that it must have been the refraction of the light in the water that made her body seem so outlandishly bloated. While swimming, I became aware that the woman swimming was following me. I turned again and we passed each other. And my heart stopped.

I had never seen anyone more obese. Arms and legs, in the shape of two cones attached to each other, protruded from her trunk, which was like a sack of rice. She was doing the crawl, but there was no space between her thighs, and her legs kicked the water like two fingers wiggling in one glove finger. She was swimming without goggles, perhaps to spare herself their extra weight, and her face, narrow eyes and all, was the face of a plump *hina* doll resting on a triple chin. When I caught up with this fat woman, who was exercising in apparent agony, I felt too embarrassed to watch, right before my eyes, the movement of her writhing legs, which kicked the water but produced no bubbles. . . .

When I stopped for a breather in one corner of the lane I was in, I saw Mr. Arai nearby, in the adjacent lane, teaching Eeyore how to use his arms for the crawl stroke. He was marking time with a repetition of words that must have sounded pleasant to Eeyore: "Catch! Sweep! Recover! Catch!"—in this order. This may have been a basic technique required of every coach, but the method seemed perfectly suited to Eeyore. Mr. Arai got Eeyore to learn the arm motions in a very short time, and was already trying to make him swim, while supporting his sinking legs. I immersed myself in the water to see Eeyore's underwater movements. Gently, softly, but correctly executing each step, Eeyore's arms showed proper form, as they caught, swept, and recovered. With Mr. Arai directing him, Eeyore was able to effortlessly touch the floor with his feet, after which he composedly took a deep breath and waited for Mr. Arai's next instruction. . . .

Mr. Arai then had Eeyore clasp between his thighs a pair of cylindrical Styrofoam floats, and made him swim on his own. Father once got him to try this method a long time ago. As I remember, he made Eeyore use a kickboard, but because Eeyore's thigh muscles weren't strong enough to keep it between his legs, the board slipped out and burst to the surface from under the water. But the device Eeyore was using now— two round cylinders joined together—was entwined, as it were, around his thighs, enabling him to paddle the water, and advance about two meters; and for the first time in his life, his body sank diagonally. Mr. Arai was waiting for him, and supported his torso. Eeyore spit out some water, and though he was coughing, he appeared excited at what he had accomplished. Mr. Arai was saying something to him, patting his soft, white back. He then turned straight toward me, as if to say he had known all along that I'd been watching, and called out, "Thirty minutes is enough for the first lesson. Let's go up to the drying room and discuss our future lesson plan there."

Mr. Arai himself had been vigorously moving about in the pool, but his voice was clear and bright, without the slightest panting. Eeyore had already become his ardent admirer, and was firmly nodding his head. . . .

Eeyore and I sat side by side on the lower of the two tiers that lined the walls of the wood-paneled drying room. Eeyore hadn't worked out so vigorously in ages, and so he was pale with tension, yet the same tension was already beginning to ebb and leave an unusual expression on his face. Tired as he was, he kept his neck buried in his thick, round shoulders, and I could see that he was pleasantly savoring the aftertaste of a good workout.

Mr. Arai, his upper body looking as though he were wearing armor made of muscles, continued to sit straight on the tier along the adjacent wall, beside the floats he had let Eeyore use, and some other training gear that he had placed next to himself. A girl, who could have been on a university swimming team, apparently someone he knew, came down from the direction of the locker room and gestured a friendly greeting to him, but he ignored her and maintained an expressionless countenance that seemed almost cruel.

It was only after Eeyore had fully recovered from the fatigue of the swim, the cooling-down exercises after it, and the walk up the winding stairway from the pool, that Mr. Arai broached with us the plan he had for Eeyore's lessons. Such thoughtfulness from a young man—whose body was that of a diligent athlete, but whose neck on up resembled a cross between a young boy and girl, the type the older generation refers to as the "new breed"—led me to embrace a favorable impression of him, as did his way of talking to Eeyore, as men of the same generation would talk. They may, in fact, have been the same age.

"Can you come every week?" he asked. "The same day of the week, and at the same time? Practice for half an hour each time, for five sessions, and you'll learn how to breathe, and then be able to swim the whole length of the twenty-five-meter pool. You're good because you're not afraid of the water, and you follow directions well."

"Yes, I followed directions well!" Eeyore replied, lending an attentive ear so as not to let even one of Mr. Arai's words slip by.

"He's never been told after physicals that he has a heart problem, has he?" Mr. Arai asked me.

"He has epileptic fits . . . ," I said, "but there's nothing wrong with his heart. And his epilepsy isn't all that bad, either. The fits last about thirty to forty seconds. He gets delirious then, that's all. It could be dangerous if it happened in the water— if he were alone. . . ."

Mr. Arai listened attentively, but twice the girl sitting next to him made a strange burplike noise. Alarmed, I turned to look up at her, and realized that she was stifling her laughter each time I said epilepsy. I let my eyes fall from her sweat-beaded face to her full, spindle-shaped, gloriously suntanned thighs. Then I resumed looking at my own plain white thighs, which were like sticks and weren't even starting to perspire. Although Mr. Arai certainly needed to explain his instruction schedule to me, I felt that he was being unfair to the girl, ignoring her as he was, talking only to Eeyore and me.

"All right, then," he said, "let's swim together every Saturday, from three. For thirty minutes. I'm always free then. . . . All right?"

"All right. That's three to three-thirty, thirty minutes," Eeyore replied, happy with the recurring numbers.

"How should we pay you for the instruction?" I asked.

"Please don't," Mr. Arai said. "I'll be doing it for my own pleasure." The girl with the spindle-shaped thighs, the color of persimmons with a strong reddish tint, again made a burp-like noise—which this time, I thought, was a warning to Mr. Arai to think twice.

"That's very kind of you," I said, "but you're going to coach my brother, which isn't easy. . . ."

Just then, the man opposite us, who had been lying on the tier like an inanimate object, with a towel over his head and face, and was profusely perspiring from his armpits, crotch, and everywhere—the perspiration spattering on the floor—raised his upper body to sit up.

"Never mind the fee," he said. His moonface, which had turned beet red, was smiling at us, and he didn't bother to wipe the beads of sweat that were dripping from his flat pug nose. "Mr. Arai works here part-time, but he has Saturdays free. What he does all day Saturday is kill the body with training. Some light coaching should do him good, help him get his kinks out."

Mr. Mochizuki of the Social Committee! This man had been lying in the drying room with a towel over his face long before we had come in. His appropriate counsel had therefore come after he had heard everything Mr. Arai had said and duly sized up the situation. Addressing the huffed-up girl who was sitting beside Mr. Arai, Mr. Mochizuki said, again with a smile, "Training now, Mika-chan? Or will you be teaching beginners?" The girl completely ignored him, but he retained his friendly countenance, and positioned himself to lie down again when the two doors of the room simultaneously opened. Three or four people, the unusually fat woman first, entered through the door from the pool. Four or five men entered from the door to the locker rooms. Mr. Mochizuki was roughly restrained from lying down by a diminutive man with a mustache.

"My, oh my, Mr. Mochizuki!" the man said, with an effeminate but sharp tongue. "Do your lying elsewhere! Can't you see this place is getting crowded? Go get yourself some exercise. Swim. Do something. It's not good for you to just drip with sweat. It's bad for the body."

"I wonder why," Mr. Mochizuki said, as he sat up again, looking apologetic but still smiling.

The mustached man, who spoke the way women do, then said to the fat woman, "Mrs. Ueki, have you gotten rid of some of your weight? You'll be disqualified as a woman if you don't get some of that blubber off you!"

"That's going a bit too far. Such insensitivity!" was the sentiment that seemed to unite everyone in the drying room. Eeyore, ill at ease, also hung his head down. But Mrs. Ueki herself firmly nodded back, and didn't seem to take any of it very personally. The room was soon filled with conversation, but Mr. Arai clammed up, hugging his knees, which he had pulled up to his chest.

Mr. Arai's behavior was not, however, something that surfaced above the fresh atmosphere of the room, which was now full of people. In the middle of the room was a metallic barrel-shaped device filled with black stones that radiated heat—a heat source for sauna effects, I think—and a woodwork frame enclosing it. There was also a narrow space between the frame and the tiers, where we were seated. Some people started warm-up stretches and what not. One man even lay flat on his

back on the floor right in front of our eyes. He then crossed
his feet, brought them to his abdomen, and assuming the form
a genie would take when entering a bottle, started spinning
his ankles. Having to bear this sight right before his eyes,
Eeyore turned to me with a grin, a reserved one, which seemed
to say, "Spare me!"

"Well, Mr. Arai has some more training to do," Mr. Mochizuki said to Eeyore, standing up. "Let me take you to the locker
room now. You can take a bath, or get warm again in the sauna
room there, and get dressed."

The place where Mr. Mochizuki had been sitting was wet,
as though he had violently emptied a bucketful of water. Yet
even while he was perspiring so profusely, he had been mindful of Eeyore. Realizing that Mr. Mochizuki was trying to help
us newcomers, the effeminate mustached individual stopped
needling him and sent us off with caring eyes. This was most
likely the result of Mr. Osawa having done a lot of spadework,
talking to people whenever he could, in the lobby or in the
locker room, to ensure that things went well for Eeyore.

I took a quick bath and, without even drying my hair, went
out into the lobby to carefully watch the entrance to the men's
locker room. Before long, Eeyore spiritedly emerged from the
swinging door that Mr. Mochizuki had pushed open for him.
He courteously bowed to Mr. Mochizuki, who went back into
the sauna room. To celebrate Eeyore's success at his first swimming lesson, I got each of us a can of hot black tea at a vending machine, and we drank together.

Just as we reached the bottom of the stairs of the club
building, about to walk to the station, Eeyore made a bom-
bastic gesture with a strained effort to stifle his joyous surprise.
In the already fallen dusk, through the wide windows facing
the sidewalk, we saw the glimmering swimming pool on the

first floor of the building. Lessons for adults had already started in the large pool, but some of the lanes had starting blocks with signs reading TRAINING LANE on them for regular members who had their own training regimens. In one of them, a swimmer with the entire lane to himself was fiercely practicing the breast-stroke. For every lap he did, he moved a float on the marker, which may have been how he calculated the distance he swam. After a minute's interval to catch his breath, he savagely plunged his shoulders into the water, and again pumped away. His shoulders split the water, and his wet muscles glittered like those of a marine animal. Eeyore quickly noticed that this merman was none other than Mr. Arai.

Eeyore and I leaned against the steel sash of the glass window and rapturously watched Mr. Arai and the shimmering water around him, which mirrored the swimming pool lights. He repeatedly went through the motion of hugging the water with a menacing force, and when he raced to the end of the lane near where we were watching him, he stopped, heaving his shoulders to catch his breath, like an ailing man, and moved one float on the marker as though he were rolling a log. Yet the strength of his legs—which you saw each time he immersed his whole body in the water, kicked the wall, and sprang off— was alien to the controlled, graceful beauty you saw in a young athlete. It was even coarse, and savage. . . . It didn't communicate the wholesome joy you feel when you see an athlete in motion. You felt more as though you had been made to witness a self-flagellation. I suddenly understood what "killing the body" meant, which dampened my spirit.

"Eeyore, shall we go?" I said. "I feel guilty about us watching Mr. Arai without his knowing it."

Eeyore appeared to suffer no lingering attachment either, and moved away from the steel sash.

* * *

The following week, after Eeyore's music lesson, I told Mr. Shigeto and his wife about Eeyore having taken up swimming. I told them it was formal training, something quite different from what Father had tried with him before, since now he had a competition swimmer for a coach.

"There's no better way to learn than to receive formal training," Mr. Shigeto said. "With your stature, Eeyore, I think you'll look magnificent doing the crawl, if you learn to swim well. And, of course, swimming's good for you. You may find your practice sessions hard, but I hope you'll keep at it."

"I've tried many things so far," Eeyore replied, "but from now on, let me keep at it in the water!"

Mr. Shigeto and his wife, and I too, heartily laughed, although we knew that Eeyore, as usual, had intentionally said it off-key. As though to remind Eeyore of the difficulties he encountered in his music lessons, however, Mrs. Shigeto added, "You mean in the water *too*, don't you?"

I had already written to Mother that Eeyore had taken up swimming. I never imagined, though, that while I was telling Mr. Shigeto and his wife the same thing I had written in my letter, my parents in California were panicking because of one line in it: *he has a wonderful coach, Mr. Arai.* On second thought, though, something had struck me as weird about Mr. Mochizuki's demeanor, too, when he saw Mr. Arai emerge from the locker room with Eeyore.

Outstripping the wind, a letter from Father reached me in reply to mine. Such a prompt response was unprecedented, for none had ever come within ten days. But this one had come before Eeyore was to have his third session with Mr. Arai. It so happened, Father added, that a sociologist friend of his was returning to Japan from a conference at Berkeley, and so he had entrusted him with the letter to mail me by special delivery from Narita. Though Father had started the letter calmly, it immediately revealed his anxiety, and I read it with tension. The first thing I understood from it was that he had discerned circumstances which, however pressing, prevented him from directly talking to me on the phone. The letter started with words that told me he was happy Eeyore had taken up swimming.

". . . But now, about his coach. It never occurred to me that Mr. Arai, with whom I am also acquainted, had returned, and so he was not at all on my mind when I thought of introducing you and Eeyore to the athletic club. And to be quite honest, I was shocked to know that he is coaching Eeyore. There was quite an involved and serious rumor about him when he left the club five years ago. I intend to make an overseas call, and talk directly to Mr. Shigeto about it, explain things to him, and ask him to go to the club to inquire about the situation. Ma-chan, I hope you won't take offense at my doing this without first discussing the matter with you.

"This could be, should I say, undue worry on Mama's part, but after hearing about the rumor in question from me, she asked me to convey this to you. She says that even if Eeyore is to receive instruction from Mr. Arai, she would want you to abide by the principle that you meet with him only where other people are watching. . . . As for his compensation, I will write Mr. Osawa and ask him to bill it to our home together with our membership fees."

I read this letter with a heavy heart. It left me with a negative feeling toward Father and Mother, which to be very frank I had allowed to develop in me. I was also at a loss as to what to do about Eeyore's coming session, which was going to be the next day. But then Mrs. Shigeto called.

"Ma-chan, about Eeyore's swimming practice tomorrow," she said, "how about finishing Eeyore's music lesson before

that, and then go to the club with Mr. Shigeto? K-chan recommended the club to him a long time ago, and he bought a
membership then. For a while, he got so involved in swimming
that, when we went to Warsaw via Moscow, he plunged into
that heated open-air pool in the snow, the one in which Mus-
covites swim from early in the morning. He is now what the
club calls a 'dormant member,' but he called them and found
out that all he needed to do to restore full membership was to
pay this year's facilities fee. You should see him in his swimsuit, the one he wore at the spa in Czechoslovakia—he's another Esther Williams!"

So after the music lesson, Mr. Shigeto accompanied us to
the club. When he emerged from the men's locker room after
helping Eeyore change, I laughed to myself, for his swimsuit
looked like one of those marathoner's outfits with the pants
and athletic shirt attached to each other. At the same time,
though, I felt it must have flattered him—he must have even
looked gorgeous in it—when and where he had worn it as the
latest style.

We walked down the hallway past the drying room but did
not enter it, which would have been Mr. Arai's usual way of
going to the pool, and went down the flight of stairs to the pool.
Going down the stairs, Mr. Shigeto's barefoot steps were firm.
The lower half of his body was so hefty and sinewy that, in
comparison, Eeyore's legs—and even Mr. Arai's legs, for that
matter—looked modest. Eeyore was walking beside Mr. Shigeto, and Mr. Arai was waiting for us behind the glass doors
to the full-time members' pool. Mr. Arai had been unfriendly
toward Mr. Shigeto, and toward me too, when I introduced
them to each other, but his white teeth and his rose-pink gums
showed when he smiled at Eeyore. He immediately started
doing warm-up exercises with Eeyore, and so all we could do

was stand at a distance, and, feeling like pupils forsaken by their teacher, repeat the movements that he was demonstrating to Eeyore.

Like the week before and the week before that, children taking lessons in the large pool were creating an excitement that reverberated throughout the natatorium. And in the pool where you could do high dives, middle-aged women in aqua suits floated in silence, slowly and gropingly moving their arms and legs in the water. We entered the full-time members' pool, where Mr. Arai and Eeyore practiced in the lane farthest from the entrance, while Mr. Shigeto and I watched from the lane next to theirs. The pool was practically empty, save for a few swimmers, all adult females, one of them the corpulent Mrs. Ueki, hanging on to a lane marker, dejection suffusing her classically featured face.

"This exceeds by far what I heard! Mr. Arai's coaching!" Mr. Shigeto exclaimed. Then, taking a break from his observation of Mr. Arai's instruction, he removed his glasses, placed them on the edge of the pool, and started off with an older Japanese-style lateral stroke. Without glasses, Mr. Shigeto looked like a samurai. His old-fashioned strokes made ripples that formed behind his large ears and flowed gently around his chin. On the return lap he did the trudgen stroke. Seeing him do these two strokes, both of which are done with the eyes above the water, I understood why he showed no interest in Father's goggles, which I had brought for him.

When I started off, doing the crawl, he immediately realized my level of ability and followed me, controlling the speed of his trudgen stroke and maintaining the distance that separated us, so I could continue with my laps. I did three laps this way, but given my physical condition, Mr. Shigeto's easy pace was taxing, and I had to stop for a rest. When I raised my body to look back down the lane we were swimming in, I saw no Mr. Shigeto. I was bewildered for a moment, but I soon saw him emerge from underwater with his right arm extended straight before him—perhaps another old-style Japanese swimming technique—holding a yellow swim cap, which he handed to Mrs. Ueki in the adjacent lane. The expression on her face was one of despondence, yet she gestured to Mr. Shigeto, and to me as well, that she wished the best for Eeyore, who was practicing hard.

Eeyore was now trying to swim on his own from about the middle of the lane. Mr. Arai was shouting instructions next to his ear, and was himself nodding at each word he emphasized. Eeyore—his head of short-cropped hair covered with a swim cap and looking so much larger than Mr. Arai's—also repeatedly nodded as though to demonstrate his resolve.

Pushed at the shoulders and waist by Mr. Arai, Eeyore floated and started swimming with uneven but large strokes. He didn't lift his face to breathe, but he swam to the end of the lane, effortlessly resumed his upright posture, and appeared to desperately look about for Mr. Arai, who he seemed to have difficulty spotting through his goggles. Mr. Arai gently threw himself forward into the water, butterflied—though he rarely did this stroke—to his pupil's side, and praised him for his accomplishment. Both Mr. Shigeto and I vigorously applauded. . . .

When Eeyore was commuting to the secondary division of the special-care school, he once went swimming at the club with Father, and fell into the pitlike pool, which had a net over it the last time I saw it. When they got home that day, Eeyore looked meek and gentle, as though he had been caught doing some mischief. By then, however, he had regained his spirits. Father, though, looked on the verge of tears as he reported the whole story to Mother. These, he said, were the words Eeyore had spoken to comfort him on the train home: "I sank. From now I shall swim. I think I shall really swim!"

Time has passed since then, but just as he had promised Father, Eeyore now *really* swam. I thought I should write to Father in California and let him know this. After all, he was in a "pinch" so serious—something I couldn't identify—that Mother had left Eeyore here, to accompany him to America and stay at his side. The news that Eeyore had swum should encourage him, like the words he had spoken on the train coming home after almost drowning. . . .

I told Mr. Shigeto about this as he continued to carefully watch Mr. Arai, who was making Eeyore go over the arm movements. Mr. Shigeto gave a reply that revealed his full insight into my motivation.

"Ma-chan," he said, "I thought you'd be angry at K for discussing things with me without consulting you first. But you aren't a stickler for things like that, are you? That's the best form of filial piety toward a man of K's disposition."

We went up to the drying room, and there was Mr. Arai, sitting as always, with downcast eyes, beside his training gear. Eeyore, who sat next to him that day, with a serious look on his face, also remained silent. I saw this attitude as one befitting people who had just finished a disciplined workout, though for Mr. Arai it would be only a short respite before his "body-killing" program. I was also proud of them because both gave off the air of people who frequented the pool with a definite goal in mind. Their demeanor sharply contrasted with the relaxed atmosphere of the drying room when occupied by people like Mr. Mochizuki, the perspiration-dripping man, and the effeminate but sharp-tongued, mustached individual, who I'm starting to have a hunch is the proprietor of a beauty parlor.

After a while, Mr. Shigeto, sounding like he wanted to get at least this across, broke his deferential silence, and said, "Eeyore, you swam very well. You listened closely to Mr. Arai's criticism and instruction. You even swam an extra fifteen meters just before coming out of the pool! It's amazing what you did."

"Yes, I did very well!"

"And, Mr. Arai," Mr. Shigeto said, "your coaching techniques deserve equal compliment."

Mr. Arai looked up at Mr. Shigeto, with eyes askance and red from the pool water, but bright and sharp, as though they had been honed with an emery wheel of irascibility.

"It's because Eeyore's the kind of person who does exactly what I tell him to do," Mr. Arai said. "But learning to breathe is going to be difficult. Myself, I hope he keeps it up even when it gets more difficult. . . ."

"I think I will keep it up even when it gets much more difficult," Eeyore said.

"I see that you two have established a firm coach-trainee relationship," Mr. Shigeto said. "Mr. Arai, did you talk with K much, when he was commuting almost daily to the club?"

"No, not very much," replied Mr. Arai, turning to me with a probing look. "Myself, I once even asked him if I could visit and talk with him at his home, but he said no."

"Oh, no!" Eeyore said, so ruefully that I had to put a word in.

"Father enjoys joking with people," I said, "but character-wise, he's an introvert, and he doesn't have many acquaintances he can call new friends. . . ."

"When you get to be our age," Mr. Shigeto remarked, "it's troublesome to make new friends. It's nice if it happens naturally, like the way I made friends with Ma-chan and Eeyore."

a quiet life

Mr. Arai let his head fall in a nod, and then, with a vigor that seemed almost savage, he kept toweling off the beads of perspiration that surfaced from every pore of his upper body, though frankly I thought them too pretty to wipe off.

On our way home from the pool, Mr. Shigeto treated us to some Italian food at a restaurant in the Shinjuku Station Building. He loosened the ties that bound my reserve by explaining that Mircea Eliade, whose correspondence he was directly translating from Romanian, had whetted his appetite for Italian food, for just then he was working on the letters Eliade had written as a young man traveling through Italy. He then carefully studied the menu with an attentiveness I thought Japanese seldom show. And the assortment of dishes he ordered was such as to make Eeyore, an experienced and earnest viewer of gourmet programs on TV, utter just the right exclamations of praise upon tasting each dish. Mr. Shigeto, elated by Eeyore's reaction, carefully observed, with narrowed eyes, how skillfully he used the knife and fork to eat his spaghetti. I think there was a certain grace about Eeyore's relaxed bearing that made Mr. Shigeto feel good, in the way he used his entire body to reveal the sense of satisfaction and fatigue that had come from spending a fulfilling day consisting of a music lesson and some swimming. . . .

Before long, Mr. Shigeto matter-of-factly divulged the real purpose of his having invited us to dinner. He had heard from Father about Mr. Arai's past, about an incident that had occurred when Mr. Arai was a law student at a private university five years ago, the details of which he would not relate to me at this point in time, since part of it was mere rumor. And he believed my character was not of the curious sort that would badger him with questions about it. Mr. Arai had actually been involved in a troublesome incident, but Mr. Shigeto thought that for me to know more about it might cause my feelings toward him to take a path in an unfavorable direction. In other words, Father in California, by recalling the incident, was now discomfited at the fact that I had become acquainted with Mr. Arai. However, were Father and Mother to learn that my and Eeyore's relationship with him would be limited to Eeyore's swimming lessons, and that Mr. Shigeto would accompany us to the pool each time, they would be immediately unfettered from their pressing cares. . . .

Later. I believe there is one kind of *later*, which refers not to months or years *later* but to just the ten or twenty days later in which things happen as time runs its everyday course and presents an entirely new picture of a situation. When you look back on those days, you reaffirm with much surprise that those things had actually happened.

Such was the course Eeyore's swimming lessons *later* took. It was still early March, and Eeyore's style when going to the club was to wear a navy blue half-coat, and carry a sports bag. There's a picture taken by O-chan of how Eeyore looks. With exams over for the one and only university he had applied to, O-chan now had some time on his hands, and he planned to go to our cabin in Gumma for orienteering practice. Before his departure, however, he turned his thoughts to our parents in America, and rendered a photographic service for them. He went to the club with us and negotiated with Mr. Osawa to exempt his admission fee, telling him he had come only to do some photography. Then he took pictures of Eeyore in the pool and left on his trip.

As Eeyore, breathing properly, swam all of twenty meters, O-chan kept snapping shot after shot, sighing as it were in amazement. Wonder touched my heart again, as I witnessed the feat that was taking place before my eyes. It was so awesome that I even quite illogically wondered whether Eeyore—apart from seals, otters, and other forms of marine animals—was the first mammal to descend from land to water, and swim so admirably well. Eeyore had performed so magnificently that I became restless after O-chan left the poolside, and lonely, too. So I went to the lane next to the one where he was swimming. I followed him and, through the water, watched him swim, propelling myself forward the way one practices flutter kicks.

In the water, Eeyore's shoulders, arms, and chest looked white like the skin of a white man as he slowly but accurately immersed his hands and arms in the water, caught, swept, recovered, and swam on, executing each movement exactly as he had been instructed. When he turned his head to breathe, I saw that his eyes were gently open in the water. He had stopped wearing goggles since I can't remember when, with the uncompromising stubbornness that's so typical of him. His mouth opened the moment it emerged from the water, and went back into the water closed, with chains of sparkling bubbles trailing it. Wave patterns that reflected the ceiling lights, created by the lane markers and crisscrossing ripples, were projected on his body and the flat surface of the bottom. To breathe, he twisted his large head as though he were engrossed in thought, then returned it to its original position. And he swam as though he were pulling himself up the net that had been cast in the form of the shadows of the lane markers and the ripples.

"After watching you swim like that, Eeyore, I feel like a century's gone by," I said to him when he stopped for a breather.

"A century! That's amazing!" he replied thoughtfully, with an air of composure.

That day after swimming practice, there were only the four of us in the drying room. The regular pool visitors were using the lounge—why they avoided the drying room you'll know later—to discuss a cruise to the Izu Peninsula, by way of a cherry-blossom-viewing outing. And perhaps because O-chan's picture-taking had created a solemn atmosphere, we were in a quieter mood than usual.

"Oh? What happened here?"

Eeyore, timidly raising his voice, had turned his gaze on Mr. Shigeto's back, and was hesitantly trying to put his finger on it. The top of Mr. Shigeto's old-fashioned swimsuit was somewhat twisted to one side, and part of his back was bared.

"I had an operation," he briefly explained, straightening his shirt quickly but not brusquely, before Eeyore's finger could touch it.

"Your back was sick?" asked Eeyore. "I think it must have hurt a lot!"

"To be exact, it was my esophagus," Mr. Shigeto said. "But not because it hurt."

Eeyore seemed convinced by this, but I was very upset. I happened to be in the dining room when one of Father's former classmates phoned to inform him of Mr. Shigeto's illness. Until then, my image of Mr. Shigeto had been of a friend of Father's who made frequent trips to Eastern Europe and traveled there extensively. And so as I overheard the phone call, I thought that Mr. Shigeto had met with a traffic accident, or had needed surgical treatment of some sort. But I had also heard Father worriedly telling Mother, after visiting him in the hospital, that aside from his research on Eastern European literature, which required five to ten years of toil and labor to complete one project, Mr. Shigeto would devote his energy to music composition, the results of which he could see in a shorter period of time. . . . What a fool I had been, so oblivious to everything! Granted, I didn't know him personally then. But wasn't it the height of insensitivity on my part that, even after I had gotten to know him directly, and he had done so much for us, I still failed to associate his decision to compose music with a serious illness of his internal organs? Apart from the heat in the drying room, I felt the skin on my face begin to numb. Before long, quite the opposite of *robotizing*, I found myself unable to refrain from uttering a chain of emotional words.

"Toward the end of last autumn," I began, "Eeyore and I went to Father's native village. We had to attend a funeral, and I asked you to change the day of Eeyore's music lesson to another day. Father's mother talked to me about a lot of things then. We slept in the same room, you see. And there was something she said that I didn't understand very well, and it's been on my mind ever since. . . . She said very slowly, as though tapping her memory, that when Father was a child, he had nearly met his death a number of times, each time in a manner that appeared as though he had brought the danger on himself—not because he was courageous or reckless, but, mysteriously enough, because he *couldn't help it*. And the people around him couldn't let it be. Grandmother said that if he was still behaving this way, she would feel sorry for Mother, and for us children, too. I apologize, Mr. Shigeto and Mr. Arai, for all the trouble Father is causing you with his 'pinch.'"

I myself was partly surprised at the stiffness of my speech and why I was talking so much, and worried whether Eeyore, too, didn't find all this bewildering. My words seemed incoherent, but once they were uttered, I felt that they were unmistakably the thoughts that had been on my mind for a long time now. Exhausted, I pursed my lips. Then the beads of perspiration that covered my face began pouring off my brows and temples and were joined by the tears running down my cheeks.

"What's come over you, Ma-chan!?" Eeyore timidly called to me. Mr. Shigeto and Mr. Arai looked humbled, as though they had taken my words as a protest against them.

". . . I'm sorry," I said, "Father has put this burden on you, saying that he has his 'pinch' to deal with. But you're both so good to Eeyore. That's why I feel so indebted to you, and so sorry that I . . ."

Mr. Arai handed me a towel, stretching out his arm to its full length, the way a monkey stretches its arms out, which alarmed me, for I thought the towel was going to be wet and smelly with his perspiration. It was dry, though, like bread straight from the oven. Wrapped in its fragrance, I dried my tears with it. And I even blew my nose in it, noisily.

That day, Eeyore and I parted with Mr. Shigeto at Shinjuku Station, transferred to the Odakyu Line, and returned to Seijo Gakuen-mae Station, where we were met with an unexpected welcome. I immediately wondered how on earth, with dusk having come, he was able to spot us in the crowd in front of the station. Or had he been waiting on the pale-lit sidewalk to the left, where people queue up for taxis? From there he could have seen us either way we went on the pedestrian crossing, whether toward the well-illuminated supermarket on the right coming down the station stairs, or toward the pharmacy in front. We needed to buy something for dinner, and just as I picked up one of the shopping baskets stacked up at the entrance to the supermarket, someone came up from behind, springing along in jogging shoes, and hit Eeyore on his shoulder with a forceful *blam!* Turning around, much to my amazement, I saw Mr. Arai.

"What a surprise!" said Eeyore, who appeared to be in

good spirits, though usually he hates it when someone touches him.

"I thought you'd be killing your body at this time of day," I said. ". . . Why?"

"Eeyore went through a photography session today, and he swam especially well. So myself, I thought I'd drive both of you home. Myself, I waited for you in front of the club, but"— he stopped his words short, turned his shoulders on their axis, and gestured in the direction of the liquor store, next to the pharmacy, in front of which were stacked many cases of discounted scotch whisky.

Since the entire block was a no-parking zone, he must have repeatedly circled the area in his car, now and then stopping someplace nearby to wait for us for a few minutes. A grass-green Porsche, a grimy one, started to roll slowly toward us.

"If you have some shopping to do," he said, "myself, I could come back in ten minutes." The way he had so vigorously said it, as though he were about to put his very words into action, made my blood boil.

If I had been my usual self, I would have declined his offer, saying that we always walk home from the station. Though Eeyore looked like he really wanted to do some shopping, I brusquely put down the basket, pulled him by the arm, and followed Mr. Arai, whose gait, as he walked in front of us, resembled that of a black basketball player. From the way he moved, he seemed to be a different person, so unlike at the club, where he walked in his bare feet, toes firmly clutching each stair. We walked toward the car, which had rolled slowly past us and was now halted a short distance away from the intersection ahead.

Mr. Arai had on a dark blue jumper with an emblem embroidered on it, of the kind many college students in sports clubs wear. He appeared to be a much slimmer young man, as though he had cast off the armor of muscle in which he swims. Only his neck looked strong, with the lines from the side of his head falling on a slant to his shoulders. The woman, who kept her hands on the steering wheel all the while she looked back and peered out at the darkening sidewalk, appeared to be past middle age. She was thin and diminutive, and wore plain-looking clothes.

Hastened by Mr. Arai, who promptly let the passenger seat fall forward, I first helped Eeyore in, then followed suit. I bowed to the woman, but had no time to exchange proper greetings with her. I gave directions vaguely to both the woman and Mr. Arai, not knowing exactly who to address, and as soon as the car started toward our house, Mr. Arai asked Eeyore if it was really all right that he hadn't bought anything at the supermarket.

"I think I wanted a can of coffee!" was Eeyore's reply.

We happened, just then, to be passing a rice dealer's store with a vending machine installed in front of it, and immediately Mr. Arai told the woman to stop. Not that he himself was going to hurry to the machine, for he made the woman at the wheel do it, which didn't seem to bother him in the least. And on top of this, he began some trivial conversation.

"You don't have many visitors after K-san and your mother left, or do you?" he asked.

"The wife of Mr. Y, the writer, kindly brought us some sweets, pickles, and a sweater!" Eeyore said.

"This is the Mr. Y who might receive the Order of Cultural Merit next year? Eeyore, you know some important people."

Mrs. Y, who drives up to the gate of our house, gives us bountiful gifts at the front door, and then drives back home, once said, "Your papa is so health-minded that he swims even when he goes to America. Now why doesn't he buy you a car to take Eeyore to the welfare workshop and back? Ask him, please, to buy you one, all right?" After saying this with such force that some passersby peered at us, she drove her Mercedes back home.

The traffic ahead was not as heavy as it had been on the street in front of the station, and we reached our house in no time. As soon as we arrived, Mr. Arai jumped out of the car, and alarm got the better of me.

"Thank you for driving us home," I quickly said, my language inadvertently becoming cut and dry. "My younger brother is away for training, and he won't be coming home tonight. So if you'd excuse us here . . ." I said, putting up a hard defensive battle. "Eeyore, now hurry! You're holding them up!"

Eeyore had received two cans of coffee from the woman. They were too hot to keep holding with bare hands, and he had just put them into the smaller of the bags he carried, the one he used for his wet swimming trunks and cap. Seeing Eeyore put the bag at his side on his lap, with the satchel he carries his music sheets in, and then slide toward the door, Mr. Arai coldly said, "Neither of you could have gotten out if I hadn't. Myself, I didn't get out to force you to invite me in." Then, as if to pick a quarrel, he said to the woman in the driver's seat, "Was the coffee on you? How generous! But you don't do that for your homeroom pupils in your middle school, do you?"

With her unassertive pink-framed glasses and prominent forehead, and with her face turned down, the woman presented the classic image of a bewildered middle-school teacher confronted by a rebellious pupil. I asked her to accept the two coins, which I had been holding in my hand with the intention of paying her anyway. As soon as we got out of the car, Mr. Arai violently got in and threw his head back against his seat. He just stared at our house beyond the hedge, and didn't reply to Eeyore's good-bye.

The following week, on the train we took to the pool after his music lesson, I had Eeyore sit down, and then told Mr. Shigeto, who was standing beside me, in front of Eeyore, about Mr. Arai taking us home in his car. I did not at all feel like I was squealing on him. In fact, I had inadvertently shown Mr. Arai my defensive side, which I have already said is one of Father's traits. Mr. Arai, as well, had displayed a derisive coldness toward my attitude. Even before I had entered our dark, empty house that evening, alone with Eeyore, I had started ruminating about this attitude of mine, and felt most unpleasant. I had also been feeling so helpless, with O-chan away on his trip, that I quickly closed the gate and locked the entrance door.

This was all there was to it. A week had now passed, but today, for some reason, Eeyore had been so excited about practicing his swimming that, though making sure he had his swimming trunks, cap, and goggles as he put each item in his bag, when leaving the house he had forgotten the shoulder bag he puts his music scores in. We had already put on our shoes, so I called out to O-chan, who had returned from his trip and was going to look after the house in our absence, to get the bag for him. And all the while we stood in the entrance, Eeyore kept patting me on my back, smiling as if to tell me that his forgetting the bag had been an amusing blunder of mine. That day, a week ago, when O-chan had taken pictures of Eeyore swimming—they had turned out unbelievably well, with Eeyore swimming in exemplary form, and I sent them to our parents in California—and in the drying room, emotion had gotten the better of me because of what I had been led to imagine by Mr. Shigeto's postoperative scar. With all these things happening that day, Mr. Arai had tried to reward and comfort us by offering to drive us home, and I had become overly defensive in my reaction. This was all there was to it, I thought, after the lapse of a week's time. Regarding Mother's suggestion that I not see Mr. Arai without other people around to watch us—well, Eeyore had been with me that evening. As for Mr. Arai, that woman had been with him. . . .

It was more or less after reflecting that I had acted rudely toward Mr. Arai that I told Mr. Shigeto about all this—presumptuously wishing that if Mr. Arai were still feeling offended, Mr. Shigeto would intercede for me and patch things up between us. Mr. Shigeto did not immediately show any particular reaction to what I had told him. He *sort of* listened to me, then turned his eyes to the book of Polish verse that, probably due to this farsightedness, he held at a distance in front of his chest, with his back erect; the binding of the book resembled those of some Meiji-era kimono-sleeve books in Father's library. From the corner of my eye, though, I thought I saw, for just a moment, a vivid flush appear on the flesh of his usually faded mien. . . .

Mr. Arai's coaching was no different than before. Eeyore was trying harder than ever, and his relationship with Mr. Arai, who butterflied after him to carefully correct his arm movements and breathing technique, appeared even intimate. In contrast, when Mr. Arai and I saw each other for the first time that day, his bow was but perfunctory as he cast a watchful glance around with vivid eyes that assumed the shape of apricots. While bowing, he avoided even looking at me or saying anything. Of course, I wouldn't have known how to answer him, even if he had reproached me for my attitude the previous week.

And in fact I felt relieved to be ignored. It would be best, I thought, for the time of Eeyore's swimming lesson that day to pass just this way, and next week everything would be back to what it had been before. . . .

Spirited talk among the regulars—the sweat-dripping, ever-smiling Mr. Mochizuki; Mrs. Ueki, who was depressive but wouldn't say no to anyone; the sharp-tongued beauty parlor proprietor, who as usual kept needling the other two; and a newcomer, a stalwart man whose muscles looked as though they had come from manual labor rather than weight training—filled the drying room that day, with the newcomer at the center of a discussion that recapitulated the professional baseball draft. Mr. Arai seemed to effortlessly withdraw into, and enclose himself within, his armor of muscles. Just as he was preparing himself to resume his own training, however, Mr. Shigeto, who had remained completely silent until then, asked him if he would spare him some time that evening. He asked him about how long it would take to finish his body-killing regimen, his bath, and sauna. He would be waiting in the lounge, he said, and proposed that they talk over some beer, which he would buy at the vending machine. . . .

Mr. Arai sneaked a look at me with his apricot-shaped eyes, wary under their single-fold lids, then returned his gaze to Mr. Shigeto and nodded. Eeyore appeared to want to stay longer, but I pressed him on, and as we exited the club, I thought it strange that I hadn't noticed the rare shape of Mr. Arai's eyes until then: you rarely saw such eyes on the face of an adult male.

The following week, when we visited the Shigetos for a lesson, Mrs. Shigeto, who opened the door to us, was wearing an expression that was more depressed and gloomier than the day she had returned from the hospital. Dark brown rings encircled her wide upper eyelids, half of which showed above the silver frames of her glasses. And her eyes, which had always looked so clever and bright, seemed to have loosely contracted.

"Mr. Shigeto is in a bad way, but please don't be alarmed," she whispered to Eeyore. I had sensed something ominous, but as much as she appeared concerned about me, I knew from the way she said this that she was more concerned for Eeyore, who had relaxedly greeted her and then was removing his shoes.

Mr. Shigeto, who had been sitting on the living room sofa, rose halfway to greet us, and suddenly he groaned "Uhh!" as he assumed a posture that appeared as though he were going to hang in midair, and then another "Uhh!" as he bounced back onto the sofa from this position. Eeyore saw all this, and despite the warning we had been given, he exclaimed, "Oh, no! What happened!? I am surprised!?" No other words could have been more appropriate for the occasion, I thought.

Mr. Shigeto's face was swollen, and had turned angular like a kite. On his upper right cheek, brow, and two places on his head—in the front and in the back—were patches of gauze attached with tape, through which the blurry yellow of an ointment showed. Around his bare chin and throat were reddish-black bruises as big as hands. He was dressed in a gown that had aged in a noble manner, but the odd protuberance around his chest and down his side—wasn't that a cast he was wearing?

"Recent disasters befalling our family all have to do with fractured bones," Mrs. Shigeto said, her voice sounding a bit more spirited than it had at the entrance. "I sometimes feel like asking a geomancer to divine the fortunes of the lay of the house."

"Eeyore, in my case it's really the ribs! And I'm in a perfect mood for your 'Ribs.' Play it for me, won't you? I've been told not to move my right arm for some time."

Granted, it was Eeyore's simplicity that caused him to immediately brace up and start looking for the object of his heart's desire among the music sheets in his satchel. But planted in the manner in which Mr. Shigeto had spoken these words was a plot to encourage my alarmed and heartbroken brother. I got teary-eyed, and I *robotized*, and was unable to do anything except stand at Eeyore's side. I could never respond to or help the injured Mr. Shigeto as much as my brother, who was thumbing through his music to accommodate his mentor's request.

"Have you found it?" Mr. Shigeto asked. "Eeyore, I'm sorry to ask this of you when you've just arrived, but could you play it for me on the piano in the music room? Play it a couple of times, and change the tempo each time. Leave the door open— I want my ribs to directly feel the vibration, but in a way that won't hurt. . . ."

Eeyore directed a worried and solemn bow to Mr. Shigeto, and alone went into the music room. All of which meant that Mr. Shigeto had wanted an opportunity to discuss matters in such a way that the content of what he needed to convey to me would not reach Eeyore's ears. I immediately understood this to be a proper consideration. And while listening to Mr. Shigeto, I even wished that I could have gone and hidden in Eeyore's shadow, as he kept playing his "Ribs." The catastrophe that had befallen Mr. Shigeto had, I think, been greater than the premonition that had reflexively and violently seized me a few moments ago.

That evening, Mr. Shigeto had been waiting in the lounge for almost two hours, drinking beer, when Mr. Arai emerged looking neat, with his lotion-laced short hair teased and combed so that it stood straight up. Because of the exhausting training program with which he kills his body, his cheeks were sunken and pale, and when Mr. Shigeto asked him to sit down and join him at the table, which was covered with empty beer cans, he bluntly refused. His excuse was *sort of* convincing: he didn't touch any alcoholic beverages while training for a meet. So Mr. Shigeto took Mr. Arai up on his suggestion that they go to a quieter place to talk: the parking lot in back of the club building.

"He clearly admits he was drunk," Mrs. Shigeto said of her husband, supplementing his words, "because it was almost strategic how late Mr. Arai showed up. And one reason Mr. Shigeto won't go to the police is because he was under the influence. Mr. Shigeto told me that, while walking from the lounge to the parking lot, Mr. Arai talked so much that he seemed a different person. And he had done this with a practically indecent flippancy, the exact opposite of what had been at the bottom of his stoic reticence in the drying room. "For instance," Mr. Shigeto said, "he told me about the dream you had of him." I blushed, though I was *robotized*. "He got it out of Eeyore in tidbits each time he made him take a break. Ma-chan, he said you'd dreamed of marrying him with Eeyore along. . . ."

Indeed, the dream I had was one of the variations of the dream I started having some time ago, in which the Eeyore-to-be appears, standing at my side as my attendant. The new dwelling Mr. Arai had prepared for us was a two-bedroom apartment. It was owned by the Metropolitan Government, yet in the basement was a long and narrow three-lane, twenty-meter swimming pool. It also seemed that the pool came with our room. It was for our exclusive use, and Mrs. Ueki was training in it. Eeyore, with Mr. Arai coaching him, of course, swam on and on, repeatedly making turns. Quite inappropriate for the place, I was dressed in a wedding gown, and was standing nonplussed by the very wet poolside, with a bouquet of withered flowers in my hands. I had told Eeyore of this dream, focusing on the moving scene in which I had seen him vigorously swimming.

What finally provoked Mr. Shigeto to ire was evidently the insinuating manner in which Mr. Arai talked about this dream. According to his wife—who put in her comments from the side—this time, too, just as when he had gone to have a word with the privilege-flaunting Polish government official at Warsaw Airport, Mr. Shigeto had been stirred to the point of venting his *desperate Yamato spirit*. "But Shigeto-san," added his wife, "is an internationally minded intellectual, a rare specimen in this country. . . ."

With an aching heart, I entered in "Diary as Home" the verbal exchange between Mr. Shigeto and Mr. Arai. To be fair, however, I should also say that, although it was Mr. Arai who did the provoking, it was Mr. Shigeto who started talking as though he was ready to fight.

"Don't you think it's dirty," Mr. Shigeto said, "that you coaxed Eeyore into telling you about Ma-chan's dream, and then told it to a third party, imbuing it with your own nuances?"

"Myself"—Eeyore had long since found it amusing that Mr. Arai was the sort of person who used "myself" in this way—"I find it very annoying that K-san and Ma-chan—father and daughter together—forge distorted images of me to suit themselves, and then inflate them."

"Do you interpret a modest girl's humble dream as a warped image? . . . Regarding K, yes, he did write a novel that used, as a starting point, the incident that took place on the cruiser. First, though, you gave him your book of notes after receiving money from him. Moreover, I heard that you asked him to analyze your inner thoughts and behavior through his writing, because you didn't understand them very well yourself. Second, it's clear that K intentionally deflected the setting from the cruiser. And if my memory is correct, he also wrote that the crime being perpetrated by the young protagonist was a supposition. The focus of the story is on the middle-aged man, who sacrifices himself to save the young man who, because of his involvement in some sort of crime, has fallen into a desperate situation. K wrote that if, in fact, the crime had been committed by the young man, then the middle-aged man had atoned for it on his behalf by virtue of his own self-sacrifice; and so rebirth was possible for the young man, who accepted what the older man had done for him. This is how K analyzed your inner thoughts and behavior, exactly as you had asked him to."

"First off, myself, I returned the money to Mr. K. And second, there was no crime to begin with. Aren't some members of the club secretly discussing their cruise to Izu because Mr. K fabricated a sex-offense story out of what had been a mere accident? Myself, I find this a real pain in the neck."

"You returned the money to K because you stood to benefit from the insurance policy the young girl who died on the cruiser had bought. The weekly magazines played up the case long before K's novel came out. Shouldn't you have sued them, and K, too, for libel then? You actually wrote K a letter threatening to take the matter to court, and you also sent him an offensive New Year's card. I surmise that the reason you gave K your notes was so he could write a novel about the incident, so in case you were indicted you could have expected voluntary defense activities on the part of good-natured K. But it didn't become a legal case, and moreover, you received the insurance money. After this, far from suing anyone, you simply wished that the incident would be forgotten. I have no interest in any conjecture beyond this. As I said before, I don't mind you coaching Eeyore. All I ask is that you not intrude into Ma-chan's and Eeyore's private life. What did you have in mind, anyway, lying in wait for them at Seijo Gakuen-mae Station, and then following them to their house?"

Though this, too, may have been a rhetorical question, Mr. Arai, instead of answering it, suddenly pounced on Mr. Shigeto, and thoroughly beat him up. Three of his ribs were broken because Mr. Arai had intentionally and repeatedly kicked him in the side. Mr. Shigeto couldn't help reading a criminal disposition, both into the way Mr. Arai had gone about relishing the half-kill of a decrepit dog, as it were, and into the way he had seen to it that this was so scrupulously accomplished. In this regard, Mr. Shigeto believed that, though aggressive, his attitude, in giving Mr. Arai warning not to approach us, had been fair and in line with K's request. . . .

Mrs. Shigeto did not become emotional toward the young man who had inflicted injuries on her husband. She said, instead, that it wasn't right, in her opinion, to call Mr. Arai a criminal solely on psychological grounds. From what she had gleaned from reading the newspapers, the cruiser incident of five years ago had been an unfortunate accident, and the police had come to the same conclusion. When his wife said "solely on psychological grounds," Mr. Shigeto fidgeted and moved his body, thrusting his bulging torso forward. He was using these movements to assert that he possessed both material and physical evidence, when once again—"Uhh!"—he let out a groan.

All the while I was being informed of what had happened in the parking lot, Eeyore kept playing his "Ribs" for Mr. Shigeto's injured body. Mr. Shigeto, who must have felt sorry for Eeyore, gingerly raised himself from the sofa, like an old man, and started for the music room. With the closing of the door behind him, he seemed, with the sound of the piano, to have quietly receded into the distance. And immediately, I faintly heard him begin his private lesson.

I read the copies of the newspaper articles Mrs. Shigeto had obtained through an acquaintance of hers at a news agency.

a quiet life

The incident had involved not so much Mr. Arai, but more a
fifty-year-old high school teacher named Kurokawa and a
thirty-five-year-old female travel agent named Suzaki. Mr. Arai
merely happened to join the Izu-Oshima cruise on which the
other two had gone. Mr. Kurokawa and Miss Suzaki had disappeared during the night, and later both bodies were picked
up by a fishing boat. It came to light that Mr. Kurokawa had
drowned but Miss Suzaki had been thrown into the sea after
being strangled. Mr. Arai testified that he had been sleeping
in the cabin below, it having been his night off duty, and had
learned that his cruising companions were missing only around
dawn when the shifts were changed. . . .

Magazine articles emphasized that Miss Suzaki had taken
out an enormous amount of insurance with Mr. Arai as the
beneficiary. Mr. Kurokawa, Miss Suzaki, and Mr. Arai had
met at the athletic club, and had become so intimate they went
to far-off places together, cruising, skiing, and whatnot.
Shortly before the incident, Miss Suzaki and Mr. Arai had
secretly become engaged. Miss Suzaki, much older than Mr.
Arai, and very well paid, had been the guardian of a student
who was still in college, and the buying of an insurance policy
had been her idea, she being very familiar with the business
from the nature of her work. From the very start, however,
Mr. Kurokawa and Miss Suzaki had had a physical relationship, which Mr. Arai had known about. Other people saw,
on top of this relationship, a special affinity at work among
the three. The cruise was supposed to give Miss Suzaki an
opportunity to discuss breaking off her relationship with Mr.
Kurokawa, but he pressed her to continue it, and in the course
of the argument he had strangled her and committed suicide. . . . The widow Mrs. Kurokawa lodged a protest with the
police, who had ruled the incident a murder-suicide. This pro-

test, and the discovery of the existence of the policy, had scandalized the case.

"As far as Mr. Arai's inner thoughts are concerned, K-chan's novel doesn't deviate from his notes. After all, that's how Mr. Arai asked him to write it. In the scene where the woman gets murdered in the dark of night, K-chan changed the concrete details, such as from the cruiser at sea to a children's park beside a loop highway. It's depicted in the grotesque realism that's so typical of K-chan. . . . I don't think you need to read that far, Ma-chan.

"K-chan contrived a setting that couldn't exist in reality—probably because he was being careful to avoid pulling the reader's attention back to the actual incident—wherein he has a young man kill a woman because of what transpires sexually. But then he has a man in his fifties, totally drunk, assault the woman again, and step into the role of murderer. As a result, the man commits suicide. This is the story K-chan wrote. The scene he invented, in which he has the man hang himself in a dovecote on a nearby rooftop, is one you would find only in the movies. K-chan imparts meaning to the man's motives by writing: He sacrificed his own life in such a manner as to destroy his ego and his own body in disgrace, so as to rescue a young man in dire circumstances from which there was no turning back. . . .' He also has this drunk-turned-hero reveal his peculiar resolve this way: 'All right. Then I, and who else but I, shall let him taste of grace—this youth ensnared in remorse enormous and without exit. I shall assume God's role so that the murder, which he committed, will be effaced for him.'

"Though it may be stretching it a bit, doesn't this seem a peculiar contraposition of Christ's crucifixion? Perhaps K-chan himself has a strange desire to act out this man's sacrifice. But in real life—which is exactly what his dilemma appears to be about—instead of him sacrificing anything, there's a tendency for him to have others perform sacrifices for him. Even the roughing up that Mr. Shigeto incurred stems from what K-chan requested of him. And he's victimizing you, too, by having you look after Eeyore, while he himself has taken emergency shelter in California with Oyu-san nursing him. . . ."

"I don't think I'm being victimized," I said.

"You don't? Well, you've always been a personification of conviction, Ma-chan!" Mrs. Shigeto ruefully said, tolerating the forceful way I had answered her. "I don't think it will do you harm to read at least this part of the novel, because it quite honestly reveals his feelings at the time—before this current 'pinch' of his—when he diligently swam as treatment for his ailing mind. . . ."

Before Eeyore's lesson was over, I had not only finished reading the part of Father's novel that Mrs. Shigeto had marked in red, but thinking that I ought to preserve it in the pages of "Diary as Home," I also copied it down on one of the Céline cards I always carry with me, though as I wrote, I had a feeling that I didn't understand it well enough.

One day when I was a child, which later I surmised was just before my father died, he said something like this to me. "Nobody will ever throw down their life for you. Never think such a thing could possibly happen. Never think, somewhere down the line as people lavish attention on you, remarking how clever a child you are, that someone might emerge who will think that your life has more value than their own. This is human depravity at its worst. You may say you'll never feel this way, but those who are doted upon and given too much attention tend to believe this. And not only kids. Some adults, also, get it into their heads, and continue to think this way."

I perceived then, even as a child, that my father's words, prophetically, as it were, had hit the mark. I also felt a stifling dissatisfaction from being unable to gainsay that I didn't actually possess such a character, since it was a matter that pertained to the future. In fact, in my life since then—in other words, at various times in the future I envisioned as a child—I found my father's words to be true. I even think that the shame I felt upon awakening to the worst of human depravity is one reason for my soul's depression, which in turn necessitated my present self-treatment at the swimming pool. Hadn't I, in the way I dealt with this man or that woman, thought that they were inferior to me, and would willingly sacrifice their lives for me, because their lives were lower in value than mine? Though, of course, this has never reached the point of involving an exchange of lives as such, I have sometimes thought this way regarding certain routine choices I have had to make. And so, all this time, an enormous shame has been compounding in my heart. . . .*

After the lesson at Mr. Shigeto's place, I thought that Eeyore and I would make the transfer to the Odakyu Line at Shinjuku Station and go straight home. But Eeyore hurriedly went through the National Railway gate on his own, and headed toward the platform for the Chuo Line's rapid-service trains.

"Oh, wait! Let's not go to the pool today. Mr. Shigeto didn't come with us, you know?"

"Because that gentleman is having a terrible time with his rib injury. I think I shall swim!"

So firm was Eeyore's reply that I had no choice but to go to the club with him. But then in my heart, I guess I had thought

*Ibid., pp. 260–61.

little of it. I figured that because Mr. Arai had roughed up Mr. Shigeto so badly as to cause such serious injuries and had done it all in the parking lot, some club member must have witnessed the brawl. And though the victim hadn't reported it to the police—I thought that this kind of attitude must be typical of a strange man in his fifties, the kind of person who would sacrifice himself to do something for a young man who's gone astray—the information must have gotten around. Mr. Arai couldn't possibly disregard this and come out for his everyday practice, could he? Besides, he had once before been involved in an incident the weekly magazines had scandalized. So I would take Mr. Arai's place and, while standing in the same lane, only because I worry about his epileptic fits, watch Eeyore do his laps with his newly acquired skills.

Eeyore and I opened the glass door to the members-only pool, and walked down the aisle that led to the tiered poolside. But in the open space where we usually do our warm-up exercises was Mr. Arai, with his white teeth and pink gums showing through his typically slightly parted, girlish lips, vigorously flailing his arms and motioning to Eeyore. Taking big strides, in his new pair of red-and-green swimming trunks of the most unconventional design, he walked over to Eeyore, held him by the arm as he would a friend, and fetched him away, making only a neutral bow to me.

I was left alone with warm-up exercises to do. But without Mr. Shigeto, there were no examples to follow in moving my arms and legs. At a loss, I noticed Mrs. Ueki on the other side of the pool slowly doing some preparation exercises, so I went over to her side. Weighing more than when in the water, Mrs. Ueki was all the more laboriously moving her body. Yet she greeted me with a nod that, though despondent, was friendly. After the exercises, Mrs. Ueki and I entered the pool. The only others swimming were Mr. Arai and Eeyore, two lanes across from us.

Mesmerized by the mesh-patterned shadows that the lane markers were casting on the bottom of the quiet water, I recalled, in fragments, Father's words, which Mrs. Shigeto had read to me: *this youth ensnared in remorse enormous and without exit.... which he committed . . . be effaced. . . .* Could it be that Eeyore and Mr. Arai, enthusiastically exchanging words each time they swam, were struggling together to wipe away what had been done in the parking lot, with a huge invisible eraser they kept afloat on the water?

Before long, however, I recalled with sudden fright the scar on Mr. Shigeto's back, and the decision he had made after the operation on his esophagus, most likely for cancer. I couldn't help but shudder again at the thought of the cruel Mr. Arai smiting and kicking a man of such mind and body as Mr. Shigeto, kicking him repeatedly, and aiming the kicks at his ribs in order to break them.

My small round head became unfocused and hot, as though it were being pulled apart from both sides, but I continued with my flutter kicks, feigning bravado, repeating in my heart, *Hell, no! Hell, no!* as if it were an incantation, yet no longer knowing why I was saying this. I saw out of the corner of my eye that Mr. Arai and Eeyore were leaving the pool, so I went over to the faucets used for washing the eyes and gargling, while maintaining a little distance from them. By the time I had settled in the drying room, my body was tired, as if I had swum two or three times longer than the usual thirty minutes, and my head was exhausted to the core.

In the drying room, as usual Mr. Arai's behavior was the opposite of the lively movements and expressions he exhibits at the pool. He had entrenched himself in his armor of muscles, and was sitting there motionless with his head down, not even sweating. Mr. Shigeto's absence had given Eeyore, too, a reason to sit there solemnly with his eyes cast down. But perhaps

a quiet life

I appeared even lonelier, as I looked down at my plain thighs, which resembled white sticks. As the regulars trickled in, the atmosphere of the room gradually changed into something quite different from the usually more lively one. The jovial and gentle Mr. Mochizuki, whose facial features and body are those of an artisan, sat in silence that day with a deep, pensive look, glaring, as it were, at the sauna device in the middle of the room, with beads of perspiration forming around his reddened nose. Even the mustached, feminine-sounding beauty parlor proprietor was wearing an irascible expression on his face; he looked like a young prosecutor in a colored-woodblock print from the late nineteenth century I had seen in a course on contemporary literature. Mrs. Ueki, who had finished her training somewhat later than us, had climbed to the upper tier of the drying room, with her thighs rubbing together and her shoulders rounded like a cat's, to endeavor to heighten the perspiration effect at its ever-so-slightly higher elevation; and only she seemed to have adopted the attitude that she could not be discriminatory toward Mr. Arai, which is not to say that she was a friendly woman. . . .

All the other regulars were critical of Mr. Arai, and each appeared, in their own way, to be demonstrating a warning to me for still incorrigibly associating with him. Pressured by the stiff-mannered attitudes of Mr. Mochizuki and the others, I was nonetheless starting to react to it all with a *Hell, no! Hell, no!*—though Eeyore would say, "Ma-chan, you're impossible." No doubt Mr. Arai's act of violence had been horrendous. Even so, aren't there times when the mind becomes *distressed* to the point that a person explosively resorts to violence? Instead of bawling, for not having people understand your suffering? Though the cruiser incident that had killed Mr. Kurokawa had involved Mr. Arai, the man who had beaten up her husband, Mrs. Shigeto told me that, ever since the incident Mr. Arai had been living with the widowed wife, a middle-school teacher, and she said that perhaps this was his way of atoning as best he could. . . .

After a while, though, it appeared that Mr. Arai, to my surprise, was whispering something in my brother's ear, something apparently interesting to Eeyore, who was sitting solemnly beside him with his head sunk into his fat, round shoulders. Mr. Arai then came over to the corner in which I was sitting, one corner away from where he had been. He aligned his thighs, which resembled unboned ham, right in front of me. And as heat waves of silent rebuke gushed toward me from the regulars, including an especially strong glare from Mr. Mochizuki, whose protests I had ignored, Mr. Arai fixed his apricot-shaped eyes on me and said, "Let's design Eeyore's new training plan at my condo, where we won't be bothered by rubbernecks. Eeyore thinks it's a good idea. Mr. Shigeto"— it sounded like he said Mist*a* Shigeto—"is trying his best to cut me off from Eeyore, which I don't mind. But in all fairness, myself, I don't think Eeyore should let the progress he's made go to waste. And if he's to practice on his own, myself, I have this *Textbook of Swimming* I can lend you. You can read it with Eeyore and follow it in conducting his swimming regimen. So if you would come . . ."

As soon as they saw me emerge from the locker room, Mr. Arai and Eeyore, who had already changed and had been waiting for me, hastened down to the club's reception counter on the second floor. In the staff room beyond the lockers and automatic door of the regular members' exit was Mr. Osawa, who seemed to have something to discuss with me. But because Eeyore, who usually needs more time to put on his shoes and everything, had been very quick that evening, all I could do was hurry out after him.

Night had set in, and a fine rain was falling. Both Eeyore

and I took out our folding umbrellas from our bags, but Mr. Arai, who had turned up his sweater collar, wasn't at all bothered by the rain. We helplessly followed Mr. Arai, who had the sort of gait that exploited the spring in the sole of his jogging shoes, and entered a road alongside the health club, perpendicular to the street that runs along the railway tracks, the one we always take. On one side of this road was a kindergarten and several posh condos, and on the other side, which had night lamps, ran the carefully built high concrete wall of a prewar residential area. It wasn't that long after dusk, yet the road was empty of human figures, probably on account of the rain. Mr. Arai kept walking, even after we had passed the signboard marking the club's parking place for bicycles, and so I asked, "Is the parking lot far?"

To this he clasped the collar of his sweater like an eagle, turned, and replied curtly, making light of me, "My condo's very near this place. Why should we go by car?" and continued walking briskly.

I too hurried along, abreast of Eeyore, who was resolutely stretching his strides to keep up with Mr. Arai, and while walking I was seized with a sense of fear and a feeling of nausea that chilled me to the core of my body. It occurred to me that, if he didn't keep his car at the club parking lot, then he must have gone there from the very outset, in search of a place to beat up Mr. Shigeto. Unable to bring myself to tell Eeyore that we should turn back, I kept walking along the road between the wall, which grew progressively taller, and structures that showed no sign of people in them. I was intimidated by the fact that the road, which up ahead turned down to the right, was of an antiquated style that consisted of placing on a slant one thick, blackish, hardened-gravel slab on top of another, for never before in my life had I taken such a road. I tried to walk its full stretch, while bringing myself so close to Eeyore that our umbrellas hit. On the right hand side of this slope, which felt like we were descending one oddly long step at a time, was a garage that cut into the backyard hedge of a stately old house. In the darkness were two cars. One of them was the Porsche. Mr. Arai hopped onto a narrow walkway by the garage. At the top of a steep flight of stairs that led up from the path was a long and narrow lot on which stood the three-story building that housed Mr. Arai's condo, on one side of which was a high concrete wall, and on the other a structure, most likely a public building, fringed with beech and zelkova trees that had shed their leaves.

On the second floor—reached by ascending a flight of stairs on the outside of the building that was narrow like the passageways adjoining a ship's cabins, and had chest-high panels that served as blinds—were two residential units, side by side. Mr. Arai unlocked the two doors with a gesture that boasted he owned both units. I then realized that, if Mr. Arai had left the place with both keys—one for the unit closer to the stairs, which had KUROKAWA on its nameplate, and one for the other unit, marked ARAI, which Eeyore and I were being led into—then Mrs. Kurokawa wasn't home, and this prompted me to assume a firm defensive posture. Yet I failed to turn back, despite this situation, not only because Eeyore had quickly gone in, but also because my attitude that day on the whole had been one of confusion. And my memory of what happened after I entered Mr. Arai's condo is just as confused. Indeed my comportment, as I tried to somehow hold my ground against fretting, fearing, almost *robotizing*, must have been far from natural. . . .

This, ironically, must have been a factor in causing Mr. Arai's actions to escalate in the direction of utter unruliness. Although I could never match Mrs. Shigeto's efforts to be thoroughly fair, I want to write about what happened in Mr. Arai's room without imparting any emotions, lest I be overly unfair to him. I'll be brief, like I would in presenting an outline. While I have reservations about presenting conclusions beforehand, I would say that the most distinctive feature of the incident, which began to gel in my mind as I later repeatedly replayed what had happened, is that Mr. Arai's attitude in his condo, even after he became overtly hostile, indeed even before that, was such that I could not really tell whether he was serious or joking; and in spite of this, or because of this, his behavior was overly and flagrantly exaggerated. In a sense, you could interpret the ambiguity of Mr. Arai's attitude as something he intended to serve as an alibi, so that later he could insist that it had all been a game, for no man in his right mind could have seriously attempted to translate into action anything so outrageous. . . .

Mr. Arai's condo was typical of a young man's habitat, with new-model audio components, a TV set with a videogame gadget attached to it, CDs and videos piled on shelves next to a big bed. Pinned to the wall, like a collage, were a slew of bright, gaudy posters and pictures of himself swimming. For books, all he had were, I don't know what you call them, new science or new religion books with psychedelic covers on them, books on swimming, and textbooks of sports theory, all jumbled together with magazines, which made me feel that I didn't belong there, accustomed as I was to life in a house filled with Father's books. Eeyore, who proceeded straight to the CD shelf to see what it held, said reservedly, but with bewilderment and dismay crossing his face, "Rock and new music aren't my favorites. . . ."

Whereupon Mr. Arai, saying that there was plenty of classical stuff in the adjacent room, opened the large steel door connecting the two units from inside, and took Eeyore into Mrs. Kurokawa's living area. Almost immediately after this, Brahms's

First Symphony came through with fine sound quality, and I heard Eeyore's joyous exclamation, "Furtwängler, is it? Hoh!" Mr. Arai came back alone, sat down on his bed with a thud, and suddenly, with an attitude that was almost rude, told me to come to his side. I feared that if I *robotized* I wouldn't be able to put up any resistance, and while desperately bracing my feelings, I tried not to listen to the unbelievable words he relentlessly spewed at me. . . .

I quote Mr. Arai's words. "If you want to make your dream of marrying me and bringing Eeyore along come true, you could very well move in here, right now. Eeyore could sleep in Mrs. Kurokawa's room at night. . . . You sit there as prim as a princess, but myself, I've seen what yours looks like, good and hard, from behind your crotch when you, in your swimsuit, were doing the breaststroke. . . . Myself, I could give it to you now if you want, but Eeyore's quietly listening to music, and he would be bothered if you started moaning and groaning with pleasure. But as a token of us having arrived at a new relationship, you could show me just the part that your swimsuit conceals . . . never mind your breasts—myself, I could see from looking at you in your swimsuit that you hardly have any. Myself, I want to see your lower body. . . .

"Mr. K wrote that myself, I had the woman bare her lower parts, and tied her legs to both sides of her hips in the shape of an *M*, so as to expose her c——. He just let his imagination go wild, and branded me with infamy. . . . It would be mighty fun if myself, I experimented with you, his daughter, to see what shape it really looks like. . . ."

I screamed at the top of my voice in the direction of the living area next door, and I heard what sounded like Eeyore quickly rise and approach the door and repeatedly pull at the doorknob, for Mr. Arai had locked it. I sprang to my feet to rush to the door, but Mr. Arai caught me by my arms and twisted them upward from behind with the force of a machine. He stood like this for a while, chuckling behind my ears, but soon he dragged me backward with one forceful pull, and threw me onto his bed. I fell on my back and tried to hide my face in my hands, but he pushed my arms open, from in front of me to my sides; and with his flushed smooth face mixed with an expression of rage and amusement, he kept looking down at me with his apricot-shaped eyes. . . .

Pinned down, and utterly helpless, I suddenly found myself free, standing by the bed in blank surprise. Eeyore, with power suffusing every fiber of his body, like when he's angry at a barking dog, had his hands clasped around Mr. Arai's carotids, and the two, entangled together, cascaded down between the bed and the sofa. . . . Eeyore had exited Mrs. Kurokawa's condo to the road, and then entered Mr. Arai's unit through the front door. As soon as I realized this I was running to the door, which was still open, and I fled outside without even putting my shoes on. . . .

The direction in which I ran, trying to get back on the road we had come on, turned out to be wrong, and I found myself on the block of the Women's Community Hall and the Elderly Citizens' Welfare Hall, where there were neither any lighted houses nor passersby I could ask for help. I slipped and fell as I panted and raced up the slope with its sturdy, cemented-pebble slabs, and just like that little girl in our neighborhood, I wobbled on my knees to get away. I even sobbed and cried. When at last I was on my feet again, I was seized with the blood-curdling thought that I had fled without Eeyore, that I had left him in the hands of a person like Mr. Arai, who could kick at, and break, his ribs. I cried out loud as I thought of Eeyore, who had been forsaken by Mother and Father, and by me too—

undoubtedly an "abandoned child"—yet was fighting bravely to save me. . . .

Despite all this, I somehow managed to get back on the street that ran along the railroad tracks, and heedless of the penetrating stares of the passersby—it was drizzling, I had no umbrella over my head, I was barefoot, and my knees were bleeding—I walked back toward the health club. Feeling helplessly desperate, I thought of asking Mr. Osawa to come to Eeyore's rescue. But as I passed and happened to peer up the alley we had taken when going to Mr. Arai's condo—the road right beside the club building—I saw Eeyore walking with Mr. Arai, who was carrying the bag and umbrella I had left behind. I stood there, rooted in fear, but Mr. Arai, upon recognizing me, handed my belongings to Eeyore, and leapt back on the road he had come, as if he were jogging.

I walked in Eeyore's direction, and he hurried toward me, squinting his eyes as if to peer into the drizzling dark, and said with a calm and gentle voice, "Are you all right? Ma-chan! I fought!"

The next day, I started running a fever again, and I couldn't get up for some time. I couldn't even write to Mother, though it bothered me that I didn't. All the while I was in bed, O-chan did a great job not only with the household chores but also with various other things he had searched out that needed to be done. As for things that concerned him personally—such as going to the university to check the bulletin boards and see whether or not he had passed his entrance exams—he did them after taking Eeyore to the welfare workshop. O-chan locked the front door so that I could sleep without being disturbed. Returning home with the makings for dinner, he busied himself in the kitchen with this and that, and at long last he peered in through my door and said, "Sister, thank you for your cooperation." It was an impersonation of his younger self, but with an adult voice that was nothing like the clear, crystalline voice he had when he passed his elementary school entrance exams. "Thanks to you, I passed."

O-chan had gone to pick up Eeyore, and later, bearing in mind the time difference, made an overseas call to our parents in California. Eeyore was beside him, probably thinking he would substitute for me, since even if I could have gotten up and walked to the living room, given my unstable emotions my voice might have become all teary. So after O-chan had made his *sort of* passing-the-examination report, Eeyore switched with him and said, "Ma-chan was in big trouble, but I fought!"

This prompted Mother to get O-chan on the phone again. He, sounding irritated, bluntly but correctly related to Mother an account of what had happened, as I had briefly related it to him. He also reported to her that, after listening to my story, he had *sort of* contacted Mr. Shigeto, upon whose advice he had called the health club and discussed the matter with Mr. Osawa. It seemed that Mr. Osawa was taking action to prohibit Mr. Arai from coming to the club. For the time being, Eeyore wouldn't be swimming, but what the body has learned it won't forget, so when he resumes, he'll swim all right. I was in bed with a headache, but my fever seems to have gone. Soon I should be able to recover the quiet life I love. In other words, Mother need not worry about us here. . . .

But when Mother heard this on the phone, she got to worrying, and before the week was up, she was already back in Japan. What first shocked me was that, during her roughly six-month stay in California, something had made the texture and movement of the skin on her face project the impression of a nisei woman in her early sixties. And though Mother herself had decided to go with Father in order to help him cope with his "pinch," she now embraced not so much a cold attitude as one that placed a clear distance between herself and Father— perhaps because she had decided that, for her part, she had done all there was to do and could do no more. She did say, objectively, that he might stay another year at some UC campus, for toward the end of last year, through the auspices of some friends at Berkeley, he had received the Distinguished Service Award; and, though not because of this, he could expect a grant from the Japan Foundation if he earnestly asked for one. And just about this time, when Mother returned to Japan, a freelance photographer who had signed a contract with a Japanese magazine had taken some pictures of Father, several of which had been forwarded to us. Some showed Father in the shade of a California live oak tree on the UC campus, standing in his black-collared raincoat with ornamental cuffs on it, his eyes closed and his hands cupped behind his ears; others depicted him lying on a slope studded with oak trees that had trunks as big as elephants' feet, looking up at a shoot of grass right in front of his nose, one that looked like a wood sorrel grown tall. . . .

"I didn't know the man could pose before a camera," O-chan said in astonishment, a sentiment I shared.

"I don't think there was any posing as such," Mother said. "He simply wasn't aware that there was a photographer looking at him when the pictures were being taken. About this time, he almost always had the same expression on his face when in the faculty quarters, and said nothing for days on end. He hasn't written you for some time either, has he? He was stirred to action, as if he had just awakened, when he had to deal with that swimming coach, but it didn't last long. Besides, he's found himself some new reading matter to concentrate on. . . . The place we stayed at had several rooms, and because he kept reading in his bedroom, day in and day out, he forgot that I had come with him. There were times he even prepared his own meals, and ate them alone."

"I wonder if he'll be okay, with so many live oaks, and branches he can hang from," O-chan said, although reservedly. I had told him about what Mr. Shigeto had said about Father.

"I don't think we need to worry about that," said Mother. "Basically, I returned because that worry has gone. He's found a wonderful professor on the campus. He takes private lessons from him once a week, for four hours, and he's thoroughly engrossed in them. He's pouring all his energy into preparation and review, and that's why he's so easily distracted."

"Is this professor a priest?" I asked.

"Why? . . . He's a specialist on Blake. Papa's now reading his Prophecies. 'The Four Zoas,' mainly. He's using a facsimile version. But despite all the time he spent reading Blake, it seems he was able to go just so far by self-study, and had no way of knowing how the Prophecies had been rewritten, let alone know the importance of their revision. He was grumbling to himself that his failure to fully understand Blake's vision of rebirth, too, was due to his half-baked study methods.

"I couldn't help him read Blake, so I was ready to come back. Our life on this side is important, too. . . . Before Papa met us"—I thought this a rather strange expression for Mother to use—"from the time he was fourteen or fifteen years old, he'd been living alone in a boardinghouse. And this was how he managed to surmount the 'pinches' that came at the various stages of his development. I've learned this time that, in the end, he's the type of person who has to deal with his 'pinches' this way. In any event, if he's so determined to cope with them by doing things his own way, I think there's no other place to do it but there, where he can learn about Blake. . . ."

diary as home

Of course, Mother hadn't given up on Father restoring himself to us, which you might say is a matter of course, she being his wife and all. But I have sometimes thought that, if a person of her character had done her level best for six long months in her life with Father, just the two of them together—and had, from this experience, come to reconsider their relationship—then whatever conclusion she had arrived at must be one that indeed *couldn't be helped*. . . . One morning, some ten or so days after her return, Mother said that she had finished reading "Diary as Home," which she had borrowed from me. I was watching her make up her face, amazed at her skin, which was recovering with such vigor that it seemed to be at one with the swelling of the buds on the cherry trees along the street in front of the station. And she suggested that I send the diary to Father in California.

"Because," she said, "you've written not only about Eeyore, of course, but about O-chan, and yourself, too . . . and even about me, which I didn't expect; and it reads as though we were living one life together. If Papa reads this, he might remember he has a family, though it be in his typically serious, yet off-key fashion. He might come to realize that, just because he's rowed himself out into the stormy sea of a 'pinch,' it's shameful to be so absentmindedly concerned with only himself. . . . In her last letter to me, Grandma wrote that Papa, after being spirited away in the forest, suddenly couldn't remember his own name. The other children got a big kick out of this, and teased him whenever they needed a laugh, saying, 'Hey, you there! What's your name?' If he reads 'Diary as Home' he might relearn the names of his real family."

I never imagined that Mother would utilize the "Diary as Home" this way, this diary that I continued to write in the midst of our real-life 'pinches.' I thought I had been impartial in my writing, but I was anxious about Father reading it. While trying to suppress this sensation, I found myself again shouting in my heart, *Hell, no! Hell, no!* Nevertheless, I went out to look for something to send it in. When I returned and was about to do the packing, Mother made another suggestion.

"Ma-chan," she said, "'Diary as Home' sounds bland and dull. How about giving it a title that best describes your life over the past six or seven months?"

"I haven't got that sort of talent in my small, round head. . . . But Eeyore, you're a master at titles. Can you think of one for me?"

Eeyore, who was lying on his stomach on the dining room carpet, writing music on staff paper—with a composure I never saw in him while Mother was away—took his time, and then replied, "How about *A Quiet Life*? That's what our life's all about!"

Kenzaburo Oe was born in 1935 in the remote mountain village of Ose on Shikoku, the smallest of Japan's four main islands. He began publishing short stories while studying French literature at Tokyo University and won the coveted Akutagawa Prize for "Prize Stock" when he was twenty-three.

Since that time, Kenzaburo Oe's prolific body of novels, short stories, critical and political essays, and other nonfiction has won almost every major international honor, including the 1989 Prix Europalia and the 1994 Nobel Prize for Literature. His many translated works include *A Personal Matter*, *Teach Us to Outgrow Our Madness*, *The Silent Cry*, *Hiroshima Notes*, and *Nip the Buds, Shoot the Kids*.

Kenzaburo Oe resides in Tokyo with his wife and three children.